Nowle's Passing

A Novel

Edith Forbes

Seal Press

Text and jacket design by Clare Conrad
Jacket painting, "Barn with Snow" by Georgia O'Keeffe, courtesy of the San Diego Museum of Art, gift of Mr. and Mrs. Norton S. Walbridge

Library of Congress Cataloging-in-Publication Data
Forbes, Edith, 1954-
    Nowle's passing : a novel / Edith Forbes.
1. Brothers and sisters—Vermont—Fiction. 2. Women teachers—Vermont—Fiction. I. Title.
PS3556.0662N69   1996   813´.54—dc20   95-42658
ISBN 1-878067-72-9

Printed in the United States of America
First printing, March 1996
10 9 8 7 6 5 4 3 2 1

Distributed to the trade by Publishers Group West
Foreign Distribution:
In Canada: Publishers Group West Canada, Toronto, Ontario
In the U.K. and Europe: Airlift Book Company, London

for Franklin
live in us

ALSO BY EDITH FORBES
Alma Rose

Nowle's Passing

1

"ANOTHER CASUALTY OF HARD TIMES." The head-
line drew her eye, and then the photograph, which she recognized.
It was an old newspaper file photo of Vernon with his top cow
Nutmeg, the year the farm won an award as the highest producing
Jersey herd in the state.

She slid automatically into the booth her husband had chosen
and spread the newspaper to read.

"The cost squeeze that drove a third of Vermont's farms out of
business in the last decade has brought tragedy to the Owens River
valley. Authorities now believe the gunshot wound that killed Vernon
Nowle, 67, of Worthing, last Saturday, was self-inflicted. 'All indi-
cations point to suicide,' said a spokesman for the Vermont State
Police.

"Nowle's body was found in the kitchen of his farmhouse late
Monday afternoon by the fuel delivery man, Orville Baines. Police
say that Nowle was despondent after the auction of his dairy herd
and equipment two weeks ago. Friends say, also, that he had never
recovered from the death of his wife Phoebe in a tractor accident
more than a year ago."

"Nineteen months, to be exact," Vincie thought, quarreling with
details because the whole was still too grim and incomprehensible
to take in. She felt numb, and the detached language of newsprint
made the people in the story into strangers, not her parents. "Vernon

Nowle, 67, of Worthing," could be anybody. Her brain was trained to skip across news stories, like a skipped rock, not breaking the surface.

She stared at the photo, trying to connect the unsmiling face under a New Holland billed cap, any farmer, anywhere, U.S.A., with her father. She couldn't believe he was dead.

When she had heard that her mother was dead, she had believed it immediately. Phoebe had been vibrant, flickering, laughing, a small darting person one could imagine snuffed in a moment by death. But not Vernon. Her father had had a kind of inevitability about him. To imagine him dead was to imagine a great river dammed up and still, or a granite mountainside split wide open and cascading in rubble.

She could not make it real to herself. It had not been real when she heard Darrell's voice on the phone, quiet as always, wasting no words. "Dad's killed himself. I guess maybe you should come." It was not real now, sitting in Bev's with coffee and a Danish pastry, barely tasted, and the black and white type marching in neat rows across the page, as if the neatness of the print and the dispassionate tone of the words were a certification of truth.

"This is not cream."

She heard Gifford's voice, each word clipped off from the next. He hated sloppiness, in speech or anything else. He was holding the metal pitcher for the waitress to take.

"If all you have is non-dairy creamer, then please bring me some milk. And I will need a fresh cup of coffee. I poured some of that synthetic liquid into this cup before I thought to taste it. Thank you so much." He finished with a smile that was meant to forge a bond of common humanity, even across the chasm of class, education and taste that separated him from the waitress. Gifford saw Vincie looking at him and became aware that his behavior might look petty, under the circumstances. "Your father thought non-dairy creamer was an abomination," he said, as if his complaint had been answering an affront to Vernon's memory rather than to his own palate.

4

"You can send the coffee back if you want," said Vincie. She did not want to squabble with her husband.

"Of course, your father thought I was an abomination, too," he added.

He took a bite of his pastry and grimaced. "Sugared cardboard. I should have known by the decor that the food would be atrocious." His gaze swept around the diner, taking in the vinyl seats, the Formica table tops, the yellow and brown plaid wallpaper, and the bony, scowling woman who was tending half a dozen mounds of egg on the griddle. "Bev looks like a gorgon, if that's Bev. One look from her would turn a Danish pastry to stone. I don't suppose there is any other place in Worthing where we could eat."

"No." Vincie was still absorbed in the newspaper. She did not have to look around to know what Gifford was seeing. The diner had not changed since her short stint working there when she was in high school, except that the vinyl seat covers had worn through and been replaced by a different shade of tan.

Bev had greeted Vincie without surprise, and with a welcome visible only to someone who had known Bev long enough to distinguish among the shadings of her scowl. "Morning, Vincie. Sorry to hear about your Dad. Guess you must be back for the funeral." She was, as Gifford had perceived, uncordial, and she was not even a good cook, but her restaurant had been there half a lifetime and people had the same attachment to it that they would grow to have for anything if it stayed in one place long enough. At this hour, midmorning, many of the seats were filled.

Vincie stared at the photograph. Her father's face was indistinct, shaded by the bill of his cap, but Nutmeg's face stood out clearly, the wide forehead, the dished face and soft doe eyes, the dark shading down the nose ending in a pale highlight around the muzzle. It was the face of the creatures her father had loved without any complicating responsibility for the shape of their character.

"... despondent after the auction of his dairy herd and equipment...." No doubt it was true, she thought, but the image seemed too small, a boy who has dropped his ice cream cone. She still couldn't connect it to Vernon. His was a figure large, serious, and sometimes frightening.

She saw him suddenly, outdoors in the predawn twilight, lit by a flashlight he had propped on the ground. The light, shining upward, cast strange shadows. In front of him lay a cow, flat on her side, unnatural, her belly a huge mound, her neck arched back, her body twitching. Vernon was on his knees, bending over her. He could have been praying, except that one arm was raised and held a plastic bag with tubing down to a needle in the cow's neck.

He did not notice Vincie watching him, though she was barely ten feet away. His eyes were on the cow, fixed with a furious intensity that willed the animal to keep fighting for life. Vincie stood still and watched. Her mother had sent her out with some message for Vernon but she had forgotten the message at the sight of the cow.

As Vincie watched, the cow shuddered and her neck arched back convulsively. Her brown eye blinked and three drops squeezed out of the corner and rolled across her cheek, and then she stopped moving. Vernon's shoulders sagged. For a moment he sat slumped and still, and then it was his body that shuddered as he broke down in sobs. Vincie had been motionless with awe and curiosity before, but now she felt afraid. She had never seen her father in tears, not when her aunt, his sister, died, not when the president was shot, never. She could not grasp the magnitude of a catastrophe that could bring her father to tears.

She began to back away and her father must have sensed the movement. He turned abruptly and saw her. His face was contorted, made strange by the deep black shadows cast by the flashlight.

"What are you doing there?" he asked and his voice was rough and unfamiliar. "You should know better."

She turned away and fled toward the house, stumbling over the bumpy ground. She would have screamed but the screams were locked down in her throat by fear of this man she barely recognized. He had sounded angry and she did not know what she had done wrong.

In the kitchen, Phoebe was making coffee and putting out the breakfast dishes. Darrell hovered just behind her, still in his pajamas, tracking every move she made. Chad was sitting on the floor in the corner, knocking over toy soldiers with a bulldozer and crooning to himself. The room looked the same as it did every morning.

For a moment, Vincie almost thought that the cow and her father had been a nightmare, except that her heart was still racing and her hands and face were cold from the early morning air.

"Did you give him the message?" Phoebe asked.

Vincie shook her head but didn't speak.

"Why not? He needs to know before . . . ." Her mother stopped and looked at her more closely. "Vincie, what's wrong? Has something happened?"

"There's a cow . . ." she began confusedly. What had happened, in fact? "There's a cow . . . he was busy . . . ."

"Does your dad need help?"

"I don't know. There's a cow . . . ."

The door opened behind her and Vernon came in. He looked exactly as he always did, calm and serious, no sign of anger in his face. Again Vincie wondered if she had been dreaming.

"I'll be late in for breakfast," he said. "Juno went down with milk fever. I thought I got the calcium to her quick enough but I didn't. I'm afraid I lost her." His tone was matter of fact, and he added, "Could you get ahold of Jim Maynard and see if he can come dress her out?"

Vincie saw her mother's eyes widen and well up with tears before she turned away to pick up the phone book. The two boys were staring in curiosity, Darrell silently from across the room, while Chad had jumped up and run over to his father.

"Is that blood?" Chad wanted to know. He was looking with eager interest at Vernon's hand.

"Yes, Chaddy, it's blood." Vernon's voice had softened toward apology and affection, speaking to his youngest, who was only five and whose brown eyes had the same sweet velvety depths as the eyes of the fawnlike Jersey calves. The change in Vernon's voice

7

was a bare half-tone, hardly there, but Vincie heard it.

She looked too and saw the blood, just one small smear across the back of his hand.

"Is there a new calf?" Chad asked.

"No, not a new calf this time," said Vernon.

He turned and went out the door. He had not once looked at Vincie, and she trembled, wondering if he was still too angry with her to speak.

Later, as she walked with Darrell down the driveway to wait for the school bus, she paused to look longingly toward the barn, hoping she might catch sight of her father letting the cows out to pasture after milking. Instead, she saw an object that froze her where she stood. Outside the barn, the blue Ford tractor was parked with diesel idling and front-end loader raised to its fullest height. Dangling from the loader, hung with chains by her back legs, was the cow. Her round belly and pale udder looked exposed, ungainly, helpless. Her eyes were open and staring, her nose stretched toward the ground below, her throat and jaw were dark with draining blood.

"Why does anyone choose to eat in a place like this?" Gifford's voice broke in on her. "Have they forgotten what food tastes like?"

Vincie's eyes came into focus on her husband, with his high domed forehead fringed by black hair clipped short. He scorned men who grew a long lock of hair to comb across their baldness. People should meet reality squarely, he said. Every action should be an authentic expression of the self, applied to a world viewed without illusion. He was frequently annoyed by the sensitivities in Vincie that made her tentative and confused, inclined to bend herself to fit the wishes of others, to smooth over rough emotions and moderate disagreements and in general, try to make other people feel better.

"We can drive to Huntsbury for dinner," she said, to quiet her husband's discontent.

"You could have thought of that for breakfast, too," he said. "Every time you tolerate mediocrity, you are helping to perpetuate it."

He'd expressed that sentiment many times, but this time Vincie

8

heard him with a start. It sounded like something Vernon might have said, except that Vernon would not have chosen those particular words nor thought to apply them to Bev's Diner.

A man had stopped beside their table on his way to the cash register.

"It's Vincie Nowle, isn't it?" he said. "I'm Roger Cobb. Don't know if you remember me. I dug out a bunker silo for your dad years back."

"I remember you," said Vincie. He ran bulldozers and backhoes for an excavation company in Huntsbury, and kept a few beef cows in his spare time.

"Awful sorry to hear about Vernon. He sure kept that place up. A person could have invited his cows into the living room, he kept his barn that clean. I bought an old Haybine off him once, when he switched over to the new disc mowers. Fifteen years old and it worked like new. Best deal on equipment I ever got."

Reminded of that mower, Cobb began a long and loving catalog of its gears, bearings and bolts, every one of them perfectly maintained for fifteen years by her father. Gifford sat gazing out the window in boredom, but Vincie listened, thinking that it was as genuine a eulogy as any.

2

JUST THINK, you could have been part of all this," Gifford said, when Cobb had gone. He swept his arm in a circle, taking in the diner and its customers. "You could have succeeded your father on the farm and become one of the leading citizens of this fine community."

"No, I couldn't have. I could equally well have become an astronaut."

She felt irritable. Gifford's favorite game was to diminish the world to the size of a tennis ball and bat it about with irony. She was not in the mood to play her half of the game.

Back when she was a student, she had been dazzled by the witty eloquence and sophistication of his lectures. Though still a junior professor, his demeanor had conveyed certainty that his climb to the heights was only a matter of time and a few tedious formalities. Now that he had reached the heights, and brought her with him, she sometimes found herself looking wistfully toward the humbler creatures below. She knew, too, that Gifford sometimes questioned his own choice of wife, and doubted whether her mind, for all its quickness, was truly profound.

"Why couldn't you have followed him?" he asked. "Because you were a girl and girls don't run farms?"

"It wasn't that simple," Vincie said. Why was the idea of taking Vernon's place so unimaginable? Was it only that she was female, and had to use a crowbar to lift things her father or Darrell could lift with their backs? She had worked on the farm, as a matter of course, until the year she finished college and moved in with Gifford. She knew enough. She was smart enough. Yet the idea of becoming

Vincie Nowle, that lady farmer just this side of Five Mile Road, old Vernon Nowle's daughter, was unimaginable. She could not bring the corresponding image of herself into focus.

"Because you were a girl?" Gifford's words reduced the difficulty to its obvious explanation, dismissed the obstacle as trivial, and then dismissed her as weak for not having surmounted it.

She remembered the first time she had walked into Hatcher's Equipment by herself, sent by Vernon to pick up a part. She remembered the dim interior, the pyramid stacks of five gallon oil cans, the racks of cotter pins and grease fittings, the brownish walls decorated with promotional posters for John Deere and International, green fields with red and green and yellow machines as shiny and enticing as toys. She remembered the long aisles between shelves full of parts, and the long battered wooden counter in front of the shelves, and on either side of the counter, men in work clothes, casually leaning on elbows, exchanging friendly grunts of opinion about some black oil-smeared piece of metal that had been extracted from a tractor or mower and now lay on a grease rag on the counter to be probed and discussed. When she walked in, there was a pause, like an intake of breath, and then the conversation resumed.

Like the men, she wore pants that were smudged with grease and her fingernails were dark in the corners from grime it was too much trouble to scrub off more than once a day. Like them, she carried a black, oily chunk of metal wrapped in a rag. But she was sixteen, blonde, female, and as she now recognized, pretty. There was that moment's pause, a few of the men glanced at her, and then the conversation resumed, as if she weren't there. She found a space at the counter and laid out her piece of metal, a bearing off the baler. Around her the conversation went on, barely rippled by her presence.

She waited and began to grow agitated. Vernon had been in a hurry. He had sent her so that he could go on working himself. They needed the baler fixed, quick. She looked first at one counterman, then another, trying to catch someone's eye.

Finally, reluctantly, one of the countermen began to make the noises preparatory to ending a conversation. He wrote up a sales slip, said good-bye and moved down the counter to where she stood. Could he help her, he asked skeptically. Then, without saying another word to her, he picked up the bearing and examined it. In her hands, it was not a battle trophy laid out for admiration. It was a confession of helplessness, a puzzle brought to the oracle for interpretation.

"It's the bearing on the left side of the knotter," she said. "I have the model and serial number of the baler, if you need it to find the part."

The man did not appear to have heard her. "Must have come off a baler," he murmured to himself. He was busy measuring, turning it over in his hands, fingering the deeply scored rings of metal, one of which had cracked in two.

"My dad says it's shot. He said to pick up a new one. He has an account here, Vernon Nowle."

The counterman looked up. She had spoken the magic words. The veil dropped, the man saw her and smiled. "You're Vernon's girl. Shoulda known you right off. You've grown up a little since the last time you came in with him."

Suddenly everyone in the room was smiling at her, asking how the haying was coming along, how her mom was, whether Vernon thought milk prices were likely to come up at all next winter.

She was Vernon's girl. Suddenly, she existed. Always after that, she was greeted with nods and hellos.

So why couldn't she have slid from that existence into an existence as Vernon's successor? The barrier was not her femaleness. Gifford was right, her sex was an obstacle but one that determination could overcome. The men in Hatcher's had not been hostile. They behaved the way they might have behaved toward a person with two heads, with uneasy avoidance, because they weren't sure which head they should speak to and couldn't pretend not to notice the oddity. Once one of the two heads spoke, they could begin to unbend. At least then they knew where to look when they replied. As a woman, she would always have to be the one to speak first. She would always have to overcome her own self-consciousness at being out of place and extend that bridge across the gap. But it could be done.

What could not be done, what she could not imagine, was trying to live in the place where Vernon had been. She had tried once to explain this feeling to Gifford and he had laughed at her. He told her she idealized her father and made him larger than life, just like every other little girl.

The two men had disliked each other almost on sight, so neither had ever really known the other. Around Gifford, Vernon became silent and watchful. By nature, he used words sparingly and methodically, and he distrusted the quick, fluid speech of his son-in-law. Gifford, in turn, was made nervous by someone who did not smile at his turns of phrase. Nervousness made him retreat even further behind his sarcastic wit. He would have liked to dismiss Vernon as an inarticulate peasant, but he was perceptive enough to recognize that in this case a lack of speech did not mark a lack of thought.

Vernon had a massiveness about him that was unconnected to physical size. He followed his beliefs as the tide follows the moon, its motion slow, barely visible, but unstoppable. Vincie felt small and changeable, a windblown leaf compared to him. If she tried to come after him, she would be engulfed and disappear. She had found her place instead among others like herself, who swirled this way and that until they collected in drifts against any hummock that rose above the flatness of terrain.

Now Vernon was dead. Perhaps it was fitting that he had chosen the time and place of his death, and not waited until physical decay made a path for some fatal microorganism or malfunctioning clump of cells. Death seemed less impossible, if he had chosen it. His own will had collided with itself, a worthy adversary, and so had avoided the indignity of imprisonment in a failing body.

This thought almost made her believe in his death, but not quite. His body had been many years away from failure. So why had he

13

chosen this moment? Was it indeed, as the newspaper said, the loss of his farm? ". . . despondent after the auction of his dairy herd and equipment . . . ."

She could not picture Vernon broken in this way, not by a tragedy purely personal. He had had a curious indifference to the fate of human beings, including himself; or most particularly, himself. He did not go to church, because he thought Christianity was too driven by human egoism, too preoccupied with individual fear of death. Yet he was religious. He had the calm that comes from the certainty that humans are not the summit of what exists. If he objected to Christianity, it was for being too narrow. It reduced god to the shape of a human being, and to Vernon, god was a being vast, mysterious and fascinating, far more complex than a mere human, and far too large to be confined within any human's attempt at definition.

Vincie thought he would have recoiled at the prospect of becoming a burden, but beyond that, she did not think he much minded what turn his life took. He would not have been destitute. Debt had swallowed the cattle and equipment, but not the house and land. He had said sometimes, half-jokingly, that he could easily earn more money fixing other people's machinery than he would ever earn milking fifty-five cows. Nor would he have been alone. Darrell and Georgeanne lived in Worthing, with his grandchildren. He knew everyone in town. His plight was not nearly so desperate as the newspaper wanted to make it sound.

Yet he had killed himself. Wriggle as she would, she couldn't elude that fact. She turned back to the newspaper and read more of the article, as if an answer might lie there.

". . . survived by three children, Vernice, Darrell, and Chad, and two grandchildren . . . had worked the farm for thirty-six years . . . was negotiating with a land trust to preserve his land permanently in agricultural use, but the agreement had not been finalized . . . ." Here she stopped. Possibly that was the action of a man thinking of ending his life, that impulse to leave a legacy of good. But then why had he killed himself before the agreement was final? She read on.

". . . killed by a single bullet to the head . . . at close range . . . gun his own . . . found seated and fallen forward onto the kitchen table . . . near his left hand was a photograph of his wife and children with a tractor. . . ."

Was it because of Phoebe, then? But why had he waited a year and a half? Why had he waited so long and then left a lot of loose ends?

"I don't understand why he did it," she said. "The things it says in the newspaper don't fit together. It makes no sense."

"People don't make sense," said Gifford. She had been lost in thought for too long and he had grown restless, too restless to apply his mind to her question.

"You won't find the answer sitting in this booth," he added. "Maybe you will never know for certain. But I do know for certain that Bev's coffee is going to exact a prolonged penance. Possibly lasting into old age. Let's get out of here."

He picked up the check and calculated the five percent tip he left when he was displeased. On a check of $3.80, it came to nineteen cents. As he laid two dimes on the table, he seemed torn between annoyance at the extra penny, and an awareness that leaving a nickel and four pennies to make the exact amount would only make him look cheap and would not reinforce his message of displeasure.

When he had gone to the cash register to pay, Vincie surreptitiously slid three quarters under the edge of her saucer. The first two expressed her own theory that cheap food and bad coffee were just as much work to serve as any other kind. She added the third out of a feeling that anyone caught between Bev's temper and Gifford's opinions deserved a gesture of consolation.

3

OUTSIDE, THE AIR WAS WET, though no rain was falling. Moisture hung dispersed in the air, condensing on every object, dampening Vincie's hair and face. She could hear the rush of the Owens River, behind the diner. The building was perched on the riverbank between the firehouse and the one-room public library. All three buildings looked as if the next high water might send them sliding down into the river, but the firehouse and library had been perched there for a hundred fifty years and Bev had thought that was a pretty good guarantee thirty years ago when she decided to locate her diner between them.

Worthing didn't offer many places to put a building. The whole village was wedged onto a narrow strip of land between the river and the steep wooded hills that rose on either side of it. Back in the early 1800s, when the town was settled, the hills had been clear and grazed by sheep. There had seemed to be a good reason to put a town in that spot, where Quail Brook tumbled down from the hills to join the Owens River. A miller named Amos Hood had dammed the brook and built a small mill to grind flour for the farms up and down the valley, and the town had grown up around him.

Later in the century, the farms and sheep both moved west to better land. Worthing shrank to half its former size, which had never been very large. Hood's Mill struggled along for a few more decades, until the Depression sank it for good. The few farms remaining in the valley now were dairies, like Vernon's, that tilled only the choice river bottom land. Left alone, the hills had mostly returned to woods.

This part of the Owens River ran north to south, from Owens Falls through Worthing to the town of Huntsbury. Much of the valley was so narrow and the hills so steep that even in summer the sun rose after breakfast and went down before supper. At all seasons there were long hours in morning and evening when the sky was light but half the valley floor lay in shadow. At most seasons, too, there were days like this one, when the clouds crept halfway down the hillsides, when the light was flat, the air wet, and the valley closed down to a narrow gap between walls of trees that could have gone on upward forever, as far as a person looking from the valley floor could tell.

Now, at the beginning of April, the dullness of sky was not brightened by any color below. It was the grim season, when snow lay in dirty patches here and there, when fields, woods and dirt roads were impassable mud, when color was reduced to the range from gray to brown. The landscape was littered with the debris of departing winter but was not yet tinted with any sign of coming spring. This season, coming as it did after months of sleet, ice and snow, seemed like one last test of fortitude, or possibly one last mocking insult. It was the season that spawned puritanism, and the sourly joking attitude that no matter how bad things were, they could always get worse. New England pessimism was like the black humor of soldiers, an attempt to stay sane. Visitors from other regions often did not understand that the locals were speaking with irony and simply concluded that New Englanders' dispositions had curdled from staying in one place too long.

Those visitors did not come in March and April. They came in more cheerful seasons, particularly in early autumn, when for a week or two the frosted leaves turned the hillsides into a picture postcard of flaming red and orange. At that season, the locals' conviction that "we'll pay for it later" sounded like gloomy ingratitude for blessings received. A person had to stay on for the six months of cold that followed this last burst of color to understand how it could look like the last fall of glowing coals before a fire sinks into ash, or the last gush of lifeblood before death.

"Why does anyone choose to live in this place?" Gifford's question echoed his earlier assessment of Bev's cooking. He was looking at the house across the road, at the bank of grimy snow now melting into rivulets across its driveway, at the brown matted grass of its lawn, still too muddy to rake, at the wall of hillside shoved almost against its back porch and its front door still sealed over for winter with a sheet of plastic and strips of lath.

"It's not as if it offers the romance of the frontier, like Alaska," he said. "Christ, at home the cherry blossoms are out, and look at this place. It's no wonder a man might kill himself. Does spring ever come?"

"Eventually," said Vincie.

Why did people choose to live here? The answer flashed across her mind—because people like Gifford and me don't choose to live here. Why do lichens live on the windswept granite of Mount Washington? Why do iguanas live in barren desert dust, and cypress trees in steaming swamps? As much because of what's not there as because of what is.

In the car, Gifford turned the heater up high, trying to clear the mist that clung to the windows.

"A person's brain would grow mildew in this climate," he muttered. "Which way to the farm?"

She pointed left and he turned. Gifford preferred to do the driving, even when Vincie knew the roads. If he was in the car with her, she drove in spurts and hesitations, distracted by their conversation or by the scenery. Her style annoyed him, and she couldn't learn to keep driving and conversation in separate compartments, so it was simpler to let him have the wheel.

At first sight, the farm had not changed. On the left stood a massive three-story post-and-beam barn, built in the last century, and

19

two low, modern sheds. On the right stood the house, a white clapboard structure in the farmhouse style, which began as a simple two-story box with a steeply pitched roof, and then, over a span of one or two centuries, sprouted ells, dormers, chimneys, sheds, and porches in response to each new inhabitant's desire for more space, light or heat. Such farmhouses were as common yet distinct as so many wild-growing trees, all of which had begun life as a neat single shoot, but after a century had grown into a multitude of shapes according to the vagaries of wind, sunlight, rainfall, and whatever unseen impulse it is that decides to send out a branch here rather than there.

The place looked as it always did at the end of winter, the lawn brown and littered with twigs, the dooryard churned into mud, the cattle and machinery out of sight, still under cover from the weather. It looked a bit disheveled but not disorderly. Only when she stepped out of the car did Vincie feel the change. It was too still.

The silence was eerie. Gone were all the small sounds and movements and smells that would have greeted her in the past. She would hardly have noticed them, they were so familiar, but their absence was as stunning as a deafening din. Gone were the small grunts and sighs of the cows, as they shifted position or belched up a fresh cud to chew. Gone was the warm fragrance of hay, silage and manure. No dogs barked. No cats wound themselves around her ankles. Even the hum of the refrigeration motor on the bulk tank was still. The whole place was still, except for an occasional drip of water when enough wetness had collected on something to form a drop and fall. The only warm-blooded creatures to be seen were three robins, their feathers fluffed against the chilly mist, rather disconsolately poking about in the grass of the lawn.

Vincie looked around at the empty, silent farm and a shiver ran down her back. In a few weeks, her mother's daffodils would be up, the rhododendrons would flower, the grass would turn green, birds would be chattering from every branch and wire. Nature, at least, would be alive. But right then, everything seemed dead. The three robins looked like a forlorn trio of mourners, discouraged by the weather, dismayed at the meager turnout, and perhaps even wondering if they were at the right funeral.

Nothing else moved. Nothing grew. Without cows, the barn was a cold, damp shell. Hidden in mud, the roots were quickening, but above ground no human eye was waiting, yearning for the first small shoot of green. Above ground, everything was still.

Vincie knew then, as deep down as if she were looking at his cold body and stiffened face, that her father was dead. She felt the tears start up in her eyes and walked away by herself toward the barns. She walked through the milkroom, bare, damp concrete stripped of equipment, disconnected electric wires and water pipes dangling from the walls. She continued into the cow area, the bottom floor of the old barn. This area had always been warm in winter, full of smells, with half a dozen cats perched on window sills and railings. Now it was clean, odorless and tidy. The manure and shavings had been scraped up and hauled away. The feed bunks were empty and swept. The cats must have been taken somewhere, she didn't know where. Darrell was keeping the dogs, but he couldn't keep half a dozen barn cats.

She stood alone at one end of the barn, weeping. Gifford had guessed, correctly, that she did not want his comfort and had not followed her into the barn. After a time, when all the tears were wrung out of her, she went back outside to join him.

They found the back door of the house locked, and that jarred her almost as much as the stillness. She did have a key with her, but only because Gifford had had the forethought to suggest she hunt down and bring the copy she kept in a desk drawer. This was the first time she had ever used it. A dairy was never empty of people for more than a few hours, and there had never been a need to lock the door.

Unlike the barn, the house was warm, the furnace set for sixty-five as it would have been when Vernon was there. The refrigerator hummed, the clock showed the right time, Vernon's jacket still hung on a hook beside the door. Nothing had been touched, it seemed, beyond what was required to remove the body and clean up the mess and perhaps look for a suicide note.

Vincie expected to find the house in good order. When it came to inanimate objects, her father had been systematic in his habits. Everything had a place and a use. Anything that didn't have a use, he got rid of. In this regard, he departed from local farming tradition, which held that just about anything might turn out to have a use someday so nothing should ever be thrown away. Most farmers had enough ingenuity with hacksaws, welders and wrenches to prove the tradition right every once in a while. When a machine broke, they would rummage through their collection of rusty metal until they found a piece that could be hammered or cajoled into replacing the broken part. They would then return to work with renewed faith in the value of holding on to things.

Vernon had as much ingenuity as his neighbors, but he couldn't stand the mess. The sight of metal rusting or wood rotting frayed his nerves, so he refused to keep any object he couldn't maintain properly. He was a perfectionist, and his neighbors might have said that was why he had gone broke while they were still in business with their weeds and sagging fences and heaps of old rusty machinery.

Competing against the richer soil, easier terrain and gentler climate of other regions, farmers here felt they could not afford the time to keep weeds clipped and the money to keep barns freshly painted. The steep hillsides and narrow valleys, the soil, either stony or sandy or dense clay and all of it acid, the rain that fell in midsummer when they needed sun to dry the hay and in midwinter when it turned fields of snow into sheets of plant-smothering ice, all these things together bred an attitude that getting by was as much as a person could expect.

Sometimes it came to a choice between sentiment and survival. A favorite cow could not be kept on into a peaceful retirement after her milk gave out. The feed cost too much. She would be shipped off with the others to slaughter, because the difference between a few hundred dollars spent on feed and a few hundred dollars earned by the salvage of her carcass might be the difference between surviving and not.

On the days when Vernon called a trucker to haul some of his cows away, he became morose and unapproachable. As a child, Vincie simply stayed out of his way. Only when she was older could she understand that the mood arose from his hatred of the decision he had had to make. When she was older, he could explain all the reasons to her. The decision was just his share of the inexorable equation of a finite planet. For every living thing born, some other living thing must die to make room for it. If one species gained a member, a human, a cockroach, a stalk of wheat, then some other species somewhere must have lost one, a wolf, a clump of prairie grass, a caterpillar. He saw each piece of existence as part of a larger whole, his family as part of a culture, his farm as part of an economy, his land and livestock as part of nature, and all of them part of a vast mysterious creation. Possibly his farm would have survived better if he had been less fascinated by large mysteries and more fascinated by the small facts of income and expense.

Vincie wandered from room to room, and for these first moments, she was as circumspect as the police had been, not rummaging or prying. It was all very familiar, the furniture, pictures and wallpaper almost the same as when she was young. The sound of each light switch and doorlatch was recognizable to her blindfolded. She caught faint whiffs of remembered smells, old wood, cow manure, stored apples, dogs and wood smoke.

Vernon had not lived as a widower gone to seed. Things were clean and in their places, as Phoebe had arranged them years before. If anything, the house seemed almost too perfectly neat and unchanged, as if he had withdrawn himself to live in the kitchen and tended the rest of the house like a museum curator, dusting the knickknacks and straightening the pictures.

Curious, Vincie opened a bureau drawer in her old bedroom. It was empty. She opened the other drawers and found them empty, too. The closet, the bedside table, the desk, all were empty. Everything visible, the lamp, the pictures, the embroidered bureau scarf, the two porcelain chickadees and vase of dried flowers, these were in their places. Everything ever stored or abandoned in drawers and closets was gone. She found the same in her brothers' rooms and in the old spare room. Everything visible was unchanged. Everything out of sight was empty and clean.

In her parents' room she found clothes and a few photographs and papers, but surprisingly little else. The clothes were Vernon's and there weren't many of them. Phoebe's things were gone, except for the letters and photographs, and all the small pretty objects with which she had made each room cheerful, paintings, dried flowers, wood carvings, embroidery, lacquer boxes, porcelain figurines. She had loved anything delicate or fanciful. She collected bits of color, fragility and whimsy, and scattered them around her house, like so many tropical butterflies scattered among the massive austerity of the larger surroundings, the granite hills, the slow-growing forests of maple and oak, the gray damp climate and the dignified white clapboard architecture.

For a moment, Vincie felt it as callousness that her father had disposed of her mother's everyday belongings. So matter of fact he was, just as he had been when a cow died unexpectedly, draining the blood and calling a butcher so that the meat would not go to waste.

Then, as she walked back through the bedrooms and looked at the pretty objects he had kept, dusted and tidy and cheerfully displayed, she began to feel what Vernon must have felt, that clothes, books and toilet articles were as impermanent as her mother's body. He had kept what he could of Phoebe's soul, her brightness, liveliness and charm, but he had not tried to embalm the mundane details of shared daily life. If anything, he must have felt that clearing away those details would leave a closer companionship with her spirit.

Vincie often wished she had inherited her father's ability to shed details. She felt her own life to be a conglomeration of details, a swarm of gnats, trivial but insistent—errands, appointments and phone calls; fitful attempts at one career and then another; a multitude of acquaintanceships that never matured into friendships; a kaleidoscope of ideas and beliefs that never resolved themselves into a coherent whole. The gnats nibbled and buzzed and she longed for the gale that would sweep them away and sweep her into motion in some definite direction.

"What will you do with all this stuff?" Gifford asked. "We certainly don't want it in our apartment."

He was holding up a ceramic bird, with the analytical attitude of a biologist holding up a specimen insect.

"I suppose some people like this sort of thing," he added. "But it doesn't exactly fit with our taste."

"I don't know. I've hardly begun to think…" Vincie said.

"Perhaps Georgeanne will want some of it."

"Perhaps."

She could not yet bring herself to confess to Gifford that she too might want some of it. Of course Georgeanne would want some of it, Georgeanne who taught high school accounting and probably wore polyester. But so might Vincie, Vincie who was halfway towards a Ph.D. in English literature, who wore natural fibers, and who knew that her mother's collection did not express sophistication of taste. Anything Vincie did take would either have to be stored in a drawer or else pointed out and mocked as a family artifact to every guest who came into their apartment, so that no one would ever think they had chosen it for themselves.

Up to now, her farm background had been assimilated into their lifestyle without disharmony. Properly presented, it even had a certain chic, a spice of the exotic. When he talked about it, Gifford somehow managed to imply that she had grown up in a mountain wilderness where rugged men and women battled nature at its most elemental. He called forth images of blizzards, floods, predators, and bare-chested men with scythes and pitchforks sweating in the summer sun. Like a conjurer, he made manure, bank loans, herbicides, and ruinously expensive modern machinery vanish, leaving behind an image of simplicity and struggle that matched their acquaintances' daydreams of owning a summer place in the country. If she started bringing home cheap ceramic bluebirds and a glass-enclosed diorama of deer in a meadow, the whole conjuring trick might unravel. The manure and herbicides might re-materialize, and Vincie herself might suddenly appear before their friends in greasy coveralls and malodorous boots, or worse yet, dressed in a polyester pantsuit and holding a tray of hors d'ouevres manufactured from Ritz crackers, Velveeta cheese and canned pimentos. Her family and the farm were fine, as long as they stayed in soft focus, somewhere in the distance.

The trouble was, she wanted to keep some of the ceramic birds. The more she imagined Gifford's disdainful reaction, the more she wanted them. The birds had begun as a childhood joke among Phoebe's sisters, and then became a game that went on for nearly fifty years. When her sisters learned that a phoebe was a kind of bird, they started giving her birds for every birthday. At first, the birds came in all forms, from Audubon prints and bracelet charms to wooden duck decoys. Over time, the small ceramic ones came to predominate. They were cheap and easy to find in gift shops. The game was passed down to Phoebe's children and it became a friendly competition among them, to see who could find something new or exotic. Though they tried, none of them ever found an actual phoebe. The bird was too gray and inconspicuous to become the model for a bright china trinket. Perhaps they didn't really want to find a phoebe, because then the game might have ended.

Now, looking objectively, Vincie could recognize that the birds were cheap, tacky, mass-produced knickknacks. At the same time, she was fond of them, because her mother had been fond of them. The game had been a ritual of affection, and although Phoebe had poked fun at herself about the birds, she would have been disappointed if no one had remembered to find her a new one on her birthday.

Gifford had only one point of view on the subject, the objective one. He did not want his apartment cluttered with ugly knickknacks that would require an explanation to every guest to forestall misinterpretation.

"Now this, on the other hand, is nice," he said.

He was opening the drawers of Phoebe's desk. The desk was made of rosewood, deep blood red, finely crafted. It was the only true antique in the house and probably the only object of substantial monetary value. Phoebe's parents, who had lived in a substantial house in a substantial Connecticut suburb, had given it to her as a wedding present. At the time of her wedding, Vernon still worked at a substantial Connecticut engineering firm, and her parents assumed he would someday own a house proportional to the desk.

Barely a year later, Vernon's father suffered a paralyzing stroke. Vernon abandoned his engineering career, and he and Phoebe moved north to take on the farm. The desk and all their other belongings were squeezed into the bedroom that later became Vincie's. For two years, they lived in that room and Phoebe helped her mother-in-law look after Vernon's father, who could do very little for himself. When the old man died, she and Vernon expected that Vernon's mother would go on living with them. Phoebe was pregnant by then, and they thought his mother would want to be near her new grandchild.

Instead, old Mrs. Nowle announced one day that she was done with looking after helpless creatures, whether they be infants, old people, calves, cows or kittens. She said she was too old and tired herself, and she meant to go live in a rented cottage in the middle of Worthing village, where she would have neighbors to talk to and all of her business within walking distance. The moment she moved, she became a lot less old and tired, and before long she went to work part-time at the general store. She wasn't actually that old, only fifty-eight, and she went on working at the store for another nineteen years, until the winter she broke her hip. Finding herself bedridden and likely to be on a downhill slide to the end of her life, she told her family she meant to catch pneumonia and die. It seemed that whatever she made up her mind to do, she did, because two weeks later, in defiance of antibiotics and the efforts and predictions of the doctors, she was dead of pneumonia.

Vincie had known Granny Nowle as a steely, blunt old woman

who liked her grandchildren well enough, but was determined not to like them more than they deserved and certainly not to fall into the doting absurdity of other grandparents. Phoebe's parents, the Holdreths, had more than made up for Granny Nowle's refusal to dote. Perhaps because they saw these grandchildren much less than the ones still in Connecticut, or perhaps because they viewed them as impoverished rural ragamuffins, their rare visits were always accompanied by showers of presents and effusions of admiration for every trivial accomplishment. They also managed to convey their opinion that Vernon had selfishly and irresponsibly sacrificed his children's future by returning to the farm, thereby depriving them of the good schools, educated neighbors and cultural advantages that Connecticut had to offer.

When the time came, they backed up their opinions with money, helping to pay for all three children to attend the state university. They never gave Phoebe and Vernon another gift like the desk, however. After one Christmas visit to the farm, their gifts ran heavily in the direction of long underwear and wool sweaters, or else fresh fruit, classic works of literature, Darjeeling tea, and other basic necessities they believed must be unavailable so far from New York City.

As a child, Vincie had known how to feel about Granny Nowle. She was awed, and eager to merit Granny's good opinion. About the Holdreths, she was confused. She did not know how to take these genial people, who came for a week every couple of years, who dressed beautifully, brought lavish gifts, and conversed easily and graciously on any topic for any amount of time, regardless of whether the other person had anything to say in reply. As a grandchild, she was bathed in a warmth of uncritical and often-stated approval, and yet she sometimes doubted whether these grandparents would recognize her in the middle of a crowd if they weren't expecting to see her. Their approval seemed to have nothing to do with her, only with her genealogy.

"Are your brothers likely to want the desk?" Gifford asked. He had sat down and was testing the height of the writing surface. "I can imagine writing a book at this desk. It has a history. People have sat at this desk, thinking, and their thoughts might pass down into my thoughts. Did your mother ever use it for writing?"

"She never had time to use it for anything, except doing the accounts for the farm. If her thoughts pass down into yours, then you will be seeing long columns of numbers that mostly add up to bad news. Any other kind of thoughts will have to come from the people who owned it before her."

"That's good enough," he said. "The poets I write about predate your mother, too."

"Don't assume we can have it. We have to divide things fairly and it's far more valuable than anything else in the house."

"As far as I'm concerned, your brothers can take everything else, if we can have the desk. It's the only thing worth having."

"Until I talk to them, I don't know what they'll want."

In fact, she had a good guess, but she didn't want to get embroiled in a debate with Gifford until she had more than a guess. Chad, she thought, would be indifferent, as glad to have cash as momentos. Darrell would want the desk, not because it was valuable, or skillfully crafted, or full of history, but simply because it was Phoebe's.

Darrell had worshipped his mother, with the mute unswerving devotion of the unremarkable child, the one who stays unnoticed in the background, the one who rarely gets petted, rarely needs scolding, whose easy disposition gets taken for granted and whose true thoughts rarely get spoken because no one thinks to ask for them. When Phoebe was killed, he had helped make arrangements, helped straighten out business affairs, but remained silent, withdrawn into a stoicism that was impenetrable. Neighbors commented on how well he was taking it and how his grieving family must be grateful to lean on his strength. To Vincie he seemed like someone who had simply unplugged every nerve in his body, because the pain was too great.

"I suppose Darrell will want it," Gifford said, almost as if he had read her thoughts. "Since he adored your mother so. He'll make it into a shrine to her memory. He'll burn votive candles every day and the dripping wax will mar this exquisite finish. However, if Darrell wants it, he shall have it. He has exhibited a greater sense of filial duty than either you or Chad. My book can find inspiration elsewhere."

"How very generous of you," said Vincie. "I'm going back downstairs to look in Dad's files." She hoped he would not follow her. His manner was getting on her nerves today. She did not want to be prodded into a duel of sarcasm any more than she had wanted to argue about the desk.

The farm had often been the scene of quarrels in the past. Gifford felt out of place there. His wit was not understood, and his learning was not fully respected. He despised her parents' lack of sophistication and yet he cared what they thought of him. Since he couldn't make them think as well of him as he wanted, he grew defensive, pompous and irritable.

Vincie, for her part, became even more vacillating than usual, which compounded Gifford's irritation. At all times she felt herself to be divided between two contradictory selves, but here on the farm, the division widened to a chasm. At home, she put aside the half still tied to her past. She became clever, educated and urban, the professor's wife. Her speech became quick and sprightly, matching her husband's. Her conversation darted back and forth among the topics of the day, dropping baubles of wit and observation, even as her physical self was darting about, refilling glasses and offering finger foods to their guests.

In her parents' house, the past resurfaced. Something slow and serious emerged in her. She ceased to sparkle and became meditative. Her thoughts were drawn toward the physical world, toward rocks and trees and tractors, and away from the intricate constructions of speculative dinner conversation. Her words were spoken too earnestly, out of belief or feeling, and not for the sake of discussion.

The farm girl reappeared, but could not entirely displace the professor's wife, so she flipped back and forth between the two, like a double-image hologram seen first from one angle, then from the other. Gifford never knew which angle to expect at any given moment. Although he enjoyed keeping other people off-balance, he did not like to feel off-balance himself. So he grew irritable and quarreled with her, particularly when he encountered the farm girl he wished she would outgrow.

Vincie had barely begun looking through the file cabinets beside her father's desk when Gifford came down the stairs after her and hovered.

"It's all accounts and milk records," she said. "I don't think any of it would interest you."

"There's nothing to interest me in the rest of the house either. At least here I have your company."

Vincie sighed. "In that case, why don't you look through those and see if there is anything important." She pointed to a stack of file folders.

"I wouldn't be able to make sense of it," he said. "You know I know less than nothing about milk records." He sat down in a chair, stretched out his legs, and leaned his head back against the wall, preparing to watch Vincie work.

Vincie clenched her teeth and went back to leafing through papers. She couldn't concentrate, not with Gifford's gaze fixed on every move she made, accusing her of boring him.

"There are some magazines in the living room," she said.

"What, *Farmer's Monthly* and *The Dairy Times*? They'd be as amusing as those files."

"More likely *National Geographic* and *Time*," she said. "Just pretend you're at the dentist's office."

They were saved from an escalation of bickering by the sound of a car, slewing down the muddy driveway and skidding to a stop just short of the lawn. The car was expensive, fast and red, like Gifford's BMW, but it was a low-slung two-seater, liberated from the BMW's last vestiges of practicality such as trunk and back seat. Vincie was not enough of an enthusiast to recognize the make. Gifford enlightened her. "RX-7. Chad, I presume."

In reply, a slender blond figure, coatless, hopped out of the car and loped through the drizzle to the back door. He burst into the kitchen, and immediately, by some property peculiar to Chad, the house felt inhabited. The walls no longer gave off hollow echoes. The hum of the refrigerator sounded purposeful, as if now there were food inside it to be kept cold.

"Vincie! I'm so glad you're here." He enveloped her in a hug. "Poor Dad," he added, and the two words vibrated with a complex of emotions. Vincie felt tears start in her eyes and hid her face against his shoulder.

He stood holding her until her weeping stopped, then turned to shake hands with Gifford. His hello to his brother-in-law was friendly, but impersonal. Before she and Gifford became engaged, Chad had remarked to her that her new boyfriend was like a stuffed moose in the living room, drawing everyone's attention, provoking exclamations of awe, but giving off no warmth. Once they married, Chad kept any further comments to himself. Gifford became a rarity in Chad's life, one of the very few people he did not bother to charm.

"How long have you been here? Have you had anything to eat?" Chad asked. "I'm starved. All I've had today is coffee. I drove straight up." He was opening cupboards, pulling out crackers and peanut butter, as he would have done if his parents were alive.

Vincie remembered the last time all of them had gathered for Christmas, five or six years ago. Chad had been the last to arrive. He had burst into the kitchen, just as he did today. He had given everyone a quick hug and then begun rummaging through the cupboards for a snack, as if he were still a teenager coming home ravenous at the end of the school day. In anyone else, his behavior would have been rudeness. In Chad, it became a gesture of conviviality, a sweeping aside of awkwardness and formality, a blithe disregard for the separations of time and distance. Chad could do anything and make it seem right. In one minute, with one gesture, the family was together and unchanged.

"Seen Darrell?" he asked through a mouthful of crackers.

"Not yet. He'll be here around four."

"He still has to teach, then."

She nodded. "His biology classes are expecting a major fruit fly hatch. That's all he told me. He'd have to teach anyway, but it seems this is their big springtime lab experiment and the kids are all excited."

"Probably it's Darrell who's excited," said Chad. "He's been teaching that experiment for eight years now and it still tickles him to see a quarter of the hatch come out white-eyed recessives. But I suppose he won't be in the mood to enjoy it this year."

"No."

"He takes things so damned hard. Doesn't say a word, just eats away at himself. I wish he'd cut loose sometime, scream and yell like the rest of us. Howl at the moon. Something. It must have cut the heart out of him when Mom died, but there he was, talking to the lawyers so that Dad wouldn't have to. Probably he's carrying on with his teaching the same way. Probably the kids can't tell there's anything wrong. Though they must have read about it in the paper. What do the papers say, by the way?"

"Just that it was suicide. Plus quite a lot about what a fine person Dad was."

"Ah, yes, one of the exemplary citizens of Worthing. Even more exemplary now that he's dead. People are hypocrites. They all thought Dad was eccentric, but I'll bet the newspaper doesn't say that. Anyhow, every farmer in the state is a kind of hero these days. Struggling against the odds to keep Vermont beautiful and pastoral for the tourists. When the last farmer gives up and sells out, they'll probably make a memorial with an eternal flame, the tomb of the unknown farmer. 'We'll worship you and praise you, but Wisconsin milk is a nickel cheaper so that's what we're buying.' I'm not surprised Dad gave up. I'm maybe more surprised he kept on as long as he did. He was stubborn enough, I guess. Stubborn and foolish."

Chad was talking rapidly, between mouthfuls, not waiting for a reply or even a sign that the others were listening. He was wound up as tight as Vincie had ever seen him, and the edge of bitterness in his voice was not like him.

"The farm wasn't completely broke . . ." Vincie began.

Chad cut her off with a laugh. "That's like saying someone isn't completely insane, or completely ugly, or completely despicable. Not much comfort. It was broke enough. Dad looked after his cows a lot better than he did his bank balance. He always wanted to do things the way he thought was right, and a person can't afford to do that these days. Not if he wants to stay in business. The competition is too tough. Dad finally recognized reality and he didn't like it, so he kissed it good-bye. He was too high-principled for this world. I hope he's found one that suits him now, though I haven't much faith. I don't know why people always assume god must have done a better job designing heaven than he did designing earth. What do you think, Vincie, is Dad in a better place?"

"He wouldn't have expected to be."

"That's true, he wouldn't have. He thought earth was about as good as could be expected, apart from a few mistakes when it came to humankind. His idea of heaven would be earth without the people."

"He'd make an exception for you, Chad," Gifford interjected.

"No, he'd have been worried that one exception would lead to another and then another, and pretty soon there would be five billion of us. He'd want just the earth, and him turned into an old elm tree in the middle of a field with cows in his shade."

"Without people, who would keep the cows milked?" Gifford asked, insisting on reality.

"Their calves would," Chad said.

Suddenly the spring inside had unwound and he sat down, not in one of the chairs beside the kitchen table, but on a stool in the corner near the telephone. From the moment he arrived, he had kept a space between himself and the table, as if he could see Vernon's body still slumped over it. Vincie had done the same, without thinking. The two of them had circled at a distance, planets held in orbit by an invisible body.

She wondered if people did indeed go to whatever heaven they had envisioned for themselves. Was Chad right about their father? She felt a shiver run down her back. Instead of floating off in an abstract ether, weightless above the clouds, Vernon might be right here, his spirit rising with the rising sap in the ancient elm that stood alone in the near meadow. He might be stretching himself out through every limb and twig, feeling his new shape. He might already be wondering whether the other half of the bargain would be kept, whether cows would someday return to lie in the grass above his roots.

She shook off the thought and returned to business. "What do you think we should do for the funeral?"

Chad stirred himself, too. "I think Dad will hate it, whatever we do, so it doesn't matter. We had just as well please the neighbors, since we can't please him."

"The Congregational Church, then. That's what Darrell suggested. He was afraid you might object."

"Me? Good lord, no. I'm all for the proprieties, for everyone but me. I will even wear a dark suit and say something appropriate, since it's only for an hour. But don't expect too much more from me." He stood up. "I think I'll go look around the house. This room is giving me the creeps all of a sudden."

When he had gone upstairs, Gifford pointedly pulled out a chair and sat down at the table. "The superstition has to stop somewhere," he said. "Vernon is dead and I'm quite sure he didn't leave his ghost behind. It's a perfectly good table, though not a style to suit our apartment. And speaking of our apartment, why don't you go up and discuss the desk with Chad. If he doesn't want it, perhaps you and Darrell could flip a coin."

"I wish you would forget about the desk," Vincie said. "You're acting like a vulture."

"Vultures perform a necessary function. They clean up the mortal remains. Humans leave a lot more remains than other creatures do, so it is to be expected that they attract a larger crowd of vultures. The only difference between me and all the others is that I'm honest about being one."

"It's true, you never shrink from being honest," Vincie said. She left him sitting, making his statement in a chair that might have held a dead body.

4

SHE FOUND CHAD in his old room. He was wandering about, aimlessly picking up objects and staring at them. She picked up the bird he had just put down and remarked, "Another crow. Mom must have been given two dozen crows over the years."

"Hm?" Chad looked mystified, as if she had interrupted a daydream and he had heard only the last of what she said.

"The bird you were looking at," Vincie said. "One of Mom's multitude of crows."

"Was it a crow? I must not have been paying attention. I was thinking how the house feels the way it did when Dad was living here by himself. He was never completely here. He ate and slept here, but his mind was somewhere else. Do you know what I mean? When Mom was alive, you didn't notice. She talked and laughed and filled up the space and you didn't notice that Dad was somewhere far away. I always wondered what he was thinking about. I thought it must be something very grand and lofty. Every once in a while he would let a little piece out, especially when he thought my behavior needed correction. The clouds would part, and a ray of enlightenment would be beamed down on me. Remember when I took that raft out into the pond and dropped one of the cats into the water?"

"You said you wanted to see how far it could swim."

"I wouldn't have let it drown," he said. "But by the time Dad was done talking to me, I thought I was lucky not to be turned into a stone and dropped into the middle of the pond myself. From his tone of voice, he could have been explaining how to start the lawnmower, but he made me feel like a worm."

"He scolded you? Darrell and I always thought you were the favored child and never got punished, no matter what you did."

"He didn't scold, exactly. He explained. But the sum of the explanation was that the universe had a large and beautiful order, and I was a piece of sand messing up the gears. He never did his explaining when you and Darrell were around. He didn't believe in public humiliation. That would teach us to be shamed by what other people thought. He wanted us to be shamed by the pure awfulness of what we'd done. For years, I thought you and Darrell never got punished, and I was the only one. But then Darrell told me about something he'd done that Dad had had to 'explain' to him. After that I wasn't scared by anything Dad said. I could see right through it. He wasn't the voice of the universe. He was just a parent trying to make his kid behave. I was no different from the kids at school whose parents took a belt to them or gave them extra chores, except that I was getting off easier than they were. I always looked penitent, so that Dad would think I cared, but I didn't."

"I never got over caring," Vincie said. "I lived in dread that something I did would turn out to be a terrible wrong."

"Poor old Vincie. No wonder you were such a good girl. You were very annoying that way, leaping up to help with the dishes before Mom even asked. I thought kids should stick together, but you acted like a third parent, being so good and grown-up and leaving Darrell and me to be the troublesome ones."

"Was that how it seemed? I thought you two had it easy. You were never expected to help with the dishes. That was a girl's job, and there never seemed to be any boys' jobs, not until you were old enough to help on the farm. And I had to do that, too. And on top of that I had to look out that neither of you came to grief. When you were about four, I yanked you away from the moving chain of the gutter cleaner and afterwards I was at least as much relieved

38

that I hadn't blown it as I was that you hadn't been mangled. I thought if anything ever happened to one of you, I would be in disgrace forever. Do you remember that time with the gutter cleaner?"

He shook his head. "I do remember that you were the ogre who was always spoiling our fun. One time, you caught Pete Warrender showing Darrell and me how to dissect baby mice with a utility knife. You told us Dad would take the knife and dissect all three of us if we didn't stop."

"Did I really say that?"

"That's what I remember. You were bossy."

"I remember the mice," she said. "They were pink with no hair, and what you were doing to them was in no way scientific. I don't remember threatening that you'd be dissected yourself if you didn't stop."

"You definitely did. You also said that when Dad was done, he would fry up our hearts and livers and feed them to Sparky."

"You're making that up. I never would have said something that gruesome."

"You'd be surprised. You were quite a little despot, and very imaginative, once you got started. I tried to remember awful things you had said, so that I could use them myself when I got into fights on the playground."

He grinned at her then. His brown eyes were sparkling, teasing, and suddenly she couldn't be sure whether or not she had threatened to fry up his liver and feed it to the dog.

As a man, Chad was still ethereally beautiful. Standing in line at the bank, he had been offered a job as a model by the woman behind him, a serious offer as it turned out, from the owner of a reputable agency. He had declined, but his looks had served him equally well in the jobs he did take, in public relations and marketing. At different times, he had worked for a firm of architects, a publisher, a cosmetics manufacturer, and a startup company in waste disposal technology. He said himself that it didn't matter what company he worked for. He could promote anything. People leapt to gobble up whatever he had to offer, like fish going after a lure. He now worked as an independent marketing consultant, and since the first thing he had to sell was himself, he was extremely successful.

He had squired an array of women, of no consistent type, some beautiful, some clever, some motherly, some neurotic, some practical or artistic or damp-eyed and clinging. The only constants were the desperation with which they fell in love with him, and his haste to be rid of them once they did.

"I wish I could fall in love with someone," he had said to Vincie once, almost wistfully. "With these women, it's like trying to fall in love with a welcome mat. There's no spice in them."

Even the ones who played hard to get were too obvious in their maneuvers. They did not offer spice, only calculation. He had not yet come close to getting married. His longest involvement lasted two years, with a woman named Roxie who was almost unconventional enough to intrigue him. She made the mistake of seeking out people who shared her unconventionality. She joined a few New Age groups, and her oddities began to be predictable. Chad moved on.

When Vincie thought of her youngest brother, she thought of flames or breaking waves. Even when he stayed in one place, he did not know how to be still. Darrell could be still. He could be as calm and opaque as a sheltered pond, which shows you nothing except a reflection of yourself. Chad's very essence was to be changeable, a mesmerizing flame that draws the viewer deeper and deeper into self-forgetfulness.

"I'm not completely sorry he's dead," Chad said abruptly. He had moved to the window and was looking out across the driveway toward the near meadow, the one with the single elm. "Maybe now I'll stop feeling so small. I've always felt tiny, tagging along behind. As though Dad were the definition of a man, and I could never be that. I think I would rather have been the son of the town drunk, so people wouldn't always be measuring me to see if I was turning out as fine a man as Vernon Nowle."

"Instead they would be watching every drink you took, to see if you were going to turn out to be as no-good as him," Vincie said. "You'd be compared, no matter who your father was."

"But I might have come out better in the comparison. How could anyone ever surpass Dad when he had left everything base and human behind? He had conquered every low human instinct and locked it away in a dungeon."

"How can you know that?"

"Did you ever see him do something mean?"

Vincie was stopped, thinking about his question. She turned over one memory after another, looking for some creature of the dark and damp in her father's history.

"Not mean," she said. "Not low or petty. But he might have failed in other ways. He might have wished to be things he wasn't, more loving…" Even though Vernon was dead, Chad's attitude felt like a quarrel between them and she wanted to patch it up. But Chad did not want it patched up. He wanted his father buried six feet down, where he could no longer cast any shadows.

"It's easy, being a girl," Chad said. "No one expects you to live up to your father. No one expects much of anything from you. You're free to be whatever you want."

Free to be nothing at all, Vincie thought.

"Look at Darrell, the poor beast. He's harnessed up and well on his way to becoming Dad. I'll bet if you and I agreed to keep this place, he'd move out here and try to farm it. When he was in high school, he wanted to be a biochemist. He had some idea about making strains of ruminant bacteria that could live in a tank instead of in a cow's stomach, and digest plant waste into fuel. Probably the idea was crazy, but that was what he wanted to do. Instead, he came back to Worthing to teach bored teenagers about fruit fly genetics and help Dad chop corn."

"What does that decision have to do with living up to Dad? Being a scientist would have fulfilled any obligation to be admirable," Vincie said.

"Nothing could ever be as admirable as Dad himself. That's the whole point. It was that giving up of ambition that was the pin-

41

nacle of spiritual perfection. Becoming president would just be the pinnacle of petty striving. No, it was Vernon or nothing. So Darrell has become Vernon and I've become nothing. I'm not sure which of us is more pathetic. All I know is that neither of us can define an existence without using him as our reference."

"You hardly seem pathetic, Chad. You give up more income taking a day off than I could earn in a month."

"Ah, but Dad didn't care about money. It was an unpleasant necessity, like shitting. Once you had enough, having more just added a burden to the plumbing of the cosmos. He would see me as a septic system disaster."

"Why does it matter what he thought?"

"I've spent my whole life trying to utter that question with genuine defiance. I don't know why it matters, but it does. I have everything, but I am nothing, and that nothing is somehow connected to Dad." He shook himself, visibly. "Maybe now that he's dead, I won't feel him looming over me, sitting in judgment."

Vincie looked out the window where he was looking, towards the elm. The shrouds of vapor hung so low, they veiled its topmost branches. From the massive trunk, the bare limbs fanned upward, a finer and finer web of gray that finally vanished into the softer gray of the mist.

The hills were gone, invisible behind the clouds. The eye reached only to the far edge of the meadow before all shapes blurred and vanished. The meadow could be anywhere; the landscape around it could be anything. The visible had narrowed to a patch of muddy ground, cocooned in clouds. If the sky sank any lower, they would be breathing water, not air. It seemed the clouds might easily close down to the ground, swallow up the last trace of color, and envelop them in suffocating gray.

Phoebe had fretted at this time of year, impatient for the first sight of her crocuses, impatient to dig in the garden, weary of cold and mud. Every day she went out to clear away wintertime mulch and probe the soil to test the progress of the thaw. She rejoiced at the sight of robins, then worried that they had come too early and would starve. She fussed over seedlings in the living room window. Nothing much could be done outdoors, except maple sugaring, and Phoebe thought sugaring had mostly been invented to keep people too busy to go crazy during the long, slow weeks of thaw. Since she and Vernon did not make sugar, she fretted instead. Her idea of seasons had been imprinted further south, near the ocean, and the imprint called for daffodils to bloom at a time when the ground around her was still buckling and heaving itself out of ice into mud.

Vernon had not minded this season, a fact which Chad might have taken as added proof that he had shed all ordinary human frailties. Seeing order all around him, he saw it in this grim, gray season as well. It was an enforced pause, a moment sitting down before launching forth. It was also a time to attend to the thriving fungoid growth of paperwork that now attached to farming as it did to every business. During the day, between milkings, he would lay out the accumulated stacks of paper and settle at his desk to work, without any visible sign of bad humor.

At his death, it seemed, he had been in the midst of this annual task or nearly through it. In her quick scan of his desk, Vincie had found everything in order—a copy of his tax return, already filed; numerous other forms, all routine, concerned with loans, health inspections, soil conservation cost-sharing, herd improvement statistics. Everything past its deadline was a copy, filled out and marked "Original sent." On the top of the stack were papers related to his negotiation with the land trust. These, too, were in order, though not finalized. How characteristic, she thought, that nothing was in disarray or postponed. How characteristic, too, that he took advantage of the constraints of the season to discipline himself to this task, which he could not have enjoyed. The only satisfaction it offered was that of being done with it.

Except that he had not been done with it, she thought. The land trust papers lay there, half complete, phrased in intentions and proposals rather than deeds. They were a job half-finished, left behind to torment Vernon's spirit as any half-finished job would have done when he was alive.

"Why do you think he did it?" she asked.

Chad was still standing near her, gazing out the window in a revery.

"Because he had become an irrelevance," he said, immediately but dreamily, as if her question had fallen directly into what he was already thinking about. "A dinosaur, if you like. Civilization had moved on and left him behind, and he knew it. We even talked about it…" He stopped. "Well, I talked about it and he didn't disagree. I told him that someday there will be three kinds of farmers in this country and his kind isn't one of them. There will be the employee, who works a forty-hour week and runs a thousand nameless cows through the milking parlor on his shift. There will be the modern-day sharecropper, who leases land from the corporations rich enough to own it and sells his crops to other corporations who control the price and works a slave's hours in the illusion that he is still an independent family farmer. And there will be the hobbyist, who has money from somewhere else and buys a farm because it's a nice lifestyle as long as you don't have to depend on it for a living. Dad didn't fit the new picture. He wanted the world to be a place where you did your work and the money took care of itself. His whole way of seeing things was outmoded."

"But his farm was as modern as any in the state," she pointed out. "He kept up with new technology."

"That's just it."

"Your logic is not obvious. Why do you say 'that's just it?'"

"It was his effort to keep up with the times that made him realize he was a dinosaur. He tried to keep the farm in step with the times, and that made the farm get out of step with himself. He was trying to exist in a state of contradiction. The human race is evolving into something new, and he was becoming one of its humanoid ancestors, slated for extinction. He decided to hurry the process along, and leave his land behind, preserved like a specimen in amber. And the worst of it was, he wouldn't even resent it or rail at fate, the way any normal person would. He just shrugged and said that's how things are and made his exit."

"Do you really think someone would kill himself for such an abstract reason?"

"It didn't feel abstract to him. He was a man with one foot on the train and the other still on the ground. Being pulled in two doesn't feel abstract."

Vincie still resisted his theory. It offered enough reason to abandon the farm, probably, but to abandon life?

She heard voices, faintly, coming from the kitchen below. Gifford's she could recognize by the distinctness of pronunciation, though the words could not be distinguished. Here and there came a pause, and a word or two, barely audible, in reply. She had not heard Darrell's truck drive in, but she knew it was him.

In unspoken agreement, she and Chad stayed were they were, listening to the voices in the kitchen and waiting to see if Darrell would come up the stairs to find them. Gifford had left her alone all this time to talk with Chad. When he wished, he was capable of great tact, and she hoped it would last a few minutes longer. For a few minutes, at least, Vernon's death would belong to the three of them, the Nowle children. They could talk with their own words, or not at all if they chose. With Gifford in the room, they would become something different, adults with separate lives speaking a public language.

She and Chad waited. They listened to Gifford talking, being friendly and gracious. In the right mood, he could walk into a room full of strangers and find something to say to every one of them. They heard pauses in reply. Finally, Gifford gave up. "The others are upstairs," he said, loudly enough for them to hear.

They heard Darrell start up the stairs. He had taken off his boots, and his steps were soft, stockinged thumps, as purposeful but unhurried as the tread of a cow on the way to her usual stanchion. Chad and Vincie looked at each other, and despite the circumstances, could not help smiling. Their parents were dead, their three lives had diverged, but Darrell still walked like a cow with a goal but no deadline.

"Hello," Darrell said. He had stopped just inside the doorway. His hands were jammed in his pockets, and his head was cocked sideways and down, so that he looked at them from under his eyebrows and his smile was directed towards a spot on the floor somewhere to their left.

Vincie immediately went over and gave him a hug, which he returned, awkwardly, with one arm. To smooth over the awkwardness, she rushed into talk. She told him about the drive, asked how Georgeanne and the kids were doing, said she supposed they must be growing like weeds, the kids, not Georgeanne, though probably he didn't notice since he saw them every day. After a couple of minutes, in which he only smiled and said he guessed so, she wound down and stopped.

"So, did your fruit flies hatch out okay?" Chad greeted him.

"'Yuh." He said it the way his neighbors would. The back of his throat opened and closed for an instant and let out a small puff of air, half of which went into his nasal passages because his lips weren't open wide enough to let all of it out. Darrell's accent had grown, if anything, more pronounced as an adult. It suited his temperament, this back in the throat speech of reluctant vowels and bitten off consonants. Vincie noticed, because she no longer spoke the same way. Like Chad, she spoke television English.

"Were the kids thrilled?" Chad asked.

Darrell considered for a moment, then shrugged. "Wouldn't say thrilled. I guess they liked it."

"I thought it was the high point of the year."

Darrell paused again, shrugged again. "They like it better than the textbook, anyhow."

Darrell almost always paused for a beat or two before he spoke. A lot of people thought it meant he wasn't going to reply, so they started up talking again before he could. When he first started school, the teachers thought he was slow and needed remedial teaching. Then they discovered that his written work was as good as his quick, talkative older sister's. They found, too, that he could answer a question if they would allow him that beat or two.

His mind worked in its own way, like a methodical bricklayer who is constructing a model of the universe. Everything that happened, everything anyone said, was another brick. Before he could respond, he must first decide where the brick belonged in his gigantic model, and settle it into its spot. Considering the size of the undertaking, his replies weren't so very slow.

Chad's thoughts had already moved on to a new topic. He asked Darrell what had been done about a funeral. That was a large brick, and Darrell considered for quite a while before saying he thought Reverend Graham could probably do a service that wouldn't offend Vernon too badly.

"If he sticks to ashes to ashes and dust to dust," Chad said, "and doesn't start in about Jesus being nailed to a cross to pay for our sins."

"I told him Dad wasn't much of a one for eternal life," Darrell said. "Unless it could be as a cow."

Chad started laughing. "So that someone else could deal with bank loans and broken machinery for all eternity. If you're good, you become a cow. If you're bad, you spend eternity pleading your case to loan officers and torching out bolts that have rusted solid and sheared off."

"Darrell, did you really tell him that?" Vincie asked.

"Well . . . kind of."

"What did you tell him?"

"Just that Dad had his own ideas about religion. That he didn't believe in salvation and damnation, and didn't think it was all that important what happened to him personally after death. Except he might have liked to know the truth about god, if a person can."

"And the Reverend still agreed to do the service?"

"He said he'd have to do one that fit his own beliefs. I told him we didn't mind that, if he didn't mind that Dad would be there disagreeing with him."

Once again Vincie felt her father return from the ether and wander among them, another voice in their conversation, a comment on everything they did.

"I wonder if he does see the whole truth now..." she murmured.

"Even if he does, he won't be telling us," Chad said, with a sharpness that startled her. They had been talking lightly, familiarly, and now, suddenly, he sounded almost angry. "There's no point in wondering," he said, and the edginess in his voice shifted towards flippancy. "We're not at a séance. We're not going to hear any voices from the other side, telling us truths. I'd rather stick to answerable questions, like what are you and Gifford planning to do about dinner and a place to stay?"

Vincie had to pause, to bring her thoughts back to what was clear and material. "I assumed we would stay here. I don't know about dinner. Gifford has vetoed Bev's."

"I'll second that," Chad said. "I chipped a tooth on her pastry once. I guess I'll stay here, too. That is, if Dad hasn't given all the spare sheets away to a charity."

"The beds are made," Darrell said.

"Are they? Probably they have the same sheets on that they did when Mom..." His voice caught. His attempts at flippancy had failed him.

There was a silence, then Darrell said, "Georgeanne made the beds last night. She's expecting all of you for dinner, so you're safe from Bev's."

His voice was mild, matter-of-fact, yet Chad flinched, as if it carried a rebuke. Vincie felt the nerves in her back quiver, feeling a spirit close by. It was Vernon's voice, calmly explaining facts, and the rebuke lay in his way of being rather than what he said.

"We'll be glad to come," she said. "That is, I'll ask Gifford, but I don't see why we wouldn't."

"Me, too," said Chad. "I never pass up Georgeanne's cooking." The compliment sounded strained.

It seemed there was no refuge, nothing entirely mundane. Details like food and beds could carry a freight of significance that might spill over onto them unexpectedly. A little wearily, they looked at each other and then started down the stairs.

5

IF BEDS AND FOOD did not offer a diversion, Georgeanne, Gifford and the children together did. In the background, the children created a white noise of questions, demands and general activity. Meanwhile, Georgeanne and Gifford, who both liked to talk and who disliked each other, resumed their ongoing duel of barbed remarks. Gifford's digs were covert and clever. Georgeanne's replies were as straightforward as a bull's charge. He despised her for being obvious and she despised him for being sneaky. In truth, they may not have hated each other as thoroughly as they relished battling each other.

On arrival, they had made a few nods and murmurs of respect for the solemnity of the occasion that brought them together. The children were presented and remarked upon. Coats were hung up. Within minutes, though, Georgeanne had returned to her supper preparations, and she and Gifford had tackled each other. Vernon was dead, but they were alive and still the same two people who drew out each other's scorn irresistibly.

"Tell me, is the ICE melting in the ALPS?" Gifford asked her. ICE and ALPS were the mnemonics she used to help her accounting students remember the connections among income, cost and expense, and assets, liabilities and proprietorship. She had once made the mistake of mentioning them in Gifford's presence. He had seized upon them as a summary in two words of the simple-mindedness of her teaching. "Do you think you could help me find a mnemonic to make my students understand Yeats?" he added.

"Yeats doesn't pay the bills. Kids study Yeats because they want to, not because they have to. If you need a mnemonic to penetrate their skulls, your teaching must be in a bad way."

"Yeats pays my bills," he said. "A person doesn't have to be a grunt with an adding machine to earn a living. And surely you're not admitting there is no beauty in a balance sheet. Surely some of your students share your joy in long columns of numbers that sum up to zero in the end."

"Some of them do. And some of them are poets who wince every time I mention ICE and ALPS. And some of them are just plain dimwits who write down every single thing I put on the blackboard and who will be earning a living and supporting a family at an age when your pet students are still agonizing about whether graduate school is their proper place in the universe."

Gifford glanced toward Vincie, perhaps concerned that this jab might have struck her too close to home. As usually happened, she and her brothers had retreated to a safe distance and were listening. Seeing Gifford's look, she shrugged and smiled. Georgeanne's opinions had never bothered her. They were blunt, but not malicious. Confronted directly, Vincie could look at herself and laugh. It was the veiled criticism, the sly innuendo, that scraped across exposed nerves. It was the sideways glance and whispered remark that left her baffled, uncertain, quick to fill in the gaps of implication with all the worst things she had ever thought about herself.

"I tell my students not to write down a word I say," Gifford said. "The last thing I want is my lectures dictated back to me in a five to ten page paper. My teaching is meant to be a seed that leafs out into original thought. I try to spawn wild flights of creativity."

"And I tell my kids to save their creativity for art class, because creativity in accounting should get them three to five in a white-collar penitentiary. Since you're standing there, why don't you slice this onion for me?"

"My eyes won't tolerate it. They're very sensitive."

"I'll do it," Chad volunteered. "Mine are impervious."

"A very useful trait," Georgeanne said.

"If slicing onions is the height of your aspirations," said Gifford.

The two of them were likely to keep each other entertained for the rest of the evening. Vincie was not in the mood to spectate. She wandered away into the living room. Through one door she could still hear Gifford and Georgeanne sparring, with occasional interjections from Chad. Through another door she could hear the high-pitched chatter of Vern and Lisa, who had listened to grown-up talk for the polite two minutes Georgeanne demanded of them and then fled to their playroom.

Like the rest of the house, the living room resembled Georgeanne rather than Darrell. It was tidy and immaculately clean, despite children. The cushions had ruffles, the curtains flowers. The afghan folded over an easy chair was hand-crocheted. The mantel held a display of photographs, children and grandparents in frames. The walls were hung with a hand-embroidered sampler, from Georgeanne's mother, and a water color of an old barn with woods and snow, painted by her aunt.

Vincie was not sure what Darrell would have put on the walls and mantel, perhaps nothing, perhaps some of Phoebe's birds, although these would not have felt much different from Georgeanne's things. Vincie could not visualize the objects that would express Darrell. Like Vernon, he lived inside himself, emerging occasionally in speech, more often in what he did and how he did it. It was typical that he had already talked to Reverend Graham about a funeral, without consulting her or Chad. Probably he had deliberated for as long as necessary, and then called the minister and said, in half a dozen sentences, what he wanted. Probably the time was set, a few readings and hymns chosen, and a few blanks left for Chad and Vincie to fill if they wished. He was not an autocrat, but neither did he like committees. It did not occur to him that the others might feel slighted, not to have been consulted. He would not have felt slighted, if one of them had been the person on the scene who took matters in hand.

Vincie walked over to Georgeanne's sampler to read the stitched words, which always made her smile. The first time she saw it, soon after Darrell and Georgeanne were married, she had walked close to read it, expecting to find "Bless This House" or some similar sentiment. Instead she had found the sentence "A busy chicken is a happy chicken," and the words were spelled out by a long line of beetles, crawling head to tail toward the busily pecking beak of a predatory brown hen.

Vincie became aware that Darrell had come into the room and was standing a few feet away, looking at the sampler, too.

"Could be a life philosophy," she said.

He nodded, but it wasn't clear if he agreed or was merely showing that he'd heard.

"If only all the beetles would line themselves up so neatly," she added. "Mine go in all directions."

"Mm."

"But then, I'm not a chicken." Obviously. She began to feel irritated. Darrell was in one of his unreadable moods. He came and hovered, as if he wanted to talk, but then volunteered nothing. She asked when the funeral was. Perhaps if he was forced to speak simple facts, he might eventually speak more than that.

"Friday at two."

"Are all the arrangements made?"

He nodded. "You can still change the service, if you don't like what I've done."

"I imagine it's fine. Have you asked Chad to say something?"

He paused for longer than his usual two beats. "Not yet. Do you think I should?"

"He's the best at that sort of thing. Why? Is there some reason why not? He did beautifully for Mom."

Chad had spoken the eulogy at their mother's funeral. He had made people first laugh, then weep, recalling stories from her life. He began with a time she took her children trick or treating when they were very young, the three of them dressed as the Three Little Pigs. Unlike other parents, who stayed sedately in their cars, Phoebe

54

had dressed herself as the Big Bad Wolf and accompanied them to each house. Only Vincie had been old enough to remember the event clearly, but Chad invented embellishments as needed, to make the day reappear as the wonder it might have been to a three-year-old. By the time he was done, their lively, delicate mother had acquired long sharp teeth, huge pointed ears, blazing eyes and a ferocious roar, and all the other children in the neighborhood had run screaming at her approach while the three piglets squealed with glee.

When Chad had everyone smiling, he fell silent for a moment, then let his eyes soften and his voice deepen, and began to speak somberly the more traditional eulogy, recalling her loyalty to family, her kindness to neighbors, her unwillingness to speak ill of other people, all the qualities now vanished into the grave. At the moment when a few of his listeners were beginning to weep openly and the rest of the congregation, behind rigid faces, were beginning to sink under the sensation that virtue and sunlight both had departed the earth, he paused again. The church was still, yet his words seemed to linger as an echo among the plain white walls and tall narrow windows, and the massive beams that rose to a peak above their heads.

When he spoke again, his voice had taken on the teasing, smiling quality he had inherited from his mother. "I think right about now," he said, "my mom, if she still had a body to do it with, would poke me in the ribs and say, 'Now Chad, you're overstating things a bit, and on top of that, you're making everyone gloomy, with winter still two months away. Why don't you tell them about the bulbs?' She's probably right, so I'll just end by saying that we've put some baskets of bulbs, tulips and daffodils and snowdrops, at the back of the church. If you feel inclined to do something in Mom's memory, please take a handful and plant them somewhere sunny."

A last hymn was sung, the benediction spoken, and Vincie, crying, had taken Gifford's arm to follow Vernon and her brothers up the aisle, past rows and rows of faces with eyes cast down and jaws grimly clenched in the effort to stem a public flow of tears. At the door, she picked up a handful of bulbs and slid them into her coat pocket. Behind her, nearly everyone else did the same. Chad had said "we" but the bulbs had been his idea alone, a gesture none of the others had anticipated.

"I'm not sure he could talk the same way about Dad," Darrell said. "I don't think there was much common ground between them."

"He's expecting to speak. He mentioned it."

"Probably it's fine. He'll find something appropriate. It wouldn't be easy for any of us. Dad wasn't easy..."

"To be around?"

"No. Not to be around. To understand."

"He didn't try to make people understand him," Vincie said. "And I don't think he understood other people, either. I've always thought it was strange, how he could tell what a cow was thinking almost before the cow knew herself, but not have the faintest idea what was happening inside another human being. I think even god was less of a mystery to him than other people were."

Darrell digested her comment for a minute. "Animals didn't scare him, and neither did god."

"And people did?"

"People could reach too far inside. I suppose god could, too, but he trusted god not to do any harm. Once I asked him why we didn't go to church. He said the Christian god acted too much like an oversize human being, and he didn't believe god had any resemblance to a species capable of such cruelty and destructiveness."

"But why did he see people that way?" Vincie cried. "With such horror?"

"Maybe he was seeing things inside himself." Chad's voice broke in on them from the doorway. "Isn't that how we all interpret other people? Maybe he could still hear those demons howling from their dungeon."

He came across the room to join them.

"We'll never know how Dad saw things," he added. "And what does it matter, anyway? He's dead. We don't have to deal with him, now, and we can't ask him any questions. There's no use trying to psychoanalyze a ghost."

"Which of us would have asked him those questions, even when he was alive?" Darrell asked quietly.

"I did, sometimes," Chad said.

"You did?" Vincie looked at him in astonishment. "I never dared ask him anything personal."

"Well, I did, sort of." Chad was backing off from his claim. "Not long ago, I asked him if he regretted having given up engineering to come back and spend his life on the farm. You remember, Darrell. You were there."

"What did he say?" Vincie asked.

"He said, 'I don't regret it, but I guess I wouldn't do it again.'"

"He spent thirty-five years doing something he wouldn't do over again?" Vincie said. "What a waste!"

"He was making a joke," Darrell said.

Vincie didn't think of her father as a joking man, but the moment Darrell pointed it out, she knew it was true. The joke was more regional than personal, the kind of thing Vernon's neighbors might have said about having lived their whole lives in a place with such a miserable climate. "Don't regret it, but I guess I wouldn't do it again." They ribbed themselves with an irony so understated it was nearly invisible.

Darrell, who lived immersed in this world view, had recognized the tone immediately. Vincie lived around people whose idea of humor was different. She had to make a conscious translation, as if she were listening to a foreign language in which she had once been fluent.

Hearing the joke now, from the outside, Vincie could recognize something else about it, too, the way it lightly but absolutely fended off a probe into the personal. Did Vernon regret his choice, or didn't he, or was his state of mind truly expressed by the ambiguity of his reply? There was no way to tell, and that was the whole point.

"We are commanded to the dinner table," Gifford announced from the doorway, striking the pose of a queen's herald as he relayed

Georgeanne's instruction. "The lady of the house bids us hasten."

Vincie grimaced, annoyed that Gifford had chosen that moment to be mocking and pompous.

"Last one to the table is a rotten egg," Chad replied with a grin.

"And the rotten egg washes the dishes," Darrell added, as the two of them simultaneously made a break for the dining room.

After an instant's hesitation, Vincie dashed after them. With one stroke, her brothers had punctured Gifford's pose and reforged the alliance of shared childhood.

6

As they prepared for bed, Gifford offered Vincie his observations of the evening.

"Your brothers don't seem terribly grieved," he said. "I'd say they'll both be glad to forget your father as rapidly as possible. They think the last barrier to manhood has now been removed, but I think they'll find it's not so easy to put their father behind them. It's only the symbolic father that truly matters, and that father hasn't gone anywhere."

Gifford was standing at the sink, shaving. He had a heavy growth of beard, and it was one of his scrupulous gestures of consideration towards his wife that he sometimes shaved at bedtime as well as in the morning. He prided himself on his awareness of such details.

"The father as symbol is a creation of the child's mind," he went on. "Eventually, the child must forget about the flesh and blood parent and confront the symbol. It is the symbol that must be vanquished. Now that your father is dead, your brothers are going to discover that his physical death makes no difference, so long as the symbol is alive and well."

Gifford's own flesh and blood father was alive and well, retired to Charleston, South Carolina, but his symbolic father had long since been wrestled into submission, reduced in Gifford's mind to a shallow and vulgar household appliance dealer who represented no threat at all to his son's manhood.

His mother he treated with attentiveness and respect. She was the dedicated library and museum volunteer who had taught him his love of literature and art. His father was a crudity he had distilled out of his own character and discarded. He was embarrassed by his father's boisterous enthusiasm and eager, indiscriminate friendliness, and he kept constant vigil over his own personality to forestall any contamination by those traits. On the day he left for college, he made one final gesture of shedding his father. He dropped their shared first name Jim in favor of the grandmother's maiden name that had been his middle initial through childhood.

As he talked, Vincie stood in the doorway of the bathroom, waiting to use the sink and watching him. He was naked, except for black bikini-style Jockey shorts. He shed clothing whenever he could, as if it, like his father, were an impediment to the expression of his full self.

In their bathroom at home, surrounded by the severely modern black and white tile, the glass-enclosed shower, the shine of chrome and walls of mirrors, his nakedness suggested the elemental man challenging the steel and glass of advanced civilization. Tonight he was surrounded by flowered wallpaper, by scarred wooden wainscoting and massively old-fashioned white fixtures. Cold drafts crept through the rattling window behind him and the furnace blower answered with gusts of heat from underfoot. His body was bent forward awkwardly to bring his lathered face closer to the tiny mirror over the sink. Naked in this setting, he looked merely incongruous, like someone who has been rescued from a disaster and whose only set of clothing has been hung near the stove to dry.

With her own body wrapped in a bathrobe against the drafts, Vincie waited. Did he truly not feel the cold, or was he just determined not to concede an inch to the enveloping flannel and wool of puritanism?

"I think Chad is a good way toward killing Vernon off and freeing himself," Gifford said. "But Darrell is a big loyal ox who will be as obedient to a dead father as he was to a live one."

"I think you underestimate Darrell."

"What, does he have undiscovered depths of soul beneath that quiet, humble exterior?" He leaned down to rinse his face, then patted it dry. "Of course, Georgeanne would drive any man's soul to conceal itself in the depths. Now there is a woman without one ounce of subtlety or sex appeal. A man would feel more inclination to seduce a Sherman tank. Quite the opposite of you, my love. You are subtle and mysterious and utterly entrancing." As he spoke, he stepped across the linoleum floor, took her hand and pulled her close to kiss her. His kiss was slow, sensual, arousing. He knew her body and could mold its reactions. When her mood coincided with his, she willingly abandoned thought and let her pleasure be shaped by his skill.

Tonight, her mood did not coincide. She felt no passion, only a dull, unfocused grief for her father, defensiveness about her brothers, and the lurking thought that while Gifford might compare his sister-in-law to a Sherman tank, he never spent an hour in Georgeanne's company that was not followed by a sexual approach to his wife.

She let him make love to her, because she did not want to hurt him with a rebuff, or perhaps because she didn't want to argue with him, either about sex or about her family. Instead, she focused her thoughts on having an orgasm. Gifford was not the sort of lover who ejaculated, groaned and rolled over into unconsciousness. He was acutely aware of her body's responses, and it took her satisfaction, as well as his own, to send him peacefully to sleep.

When he did sleep, she lay beside him with the light still on. She tried to think about her father and death, but in the aftermath of sex, the image that floated in her mind was that of Gifford and Georgeanne, engaged in verbal boxing, like the biting repartee of the leading man and lady in a romantic comedy from the forties. Georgeanne was almost everything Vincie was not, a big-boned, strong-featured, strong-minded woman, handsome rather than pretty, outspoken, fearless, and unapologetic. A man might not dream about seducing her, but he might well dream about battling her until the tension of conflict reached a peak and then suddenly yielding and allowing her to seduce him.

Gifford, especially, might have such daydreams. In bed he was adventurous, inventive, and easily bored, forever seeking out new fantasies and games to fend off the creeping encroachment of routine. As a young man, the craving for novelty had made him promiscuous. Gradually, after many years and many women, he had come to the conclusion that sex was sex, and the newness of the partner no longer supplied any new stimulation. For a while, after he married, monogamy was the novelty that gave him a thrill, and he dreamed about exploring every possible variation of sexual experience with one woman. Now that, too, had run its course, and he seemed to feel himself sinking into a mire of boredom from which he could see no escape, only the occasional relief to be found in his own inventiveness or in a brief flare of attraction for another woman that he could bring home to spark desire for his wife.

Vincie was not seriously jealous of Georgeanne, because she knew Gifford's attraction to her was not serious. Georgeanne was just a moment's solid footing that would soon be engulfed by the bottomless ennui in which he was floundering. Also, she suspected that while Gifford's contempt for Georgeanne was a spice to his attraction, Georgeanne's dislike of him was genuine.

Vincie envied her sister-in-law's forthrightness, her ability to plow straight ahead with life and not hamper herself with second-guessing. Georgeanne knew that her work was useful, and her husband a good man, and it did not worry her that neither one was glamorous. She sometimes teased Vincie about her habit of darting from one pursuit to another. She said, "You remind me of my great-aunt, when she puts her house key down somewhere and can't remember where." Vincie had heard in her voice the same mixture of amusement, affection, and exasperation that Georgeanne must have felt toward her eighty-nine-year-old great-aunt. Except that Vincie was not eighty-nine and did not have the excuse of forgetfulness.

Why did she have such a compulsive need to find, not glamor, but significance in the choices she made? She had been drawn to Gifford because he seemed different from other men, more complex, more challenging, more subtle. She had never met a man who talked so readily and fluently about his inner life, who analyzed himself and other people so incisively, and whose senses were aware of such fine details. He made other men seem blundering, transparent and overly muscular.

She had chosen a husband, but the choice of a career still baffled her. Before meeting Gifford, she had intended to go into science or engineering. She was gifted in science. When not muddled by emotion, her mind worked swiftly and clearly, soaking up new concepts without effort. Even as a child, she was drawn toward concrete problems with visible solutions. When she was given a baby doll, she did not talk to it and cuddle it. At first she just studied it, twirling the arms round and round, tipping it back and forth to open and close the eyes. Having learned all she could that way, she went to her father's toolbox, found a screwdriver, and methodically pried all the parts loose, first an arm, then a leg, then an eye, to see how they worked. Playing toy soldiers with her brothers, she might spend hours building forts and foxholes and lining up her army, but once the battle began, she lost interest. It was the design of things she enjoyed.

Human drama was too slippery and treacherous, and far too real to her to be the subject of play. Her emotions were too intense and direct. She couldn't detach from them and make them into a game. Science could be a game, a place where she could be relaxed and self-forgetful. Because her own temperament was so volatile, she felt steadied by the clarity and absoluteness of numerical calculations.

But Gifford dismissed clarity and absoluteness with scorn, almost as if they were products of lower brain stem function. His mind moved in realms of ambiguity, multiple meanings, symbolic references. He considered poetry the highest and best creation of the human brain and viewed all other pursuits as lesser, valuable principally because they supplied the bodily needs of the collective genius that produced literature, music and art.

Even before she met him, Vincie had wanted to choose work that was meaningful. Once she fell in love with Gifford, her view of what was meaningful began to narrow. She tried one thing after another, and in every job, she quickly discovered for herself all the reasons that Gifford viewed that particular field with disdain. Perhaps the work was tedious or her colleagues unimaginative, the pay meager or the hierarchy stifling or the contribution to human enlightenment not apparent. One job after another, she quit.

Early on, with his encouragement, she had tried to follow him into his own field. She had finished two years of graduate school in literature, and then simply couldn't go on. She had not failed, exactly. Her work had been good, even excellent, and she was considered a promising graduate student. But she never felt that she belonged. Though she had mastered the jargon and could sound knowledgeable, she never felt that she understood down to the core, the way Gifford did. She saw what was evident and was strongly moved, but a dissertation could not be made out of what was evident. When she tried to reach deeper, into the complexities of critical theory, she began to feel her own self becoming disjointed and chaotic, adrift in elusive and half-understood concepts. The concepts did not feel real to her, and her first feeling, which had seemed real, disappeared in her confusion.

She envisioned herself spending years trying to pin down with authority her chosen fragment of the multitude of slippery ideas that were Gifford's intellectual playthings. The vision sent her into paralysis. She simply stopped, without ever being able to explain to Gifford why.

She had longed to flee to the place she felt safe, among graphs and calculators, chemical formulas, equations with three unknowns, things tangible, mechanical and orderly, that made a counterweight to the fragmentation and disarray of her own emotions. But she had come to believe, as Gifford did, that such a flight would be a confession of mediocrity. So instead, she drifted. If she did nothing in particular, at least she did nothing second-rate. She got by, hosting the social functions that enhanced Gifford's standing in the department, picking up an office job here or there, at an art gallery or a magazine or an organization lobbying the government, always making clear that it was not a career, merely a temporary arrangement while she considered what she was really going to do.

Now, lying in bed staring at the wallpaper she had stared at in childhood, she could not help seeing past the rickety facade of her "temporary arrangements." As a child, she had lived immersed in purposeful work. The tasks to be done were everpresent and rarely questioned, at least not out loud. Work lay on all sides, through every day of every season. Its final worth was tangible, the warm white milk surging through pipes and gushing into the bulk tank. Its demands were as absolute and nonnegotiable as the solution to an algebraic equation. Cows had to be fed and milked. Corn had to be planted. Hay had to be mowed. Some farmers might imagine themselves in control for a moment, driving a two hundred horsepower tractor, watching the steel behind it cutting through soil, slicing through vegetation, uprooting, chopping, crushing. Vernon, and probably most other farmers, knew that in fact they controlled very little. They were commanded by a hundred masters, and ignored those commands at their peril. The season said plow, the sun said mow, the clouds said hurry, the cows said you must stop and milk. Soil asked for lime, machines for grease; a feverish calf wanted a bolus to save its life. And always, the account books warned of the need for economy. At times, the din of requests and orders might have been overwhelming, but her parents had never had to seek a reason to get out of bed in the morning.

Vincie often found herself seeking such a reason. Even when she had a job, she usually felt there would be no measurable change in the universe if she decided not to go to work that day. The image of Georgeanne returned to her mind. How did Georgeanne see her way so clearly and follow it with such certainty? To Vincie, she looked like an object with large mass and large forward momentum, while Vincie herself felt like entropy—randomness, disorder, energy scattered into uselessness.

She turned out the light, hoping to sleep, but long into the night, she heard echoes of the place that surrounded her, the soil, the sun, the machines, animals and crops, speaking their needs and offering suggestions with the force of commands.

7

She woke to rain, and stillness except for the trickle and drip of water from the eaves. At home, she could not hear the rain falling. She would know it rained only by the change in the sound of the traffic, the high-pitched hiss of tires through water that overlaid the everyday rumble and whine.

Her husband still slept. Vincie wrapped herself in her bathrobe and went to the window. The hills were still hidden in cloud; the visible world was still a patch of mud and bruised brown grass. Water ran everywhere, cutting furrows through the mud, pooling in every indentation. The two bright red cars parked in the mud, the three bright red barns beyond, looked like a brave attempt at cheerfulness in the midst of gray.

Gifford woke up in a good mood. "Flannel suits you this morning," he said from the bed. "Maybe your New England forebears were onto something. The heightened allure of things not seen. The body's mysteries concealed beneath enveloping green plaid."

"My forebears were cold," she said. "Do you want coffee?"

"How romantic you are. You know I always want coffee in the morning."

"I meant coffee here, instead of driving to Huntsbury. It turns out Georgeanne stocked the kitchen, in addition to making the beds."

"Such a useful woman, Georgeanne. By all means, let's have coffee here."

While Gifford dressed, Vincie went down to the kitchen to see what she could find. She had not yet heard any sound from Chad's room, at the other end of the upstairs hall.

By the time Gifford appeared, she had prepared coffee, orange juice and toast. She had found eggs and bacon, too, but Gifford did not eat those. "My stomach won't tolerate such insults," he would say, if offered them.

The table still presented a difficulty. She laid her food on the counter and perched herself on the kitchen stool. Gifford set his breakfast on the table, ignoring ghosts. He had brought the newspaper from the day before, and they each took a section to read while they ate, as they did every morning with the *Washington Post* in their own kitchen.

Apart from a couple of school budget meetings and the annually repeated feature on sugaring, the front of the paper was taken up by the story of her father's death. Vincie returned to the story, reading it with closer attention than she had the day before, when she was still trying to make the death real to herself. Now, sitting in Vernon's kitchen, feeling the unaccustomed stillness of the farm all around her, she did not need a news story to force awareness on herself.

She read the story slowly, seeking understanding. The death was real enough, but still did not make sense.

"...survived by three children...and two grandchildren. Nowle had worked the farm for thirty-six years, after taking it over from his father. In seven different years, he had the state's top Jersey herd on the DHIA test. At the time of his death, he was negotiating with a land trust to preserve his land permanently in agricultural use, but the agreement had not been finalized.

"Police say he was killed by a single bullet to the head, fired at close range. The gun was his own. He was found seated and fallen forward onto the kitchen table. Near his left hand was a photograph of his wife and children with a tractor.

"The fuel delivery man who found the body, Orville Baines, said he had gone onto the porch to hang the slip on the doorknob and saw Nowle through the window. He knocked, and then tried the

68

door and found it unlocked. When he saw that Nowle was dead, he immediately called the state police. He said Nowle's two dogs, who were shut in the kitchen with him, had been without food or water for a considerable time and had messed on the floor. 'It was pretty rank, with the dogs and all,' Baines said."

Vincie stopped and stared. What she had just read was not possible.

"I don't believe he killed himself," she said, abruptly. "It's impossible."

Gifford had been reading the international news. He looked up slowly, forming words into a reply.

"I'd say you just took denial to a new level of perfection," he said. "He's dead, Vincie. He may have been your omnipotent father while he was alive, but now he's dead. Just like every other poor pathetic mortal."

The cool mockery in his tone made her shrink down inside herself and for a moment she forgot that his reply had entirely misunderstood her meaning. Tears burned in her eyes and stopped her speech, not from grief, but from raging futility, stored up for years. The tears she let flow but she could not let herself look beyond them, into herself. She feared that the last fifteen years of her existence, the whole of her adult life, might disintegrate before her eyes, like a plant whose core has dried up and disappeared while its thin, fragile shell has kept its shape.

"You have to face his death sometime, Vincie," Gifford said. His tone had softened toward sympathy now that she was weeping. "It's part of reality. Look around you. It's obvious he's gone." His hand swept in a circle through the air, and the movement unstopped her fury.

"I didn't say he wasn't dead, Gifford. I said he didn't kill himself." Each word was spoken distinctly, outlined in bitterness.

"What do you mean? How can you possibly say that? The police have looked into it…"

"The police don't know my father."

Gifford looked relieved. "You mean he wasn't the sort of person

69

who kills himself. People change, Vincie. They get into new states of mind. He had suffered a lot…"

"I didn't say that either, Gifford. I didn't say he wasn't a person who could have killed himself. He might have killed himself… if he thought he was becoming a nuisance to the world, maybe. But he wouldn't have left the dogs in. It says here the dogs were shut in the kitchen with him. He'd never have done it. No food or water. Forced to mess on the floor. He'd have put them outside, or maybe he'd have called someone to come over later. He wouldn't have left them shut in."

"That's absurd, Vincie," Gifford said. "A man who is in a state of mind to kill himself wouldn't be worrying about dog shit on the floor."

"It wasn't the shit on the floor. It was the dogs. The dogs being forced to mess in the house when they knew they shouldn't. Being left without food or water. He'd never have mistreated them that way, no matter what state of mind he was in."

"Now you're beyond absurd. You said once he left you and your brothers to make peanut butter sandwiches for two weeks because Phoebe had gone to tend your grandmother and he was too busy plowing to cook."

"That was different. We were his children, not his animals."

"You're saying he treated his animals better than he treated his children? I know your father was a strange man, but not that strange."

"If that's so strange, then I suppose he was."

The word "strange" had opened a gulf, not between Vernon and the rest of humanity, but between herself and her husband. Vernon was embedded in her. His ways had a logic that she understood, but could not make Gifford understand. She and her father stood on one side of this gulf of incomprehension and Gifford stood on the other. If normality had to stand on one side or the other, too, then she couldn't tell which. And was Vernon's way of being any stranger than suicide, an act that Gifford had automatically accepted as possible?

She remembered the worst punishment she was ever given as a

child, for having mistreated an animal. She was about nine years old, and every day she had to look after three big steers that were being fed up to be butchered. The steers were penned off by themselves, away from the milking cows and young calves. Each morning and evening, she brought their feed and dumped it through the fence into two bunks. When their water tank got low, she was supposed to fill it. To reach the water hydrant, she had to go into the pen with the steers.

The steers were slow, placid creatures, but huge, their shoulders higher than her head. One day, one of them gave her a push with its head, not mean, only playful, but she lost her balance and fell on her knees in the dirt. The steers stood around her with heads lowered in curiosity. They loomed over her, gigantic. On hands and knees, her face was level with their bellies. They stretched noses forward to snuffle her hair, and then one of them snorted, suddenly, and she leapt to her feet and ran out of the pen, leaving the water tank unfilled.

For three days, she crept about, pinned between two equal terrors, her fear of going back into the pen with the steers and her fear that Vernon would discover the empty water tank. She fed the steers, as always, but could not will herself to go inside with them. She knew they were harmless, only curious. Her fear was irrational, but she could not overcome it. Every day, she stood outside the gate calculating whether she could make a dash across the pen to the water. Every day, she was stopped by the memory of the three broad heads staring down at her and the three huge bodies looming over her. Nor could she go to her father and tell him she was scared to go into the pen. She was ashamed of her fear, because he did not seem to be afraid of anything and because he had so often said how gentle the steers were.

On the third day, the steers began to bellow and refused to eat. Their sides had a great gaunt hollow between the hip and the rib cage. Vincie lingered by the gate, knowing they needed water, knowing she should go into the pen, but now the steers all crowded around the gate, agitated by their desperate thirst, tracking every move she made on the other side of the fence. Now they really might knock her down, in their desperation.

Hearing the bellowing, Vernon came to see and found Vincie trembling outside the gate. He took one look at the steers and strode into the pen to turn on the water hydrant. The steers crowded around the tank, sucking up the water as it poured.

"How long has the tank been empty?" he asked.

"Three days." She looked at the ground, not at him.

He didn't say anything more right then. After the chores were done, he said he wanted to talk to her. They didn't go anywhere in particular. He stood with her in the barn, at one end of the line of stanchions, leaning on the rails and watching the cows with their heads down in the silage bunk, chewing.

"You must never do that again," he said. "There is nothing worse we can do than neglect an animal that's in our care. We have a duty to other people, too, but people can take care of themselves. Our tie to them is part of the way we were made, not something we chose. But these animals are our own creations. They were made one way, and people took them and made them into something else, something that depends on us for food and shelter, and gives us food in return. They are living creatures that we made, sort of the way god made us. If we neglect them, or mistreat them, then we've done the worst thing a person can do. We have sinned against the best part of ourselves, the part that is most like a god, the part that has the power to create something new and to make choices.

"We didn't choose to be human. We didn't choose to live on the earth, and to need food to live, and to pass on life by having children. Those things were given to us. But we chose to make these animals depend on us, instead of leaving them the way we found them, wild, and hunting them when we needed food. So we owe them a duty that is more than any other duty I can think of. Do you understand that, Vincie?"

She nodded. His voice was completely calm, no trace of anger, yet she felt as if her skin were on fire, as if her whole self were shrinking and shriveling like a piece of paper burning down to a puff of ash. He had not even asked her why she had left the tank empty. Probably she would not have dared tell him, if he had asked. There was no "why" that could make her crime not a crime. She felt tiny. She felt completely inadequate to the awesome task of being human, with her human's mite of a god's creative power and the terrible responsibility that went with it. She weighed sixty-five pounds, and those half-ton steers were her creation, her responsibility.

For two more months, until the steers were sent to be butchered, she had to compel herself to walk into the pen and turn on the water. Busy with their feed, the steers paid little attention to her, yet she did not lose her fear. She always walked around the far edge, staying close to the fence until she had to leave it to reach the water.

She expected to feel relieved when the steers were finally out of her care, gone to be killed. Instead, she felt sorrow. Watching them herded onto the trailer, she began to think with fondness of their eager crowding around the bunk when she brought their feed, and the three of them lying together later, like three sun-baked hippos on a riverbank, chewing their cuds. She felt a kind of wonder, that these gigantic creatures had depended on her, and a little pride, too, that she could dread doing something and still make herself do it.

As far as she knew, Vernon never mentioned her lapse to the rest of the family. It was the whole of her punishment, that she had to go on taking care of the steers. Yet the incident had scraped the hide off her conscience, leaving nerve endings bare. Even now, she recoiled from any act she thought might leave her writhing, as she had writhed before Vernon's quiet explanation of her crime.

Her father's conscience had been no less susceptible, she was sure. She could not believe in a despair deep enough to make him numb to its demands. Suicide would not have gone against his convictions, but harming his dogs would have.

"You realize what it means, if you're right." Gifford's voice interrupted her train of thought.

"What?" she answered vaguely.

"There are only two possibilities. If your father didn't kill himself, then someone else killed him."

While she was lost in memories, he had analyzed the situation and could sum it up in a sentence. His tone of voice carried not a trace of the pain that lay in either half of his neat logical proposition. If not P, then Q. It was a puzzle, and his was the brain to solve it.

"Of course, there had to be a reason," his analysis continued. "The two people most likely to have a reason are your brothers. Or possibly Georgeanne. It's most often family, and I know it wasn't you. Darrell and Georgeanne live closest by…"

"Would you stop this?" Vincie cried. "You're talking as if they're people we don't know. I can't think about my brothers that way."

"You're the one who says it wasn't suicide. You'll have to think about it sometime. It's reality."

"I just don't want to think that way yet." She had not been considering alternatives when she drew her conclusion about the dogs.

"So which is more likely, that your father would mistreat his dogs, or that one of your brothers would kill him?" He shoved his reality at her, rubbed her nose in it if necessary.

"Neither one is likely."

"But one has to be true. Obviously you don't know someone in your family as well as you thought."

"It could have been someone else." Even as she said it, she sensed this explanation was even less likely than the other two.

"Who, for instance?"

"I don't know. But if there are so many things I don't know about my family, this might be one more. Maybe Dad had some connections I don't even know about."

Having removed the problem to a safer distance, she could begin to think about it, as Gifford was thinking about it.

"Dad knew the person, whoever it was," she said, slowly. "He had sat down at the table to visit. They weren't having a fight. Someone walked up beside him and put a gun to his head."

She winced and looked out the window, away from the kitchen table that stood a short six feet from where she sat.

"His own gun," Gifford pointed out. "It was someone who knew him very well indeed."

Only her brothers would have known where the gun was kept. Her mind darted away from the thought, and returned to the police explanation, suicide. Maybe she was wrong about the dogs. Maybe he really had been so deep in despair that he forgot his responsibility. She wanted to believe it. Bad as it was, suicide was the simplest, cleanest solution. Suicide meant over and done with, no one else involved.

"...despondent after the auction of his dairy herd and equipment..." He was growing old. His wife was dead, his farm sold. What did he have to live for anyway? The question hovered, unspoken, behind every phrase of the newspaper story. The reporter was young, no doubt, and his life marched forward with youthful vigor, ever forward into a brighter future.

The question was not Vernon's, though. Once again, she ran up against that curious passivity in him. Perhaps when he was young, before she knew him, he had asked what his life was for, and what his future held. By the time she was old enough to begin to understand him, he had stopped asking such questions. He would do whatever his life called on him to do. He had learned not to argue with the weather.

If he did not strive, why would he suddenly despair?

"That photograph he was holding, with you and your mom and brothers, is it one you remember?" Gifford asked.

"I can't tell without seeing it. I remember him taking one once, right after he bought a new ninety-horse International tractor. He didn't often take pictures, Mom usually did, so that's probably the one."

And he would never have brought it out to show to a visitor

outside the family.

"Could looking at it have pushed him over the edge?" Gifford asked. "Reminded him of all he had lost?"

She tried to picture her father gazing at the photo and raising the gun to his temple. The image seemed melodramatic, too self-dramatizing for her to connect it to her father. She shook her head.

Gifford added, "But he might have been occupied looking at it, while someone else used the opportunity to come up beside him with a gun."

As he spoke, Vincie felt a chill pass through her body. Her eyes were fixed on her husband's face, but she didn't see him, because another picture filled her mind. She saw her father, many years ago, picking up their sixteen-year-old retriever Sparky and carrying him down the porch steps that the old dog had grown too weak to walk down by himself. Behind him, she saw Darrell, eleven years old then, carrying a plate of hamburger and a rifle. She had stayed in the house, with her mother and Chad, but she had heard the shot.

Later, Darrell had told her about it. They had gone out into the orchard. He set the plate of hamburger on the ground and Sparky started gobbling it down. The dog could barely stand up, but he still ate his food in gulps, if it was something he liked. When he was almost finished, but still too busy to notice, Vernon put the gun behind his ear and shot him.

Darrell? Could Darrell have put down his own father the same way?

Her brother had never forgotten the incident, she knew. It had made as deep an impression on him as the punishment about the steers had made on her. He didn't talk a lot, but he had told her about it, more than once.

"Dad didn't ever cry or anything, that I saw," he said. "He just made sure Sparky was too busy and happy with the meat to notice, and then put the gun up against his head and boom. I guess if your spirit lives on the way it was at the moment you die, then old Sparky is one happy ghost."

The method was there, laid out for use, but why would Darrell use it? She could not conceive a reason big enough to metamorphose the Darrell she knew, her quiet, gentle, somewhat plodding brother, into a man driven by rage or greed to execute his father. It made no sense. If Darrell was a creature so different from the one she knew, then her whole universe was askew and she could not trust anything she thought she knew or saw or felt.

On the surface, the facts lined up, just as they had lined up to point to suicide. Darrell lived nearby and easily had the opportunity. He would gain a lot of money, once the farm was sold. He knew where the gun was. The method was there, implanted in his brain from childhood.

She did not believe it, any more than she had believed in Vernon's suicide. The facts did not matter. What mattered was Darrell, the person he was. She could not compel the two things together in her mind, Darrell and a man shooting his own father. Her brother had a reluctance to cause pain that was almost crippling. Certainly it was crippling to ambition. Though he was big and fast, he had never excelled in sports, because he could never put out of his mind the thought that whenever he won, someone else lost.

His sensitivity may have come from being older brother to Chad, who would look agonizingly woeful when he lost a game. The two of them had played countless games of one-on-one with the basketball hoop Vernon put up in a corner of the barn. Darrell was taller, stronger and quicker than Chad, yet their games always ended in a tie, or as close to it as Darrell could contrive. Whenever he started to get ahead, he would change the rules. He might announce that he was no longer allowed to make bank shots, or he might point to a line in the concrete and say that he could only shoot from outside that line. Then the game would continue under the new rules until Chad had caught up.

Now, looking back, Vincie thought her brother might be tender-hearted to the point of self-obliteration. She remembered a time he had spent days assembling and painting an elaborate plastic model of an aircraft carrier. The day it was finished, Chad had somehow managed to sneak off with it. He pried up the deck, planted a cherry bomb inside and blew the whole thing to little bits. Vincie and Darrell heard the bomb and raced out to the backyard to find Chad gazing gleefully at bits of plastic scattered far and wide. Any normal boy, coming on that scene of destruction, would have pinned Chad on the ground and pounded on him. Darrell stiffened and sucked in his breath, but stayed still.

When Chad looked around, his eyes were sparkling with delight. "You should have seen it, Dare. It was really cool! Let's go get my B-52 and you can blow that up. I've got another cherry bomb."

"You blow it up, Chad," Darrell said. "I'll watch."

Chad scampered off to get his airplane, but Darrell just stood there, gazing mournfully at the pieces of plastic. Even if he had wanted to blow something up, the B-52 was a poor trade for his beautiful model. The bomber was a fraction the size, made of a half dozen crude pieces that snapped together. It was not painted and one engine had already broken off in some earlier day's play. But Chad had made it, and Darrell would not sneer at its inferiority. Nor would he rail at his own loss, when there was nothing to be done about it. Vernon's acceptance of inevitabilities seemed to have passed in a direct transfusion to his middle child, without the usual need for seasoning by age and experience.

Vincie had never been able to tell what Darrell was thinking, in those moments of stillness, moments when she would have been shrieking and wailing. She wondered if his calm was a product of self-control and beneath the quiet his thoughts were seething, as hers would have been. Or did that acceptance go all the way to the core? Did he really not resent injuries and slights the way other people did?

"You're not talking," said Gifford. "It's not like you, to think so much and not say anything. Has all that meditation produced a solution?"

"No, I was just remembering things I haven't thought about for years. I don't have any solutions, only some more impossibilities."

"Of which we already had a surplus."

"Gifford, do you think a person can change their character? Become a completely different person from the person you knew in the past?"

"Of course not. Whenever a person seems to become someone entirely different, it merely means that your previous perceptions were faulty. Or possibly that your new perceptions are faulty. Or both. At the best of times, we have only the dimmest understanding of other people anyway. For instance, you are still a complete mystery to me, although we have been married for twelve years. We are all little islands of consciousness, making semaphore signals to each other through the fog. It's no surprise that the message always gets garbled."

She had heard him use this description years before, in one of his lectures. Then he had been explaining to his students why one of the twentieth century poets, she had forgotten which one, was great precisely because his poems were so extremely difficult. Reality was incomprehensible, he had said, so this poet was only being more honest than his fellow poets, who tried to create the illusion of order and meaning, and thus condemned their work to superficiality.

As often happened when she talked with Gifford, Vincie was made to feel superficial herself. She saw patterns everywhere. She saw sons who grew up to become their fathers, and regions whose outlook on life was as cheerful or somber as their climate. A sunflower called to mind her Shakespeare professor, whose large round head had nodded and swayed atop a skinny, gangling torso, and whose optimistic temperament had pointed with a sunflower's reliability toward everything bright and warm. A freeway cloverleaf made her think of Stonehenge and imagine how future civilizations might come upon a symmetrical shape repeated a thousand times in concrete and puzzle over its religious significance. When she mixed batter for a cake, she wondered about the long-forgotten woman who first discovered that four inventions of nature, the egg of a bird, the milk of a mammal, the ground up seed of one plant, the extracted sap of another, could come together with such unpredictable harmony. Her own mind was frequently chaotic, but the world around her seemed a web of startling interconnections.

Gifford pointed out that the patterns she saw were simply daydreams, constructs of her own mind, with no connection to reality. If people made sense to her, it was because she did not really understand them. She lacked the depth of insight that could penetrate beyond the obvious to the murk and chaos that lay at the center of existence. Gifford was richly endowed with such insight, but all of his facility for speech could not convey the truths he saw to Vincie's understanding. It was as if he had infrared vision, while she was limited to the ordinary spectrum. He could not make her see the things he saw. He could only stop her from stumbling over them in the dark.

"I suppose my father and brothers, all three of them, might be capable of acts I can't imagine," she said. "But…" Something in her still refused to accept Gifford's guidance. If the world was chaos and humans unknowable, then why were they wasting their time trying to understand Vernon's death?

Because she wanted to know.

She was not Gifford, who saw the puzzle as a test of his wits, a brainteaser to be tackled with detachment and put aside if he grew bored. She wanted to know. She had to know. The riddle was woven out of her own nerves and dyed with her own blood. To leave it unanswered was to leave a part of her own self obscured.

"But how are we to find out for sure?"

"We won't find out from the newspaper," Gifford said. "No doubt half of what is printed there is inaccurate, as are most news stories. Perhaps the dogs weren't left in at all, and your questions will simply evaporate. We must ask the police, and until we do, I don't think you should say anything to your brothers. Why cook up a stew when the odds are better than even that the reporter got the story wrong?"

"In that case, I want to talk to the police right now. I need to know."

"They'll like the bathrobe," Gifford said.

Vincie didn't bother to answer. She swallowed the last of her coffee and ran upstairs to dress.

8

THE STATE POLICE headquarters was a standard government-issue building, a flat-roofed rectangle of cinder blocks painted light green, dropped in place with total disregard for landscape and surrounding architecture. Vincie had been inside only once before, to take her driver's test. The inside was green, too, a paler shade but still a color that looked as though it came in fifty-five gallon drums from a central warehouse.

Despite the paint and cinder blocks, the place had the same air of amiable disorganization to be found at the town hall, the post office and the local businesses, where people knew each other and the amount of business transacted was small enough to allow some slack for idle conversation.

As she stepped to the desk, it occurred to Vincie that she should have called before driving twelve miles. The dispatcher was friendly. Yes, she was in luck, the investigating officer happened to be in his office. Did Vincie remember him, Bret Leroux? They must be about the same age.

Shaking hands, Vincie realized she did recognize him. They had known each other, very slightly, from the two years they had overlapped at Huntsbury High School. Leroux was older, and hadn't thought about her for years, until he was forcibly reminded by the investigation into the death of her father. She remembered him, as a wide receiver on the football team who broke his leg and spent half the season in a cast on the sideline, acting as an energetic team mascot and cheerleader.

She had difficulty now, trying to see him as a homicide detective. He was a cheerful man with reddish-blond hair, pink cheeks and wide open eyes, a face totally unsuited to the keen-eyed squint or curled-lip sneer of movie detectives. Even more than his face, his speech did not fit the role. His Vermont accent, undiluted by travel outside the state, was a form of speech no Hollywood actor had ever mastered. Every vowel had to wrench itself out of the back of the throat and push its way past barely opened lips, so that by the time it emerged into public it was bent and twisted into a diphthong untranscribable in standard English phonetics, but loosely represented by spellings like eeyuh, ayuh, oyi, oyer, ayew, eeyew and owah. It was a speech that seemed to have evolved in the cold, when people's jaw muscles were tight and their lips closed down to conserve the warmth of their breath inside.

He briefly spoke his regrets about her father, then added, "Seems like it gets harder every year, the way milk prices are going. My uncle keeps milking more cows, trying to keep ahead, but he's getting to where he's about had enough. He doesn't mind the work, but it wears him down, being worried all the time."

Vincie murmured her agreement.

"My dad never wanted any part of Granddad's farm," he said. "He figured he could do as well selling real estate and not have to work three-hundred-sixty-five days a year. Anyhow, I guess that's not why you came in here, to hear about them. Did you have something you wanted to know about your dad?"

"Sort of, I suppose." Now that she had to explain it to Detective Sergeant Leroux, her concern sounded outlandish. She plunged ahead. "The newspaper said my dad's dogs were shut in the kitchen with him. Is that true?"

Sergeant Leroux grimaced. "'Yuh. They'd been in there two days. There was dog mess on the floor and the water bowl was dry. They were in kind of a state when Orville found them. You can see why, I guess. They were in a hurry to get out, to...relieve themselves, but then they wanted right back in. They kept nosing Vernon's hand, even though...well, you know."

She nodded. Again she hesitated, thinking she was going to seem irrational. "This may not make much sense, but I don't think it could have happened that way. My father wouldn't have done that."

"Wouldn't kill himself, you mean?"

"No. He might have killed himself. But he wouldn't have left the dogs locked in with him. He wouldn't have made them suffer that way. He thought about that kind of thing."

Leroux was silent for a while, doodling on his notepad. He didn't seem to have dismissed her suggestion right off the bat, the way Gifford had.

"I guess you know what it means, if you're right," he said finally.

"We've talked about that," she said, with a nod toward her husband.

"And you still think you are?"

"I can't be positive, obviously. But I think it is likely enough that you might want to look a little further before you close the case."

"Mmmm." Leroux was frowning, looking down at his doodles.

He felt no quickening of the pulse at the prospect of a crime to investigate. Crimes were not intriguing puzzles to him. Crimes were simply misery, for victim, criminal, and everyone connected to either one of them. He would much prefer that the death be suicide, hard as that was, because murder would be a lot worse.

Like Gifford, he had immediately seen the probabilities in this situation and he didn't like them. He knew Darrell Nowle somewhat more than casually. They sometimes played pickup basketball with a group in Huntsbury, and a while ago both of them had worked on the volunteer crew that built a new playground for the elementary school. Then, last summer, his son and Darrell's had begun tee-ball on the same team, and they had often stood together on the sidelines watching the games.

If Bret had had to nominate the one man least likely to commit a violent crime, Darrell might have come to mind. Other fathers routinely laid into their six-year-old sons for letting a ground ball dribble under their glove or forgetting when they had to tag the baserunner. Darrell would always say, "Hang in there, Vern. You'll get the next one." Only he would say it in such a quiet voice, the words could not possibly have carried out to where his son was, playing third base.

If Darrell was impossible, that left Chad, or Georgeanne. Leroux wrote the names on his pad, then absentmindedly began drawing circles around Georgeanne's. He knew Georgeanne, too, and her voice did carry as far as third base. She was as sociable as Darrell was quiet, as definite as he was vague. Both taught at the high school. While Darrell had a reputation for leading amusing and somewhat muddled experiments with fruit flies and mono-cotyledenous seedlings, Georgeanne was known as the drill sergeant of double entry accounting and keyboard operation, formerly known as typing, the teacher who demanded neatness and precision in behavior as well as homework, and who lectured with fervor on the perfect beauty and balance of a system in which the credits and debits always added up to zero in the end. Undoubtedly she was the one who kept an eye on the books at home and had a clear idea of what was needed to provide for a family.

But murder? Wanting piano lessons for your children was many steps removed from killing your father-in-law to get the money to pay for them. Was there bad blood he didn't know about? He left her name bracketed by question marks and moved on to Chad.

Chad was an unknown.

"Your youngest brother lives in New Jersey, is that right?" he asked.

Vincie started a bit at the question, coming out of his silence. "Yes. He works in New York. He's a marketing consultant of some sort."

Bret had only really talked to Chad once in his life. Chad was a senior in high school then, and Bret was fairly new on the police force. On the night of graduation, someone, somehow, had climbed to the top of the steeple on the Congregational Church in Worthing and impaled a large stuffed monkey on its spire. From below, the monkey appeared to be sitting perched on the tip of the steeple. Just below it was draped a banner for the class of '79.

Everyone in town knew that Chad had done it. No one was seriously angry, but it was felt that such behavior must, at least officially, be discouraged. So Chad was called in by the police.

Bret had done his best to administer the prescribed lecture without cracking a smile. He had explained at length that some elderly members of the congregation might have been offended, and that the prank was setting a dangerous example for younger boys who might have less luck or less agility than Chad.

Chad had listened all the way through, with those soft brown eyes looking straight ahead and solemn. Then, when Bret was done, the eyes started to sparkle and Chad grinned and said, "Yup, but it sure was a sight, wasn't it?" And there was no way that Bret could not grin back.

People fell in love with him, girls, boys, teachers, storekeepers, his own parents. He looked like a day-old fawn, but he had the spunk and resourcefulness of Huck Finn. Whenever kids caused trouble, turning over gravestones, joyriding, whatever, Chad always seemed to be somewhere on the fringe, but never the one actually committing the misdeed. Something about him made other people want to get into mischief. Bret could more easily picture him inciting someone else to commit a crime than committing one himself.

"Did anyone have any reason to kill your father?" he asked Vincie. He had to ask the standard questions. However strange a crime might seem at first, it usually boiled down to the mundane.

Vincie shrugged. "Not that I know of. Not a particular reason. We all inherit the farm, I suppose, but none of us is poor. Chad has gotten quite rich, in fact, and Darrell has a good job." She shook her head. "Probably I'm being irrational, even to question that it was suicide."

Bret went back to his doodling, then said, "You might not have inherited quite so much, you know. If he hadn't died when he did."

Vincie stared at him, and Gifford, too, turned from his scan of the sparse office decor and focused on the policeman.

"What do you mean?" Gifford asked.

"That land trust deal. It was in the paper. He was going to sign away most of the value of the land for conservation. Once you paid off the mortgage and the lawyers, there wouldn't have been all that much left. The value of the house, maybe."

"Are you sure of all this?" Vincie asked. "He never talked to me about the financial details. Maybe he talked to Darrell, but...are you sure?"

"We checked the terms of the estate. It's routine in this kind of case. He'd written a letter to the land trust saying he meant to donate all the development rights on his land. Without those rights, the land wasn't worth much."

"Is the letter binding?" Gifford asked.

Bret shook his head. "Not legally."

"Only morally," Vincie murmured.

"Maybe not even morally, if he killed himself," Bret said. "You could figure he wasn't in a state of mind to be making decisions."

"And if he didn't kill himself?" she said. "It's twice as binding, then."

"Don't be absurd," Gifford said.

"It's not absurd. Dad would have considered the promise as good as a contract, if he had lived. If someone killed him to stop the agreement, then we have twice as much obligation to go through with it."

Gifford shook his head. "That's ridiculous, Vincie. The situation is different, now. Your father was an old man, nearing the end of his life. Perhaps he felt he had no need of the money. But now the farm belongs to three young people who might make good use of that money. Darrell's kids might go to college on it. You yourself might go back to graduate school and finally finish your degree."

"Maybe I don't want to finish my degree," she said furiously. "Maybe it's just you who wants me to. We have all the money we need. You don't understand at all, do you, about my dad. He was not an old man at the end of his life. You make him sound like he wanted to dodder off into the grave. Who knows what he had in mind? Maybe he meant to join the Peace Corps and go to Africa to teach farming. He might easily have lived another thirty years. You can't just file him away like that, as if he's over and done with and on to the next thing."

"So perhaps he changed his mind," said Gifford. "You said he would never renege on a promise. Perhaps he decided he didn't want to disinherit his children after all, and perhaps he thought the only honorable way to extricate himself from the promise to the land trust was to kill himself."

"That's very complicated logic. And underhanded, somehow, like ducking out of a responsibility."

"The price for ducking out was high enough. Maybe even high enough to satisfy your father's noble conscience."

"I've never claimed my father was noble. I'm not trying to prove anything. I'm just trying to understand what he did. Or didn't do."

"So are we all. And the best way to understand is to use our brains, and not to wallow around in emotion. Your memory is full of images of your father, but how much does any child really know about his parents? You're the last person who could look at Vernon objectively and analyze his behavior."

"And you think you could? You detested him."

"And you exaggerate. We hadn't much in common, that's all."

Bret cleared his throat and shifted in his chair, reminding them that he was there.

"If I could interrupt," he said. "It's a silly question, but for completeness, I have to ask. You both live in Washington, D.C., is that right?"

"Yes." Gifford answered him.

"And both of you were home last weekend?"

"Of course."

"Not the whole weekend," Vincie said. "Remember? You drove up to Philadelphia Saturday for that symposium."

"You're right. It was utterly boring, so I forgot about it. Was that only last weekend? It's been an eventful week."

"What time did you get home?" Bret asked.

"It was after ten, maybe eleven," Vincie said. "Wasn't it, Gifford?"

"Something like that. I didn't check my watch every minute." He shrugged. "I didn't drive ninety miles an hour all the way to Worthing to shoot my father-in-law, if that's what you're thinking. Owning a BMW does not make me Mario Andretti."

"I'm not thinking anything yet," said Bret. "These police reports are a standard form, with blanks to be filled in. It's easier to fill them in than to try explaining why I didn't bother. So you were at home, Vincie, while he was in Philadelphia?"

She nodded.

"Any particular reason you didn't go along?"

"It was not the sort of event that would interest a lay person," Gifford answered for her. "A lot of discussion of European critical theory. It can be fascinating, but not everyone's cup of tea."

"Not yours, either, from what you said," Vincie reminded him. "You said yourself it was boring."

"Ah, yes, so I did." He turned back toward Bret to explain. "This particular discussion never got beyond the obvious. Fortunately, there was a very attractive, though not terribly gifted, new assistant professor from NYU who kept me company at dinner that evening. So the afternoon wasn't a total waste. Her name was Olivia Fanning, if you have another little blank on your form that needs filling."

"Can't hurt," said Bret. He made a couple of notes, with almost an air of absentmindedness.

"She gave me something to tell Vincie about over brunch on Sunday," Gifford said, and went on to repeat his thumbnail sketch of the professor's physical perfections and intellectual deficiencies. Gifford enjoyed telling Vincie about the desirable women who dangled themselves in front of him, only to be passed by because they did not come close to the standard she set.

It struck Vincie, suddenly, that she and Gifford had been laying themselves out for the policeman's inspection with almost no prompting on his part. He had asked a couple of routine questions, with no sign of pointed interest, and they had proceeded to enact a piece of their lives in front of him.

Close on that thought came another, that she had seen the same pattern happen all her life, not in front of policemen, but in front of any number of local people, in a diner, or general store, or gas station, anywhere they encountered some of the legions of tourists who came through the state. It was a pattern that had given the local population an unwarranted reputation for taciturnity. In fact, they were as garrulous as anyone else, if you knew how to turn on the spigot, but spilling out all the details of your personal life was not the way to do it. When someone else was dying to talk, as the visitors usually were, the locals were content to let them have their way. It seemed that their laconic yups and nopes were the sharpest prod they could have devised to keep the visitors chattering away, trying to find the topic of common interest that would break through the barrier and make them all friends for an hour.

The visitors never seemed to realize that describing the intimate details of their divorce provoked only embarrassment and not an impulse to respond with correspondingly intimate revelations. Only rarely did they figure out that the way to break down reserve was to drop one or two tantalizing remarks about deer hunting or the fools in Montpelier, and then shut up. An hour later they might know more than they wanted to about state government, or about the other set of fools from Connecticut who barged through people's dooryards in their brand new Chevy Blazers, as if there could be a deer stupid enough to be in sight of a house during hunting season. They might also have heard about a gall bladder operation, or troubles with potato bugs, or a new snow machine that could do eighty easy, but they'd have gotten that moment of fellowship they craved.

Vincie wondered if this manner had become a deliberate tactic on Bret's part, now that he was a policeman. Or was it simply a habit so ingrained he was unaware of it, a response with the force of reflex that the more open and confessional another person became, the more he withdrew into a noncommittal silence?

Leaving the office, Vincie thought that the police now knew much more about her and Gifford than she knew about what the police were likely to do with the information. Bret had said only that they would wait a little longer to close the book on the investigation, and that they would talk to her brothers. He said it reluctantly, though, and she sensed that he still hoped the answer was suicide.

9

GIFFORD WAS TALKATIVE all the way back to the farm. Recalling the junior professor from NYU had recalled, too, the warm glow her admiration had shed on him. He craved that glow. It had drawn him into teaching. That respectful eagerness to hear what he had to say worked on him like a narcotic.

In one moment, he was contemptuous of his students, contemptuous of their naiveté, their youthful arrogance, their fear of adulthood that made them cling to role models. In the next moment, he needed them as much as they needed him. If he guided them, he also fed off them. Their adoration electrified him. The glow in their eyes projected an image of him ten times life size, and once having seen that expanded image, he could never be quite content with the ordinary human size of his real self.

Vincie had beamed that glowing light on him once. He had married her, perhaps hoping that he could bring the light home and it would project large dazzling images of himself onto the walls of his daily life. He thought she was a rarity, beautiful and shapely, and yet gifted with an intellect that almost matched his own. She was gorgeous, and she would not bore him.

He had failed to consider certain details, however. Daily life was shaped more by temperament than by beauty and intellect, and Vincie's temperament was one precisely calculated to clash with his. She was passionate but self-doubting, intense but changeable.

Conciliation could flare into anger in an instant. Altogether, she was unsettling, and he did not like to be unsettled. Also, inevitably, the adoration of student for teacher did not survive the close scrutiny and unglamorous routines of marriage. The light faded, and he was left in a household with his human-size self and a wife he found irritating.

By any ordinary measure, he was a professional success. Unlike most harried junior faculty, he had ascended through the ranks without visible struggle or uncertainty. He knew exactly what he wanted and what he had to do to get it. Two journal articles, extracted from his dissertation, had propelled him from one-year contracts to the tenure track. His first book was hailed as "incisive," "uncompromising," "an analytical high-wire act of considerable daring," "an eye-catching performance." It had gained him both tenure and a leap to a more highly regarded university. His second book was solid, meticulous, middle-of-the-road scholarship, calculated to answer any charge that he was all flash and no substance. Together with committee work and more journal articles, it had secured his promotion to full professor.

Now, unless he became a dean, he had nowhere higher to go. There was nothing more for him to seek except the esteem of his colleagues, and that was proving to be a more elusive commodity than a title and a salary. For two years, he had been planning a third book, one which would be seen as truly ground-breaking, one which would challenge every meta- and post- theory of criticism, and even make some of his own previous work obsolete. He talked about it often with Vincie, but had not yet sat down at his computer. He said that his ideas were still evolving too rapidly to be locked into any permanent form. To herself, Vincie reflected that a word-processor file hardly represented permanence. To him, she said nothing. She could feel the anxiety the topic aroused in him and did not want to add to it, but her phrases of uncritical encouragement had been worn out long ago. So she said nothing, and left it to junior professors to give him the occasional dose of worshipful attention he required to keep up his spirits.

In the car, he talked brilliantly, first about the esoteric European critics that only he could make intelligible to the layman, then about the simple-mindedness of small town police. His brilliance made no impression on her, because she was not listening. She was thinking about what the simple-minded policeman had told her about the land trust agreement. To him, and to her, it meant one simple thing. There was a more definite motive for murder.

Until now, the reality of murder had been blocked from her imagination by a huge, unanswered "Why?" She had been saved from seeing either of her brothers as a killer, because she could not see the first step that led to the act, the why that led to who, what, when and how.

Now that barrier was gone. She still could not see the money as a compelling reason. None of them had any desperate need for money. But it was a reason. All of them would have lost future expectations if Vernon had lived, and all of them were gaining present cash because he had died. How sure was she that all of them were above common greed, which has no roots in actual necessity?

At the farm, they found Chad in the kitchen cooking an omelette for himself.

"Where have you been?" he asked. "Want part of an omelette?"

"No, thanks, we've eaten," said Vincie. "We went to talk to the police."

"The police?" Chad looked startled. "Why did you need to talk to them?"

"I had a question." Vincie paused, trying to decide whether to tell Chad her worry. Once she did, everything between them would change. Side by side with affection, shared memories, shared grief, would be questions and doubts. Did she want that?

It didn't matter whether she wanted it. The questions and doubts were already there, in her mind. She must bring them out into the open, and perhaps the daylight would dispel them.

"I wanted to find out if there's a chance Dad didn't kill himself," she said.

"What do you mean? How could he not have?" Chad was looking at her the way Gifford had, as if she were suffering from an emotion-driven delusion peculiar to females.

"The dogs were locked in with him. No food and water. Forced to shit on the floor. You know how Dad was about animals."

Now his reaction diverged from Gifford's. He grasped her meaning instantly, and drew her conclusion before she spoke it.

"Yes, I do know how he was. You're saying he wouldn't have done that. So someone else must have been here..." He paused. His eyes had taken on the melting, velvety depths they always had when he was absorbing strong emotion.

It struck her, watching him, that for all their gentle appeal, his eyes were as unreadable as Darrell's stillness. Was he shocked, grieved, or merely puzzled?

"But who do you think...?" he murmured, then added positively, "Darrell wouldn't have done it. And anyway, what reason is there?"

"Who knows what the reason might have been."

"You aren't really thinking Darrell could have..."

"He's not the only possibility," she said. "Any of us could have been here."

They stared at each other, and their thoughts made them strangers. If their thoughts were true, then someone truly was a stranger. Someone was behaving a lie and was not the person they had known from childhood.

"Have you talked to Darrell about this?"

"Not yet. But we'll have to."

The omelette, which had sat forgotten on the burner, had begun to smoke. "Damn it all, anyway!" Chad cried and yanked the pan off the stove. He dumped the frying pan full of egg into the sink and stared at it. His face looked stricken, his dark eyes bottomless.

Inwardly, she was crying, "It couldn't have been Chad!" He was too full of life and joy and fun to be the bringer of death. She saw him as a boy, blond and disheveled, a pied piper of the neighborhood, collecting all the other boys on their road for pond hockey, or fishing, or elaborate adventures in the woods, concocted with pirates, soldiers, spies, spacemen or bears, whatever his fancy decided that day. The others would do anything he thought of, and dreaded to be thought too timid or too dull. They would gather in an eager circle as Chad spun out the plan for the day's adventure. Half of them were to be a squadron of Marines in a remote tundra outpost. The other half were intelligent and ferocious aliens just landed on earth and trying to capture the weapons and radios from the Marines. A clump of white birches was the missile silo under the Marines' guard. A ledge of granite was the aliens' ship. A rusty hubcap discovered near the birches was a vital radio transmitter to be defended at all costs. The boys would scatter into the woods with whoops, and reappear at the house hours later, ravenous and exuberant, with dirt on their clothes, leaves in their hair, scratches on arms and legs, and Chad at the center, with the most dirt and scratches of anyone.

"I didn't shoot him, you know," he said suddenly, and turned from his ruined breakfast to look at Vincie. "I suppose my saying so doesn't mean anything."

"It means something to me," she said, and met his gaze, which still looked wounded somehow.

"So that leaves Darrell and Georgeanne," Gifford put in. "You have an intriguing little mystery here. In the kitchen...with the revolver...who? Professor Plum? Or Miss Peacock?"

Vincie spun around in a fury so sudden it swept aside all her normal impulses toward conciliation and tact.

"You really are vile sometimes, Gifford. Don't you ever consider anything except your own cleverness? Can't you feel even one tiny fraction of the horror in this mess?"

She grabbed a coat and ran out the door. She had no purpose in mind. She wanted simply to be away from her husband.

Only when she was outside did she notice that the coat she had grabbed was Vernon's, and that the outdoors offered no place for her to go. It was still raining, and every place she might have walked in other seasons was deep in mud, unless she wanted to walk on the paved highway. Instead of walking, she crossed the yard and went into the barn. There, under the tin roof, the murmur of rain was amplified into a roar. She climbed up into the loft and sat in the doorway at the end, looking out at the meadows. She sought clarity amid a confusion of possible truths. She sought calm where Vernon had always found it, among the intricate balance of living things, away from the humans who blundered through it all like energetic, inventive and thoughtless children let loose to play among a collection of ancient art.

The clouds had lifted a little, and she could see the lower slopes of the hills that rose beyond the narrow strip of river bottom. The farm lay just upstream from where Five Mile Brook joined the Owens River. Its cleared fields stretched from the river up over the shoulder of hill that separated the two streams, and then down the other side to the smaller brook. Over the years, Vernon's father and then Vernon had cleared every piece of land they owned that was not too steep for use. They turned more and more hillside to pasture and hay, so that the gentle land in the bottoms could be given over to corn and alfalfa. As times changed, the farm had changed, milking more cows, pushing those cows to ever higher levels of milk production, buying more sophisticated and expensive machinery, tilling more land, leasing land from neighbors, keeping up with every advance in farming technology. With every passing year, more production was needed to stay solvent. Vernon had invested, expanded and improved in a continuous, accelerating upward arc, until suddenly, it seemed, his finances and his spirit had simultaneously collapsed under the multiplying G-forces. He had declared himself broke, sold out, and resolved to salvage what good he could by putting his land in the hands of a conservation organization.

Had the collapse, once begun, gone farther than he had first meant? Had a sorrow he thought he could manage by turning it to good ended by overwhelming his desire to live? Or had those same efforts toward good driven someone else to kill him?

She wrapped his coat closer, as if it might give her answers. The material was rough brown canvas, lined with wool. It smelled like cows, like the rich smell of the oil on their hide and hair, with a faint hint of manure. She remembered having the same rich oil smell on her own skin and hair, from squatting down to wash udders with her blond hair brushing the fawn-colored flanks of the cows, or from scratching the backs of the calves as they slurped their buckets of milk. The scent was imprinted in her mind, familiar and comforting. She thought of the gamy lanolin smell of sheep, so different from cows, and to her, repellent. She wondered if it smelled rich and comforting to the children of shepherds, while to them the scent of cows was rank and repellent.

Cow scent had been part of Vernon, soaked into his skin. Only by long washing and a change into dress clothes did he shed it. The occasions for dress had been rare—town meeting, a community chicken pie supper, a funeral, an occasional night out for a movie or some event at the school. He had a different smell on those days. It had seemed synthetic, something bottled, a combination of aftershave, soap, and clean clothing taken out of storage. To scrub away the smell of cow, he had to scrub away any smell of his own, too, until nothing was left but the manufactured scent of cleaning agents.

She sat for a long time, not moving, lulled into daydreams by the rain on the tin roof. A hayloft was not the place for analytic thought. As a child, she had kept a stash of comic books in the cupola atop the ridge pole, an aerie she could reach only when the hay was stacked high enough for her to clamber onto the collar ties near the peak. For a few years, the cupola had been a hideaway unknown to her brothers. She might read a comic book or two, but more often she fell into lazy daydreams. She gazed out between the slats of the ventilation louvres at the barnyard and lawn and garden below. She watched her mother hoeing weeds, the cows ambling to look for shade, her father fixing a tractor, her brothers playing games on the lawn. She spied on all of them, unseen, drowsy, feeling sweat trickle under her clothes. The cupola was the hottest place there was in summer, a funnel for all the heat that rose three stories and collected against the roof of the barn. She would slouch there, languorous, imagining herself a sheik in the Sahara, or a tropical islander, gazing with smiling scorn at the industriousness of the northern races.

The daydream couldn't last, however. She came of a northern race herself. Eventually the heat would drive her from her perch, and she would emerge from the barn flecked with bits of hay that stuck to her damp skin and clothing. After a time, her brothers discovered her hiding place and adopted it for themselves. They constructed a rope ladder, so that access was no longer limited by the height of the haystack. Once her brothers knew about the cupola, she had no desire to go there any more. Its appeal had been its secrecy. Shared with her brothers, it was a hot, stuffy, cramped little cubbyhole with hard splintery boards to sit on and cobwebs draping every corner.

She turned now and looked up toward the opening into the cupola, a tiny hole twenty feet above the floor of the loft. She doubted her adult body could squeeze through the gap, even if she could find a way up onto the collar ties. Like the stanchions below, the loft was empty, a dim, cavernous space vibrating with the roar of rain. There was no pleasure in its tidiness, only abandonment. In April, it should hold the remnants of the winter's hay supply, a shrinking stack that Phoebe would count and recount to be sure it was enough, while Vernon smiled and said, "It's plenty," knowing exactly how many bales he had put there the summer before and how many he had fed on each day of the long winter.

From her perch in the doorway, Vincie could see one corner of the concrete bunker silo, empty too. Like the haystack, its contents would have been paced and measured over and over again by her mother, while her father simply counted up the loads in and loads out that he recorded, meticulously, in a journal.

She wondered a little that a man who planned with such exactness could have let himself be overtaken by financial ruin. Shouldn't his calculations have shown him where the ratio of income to expense was bound to end? Had he, like some of his neighbors, failed to foresee how cheaply their competition could make milk? Or had he in fact foreseen it clearly, and known there was nothing he could do, and simply waited while the end approached, like a man caught on too low a patch of high ground as the flood waters keep rising?

The newspaper had called him despondent, but he had not sounded despondent when he told her he was selling his cows. He mentioned it almost incidentally, one evening when she had telephoned to chat.

"I haven't found a way to make milk as cheap as they can further west, so I guess it might be time to retire," he had said. His voice was calm and even, almost the only voice she had ever heard from him.

"You're selling the cows?"

"'Yuh. Seems so. The auction's in three weeks."

"What will you do after that?"

He paused, then said, "I thought I might see if Darrell and the kids want to go down to Boston with me, watch the Red Sox opening game at Fenway."

At the time, she had thought his reply meant he didn't want to give her a real answer. Now, listening to it again in her mind, she heard other possibilities. Perhaps he was already thinking of death, and knew that opening day at Fenway was as far ahead as he had to plan. Or perhaps just the opposite was true. Perhaps he was contemplating unaccustomed vistas of freedom and time, and the emotion he felt was too wide and complex to be expressed by anything but understatement. All his life, he had caught fragments of baseball games, on the radio that kept the cows company in the barn. But to go to a game, to take an entire day away from the farm for a reason other than business or family, must seem like an event exotic and frivolous and enchanting, the first step in a direction that the imagination could extend all the way to taking the Concorde to Paris for dinner and a stroll along the Seine.

In none of the conversation had there been a hint of despair. He did not howl, not where anyone could hear. And yet the one time she had seen him weep, it had been for a cow. He had cried for Juno, so how could he not have wept watching every one of them, Cactus, Milky Way, Dandelion, Betsy, loaded onto trailers and hauled away?

True, he had cried, she thought, but then he had been angry that Vincie had seen him, and then he had taken a knife and slit the dead cow's throat and hung her up to drain the blood and called the butcher to prepare her flesh for food. His life was an acceptance of contradictions, that he loved creatures which must die, that their dying sustained his life, and that he would not refrain from loving them in order to spare himself grief at their death. He accepted the full price, and refused to fall into the brutality of some, who handled animals callously as a way of declaring themselves a separate, higher species, entitled to make whatever use they pleased of all the lower forms of creation. When his failure closed in, and his cows were gone, he would have met this last inevitability as he met the others, with silent, shuddering grief, and then acceptance.

Or had all the griefs of his life closed in on him together and engulfed him? Darrell had said, "He wasn't afraid of animals, the way he was afraid of people. People could reach too far inside." The thought came over her, as clearly as if someone had spoken it aloud, that when Vernon wept for his cow Juno, he was weeping for the dead president, for his sister, for his father, for all the griefs too deep and frightening to be confronted in their own shape.

What he felt flowed unseen, like Five Mile Brook in winter, shielded by ice and drifted over with snow. Yet here and there, the current tumbled over rocks, too swift to freeze, or warmed itself in a patch of swampy decay, and water appeared, to be found by deer and foxes.

10

THE RAIN HAD STOPPED. Vincie gradually became aware that there was no longer a roar on the roof. The only sounds were the drips from the eaves and the trickles on the ground below. She looked at her watch and saw with astonishment that she had been sitting for more than two hours. It was afternoon. Her buttocks were numb from the wooden floor. She stood up and circulation returned, prickling.

Emerging from the barn, she saw that Gifford's car was gone. On the kitchen table she found a note. "We have embarked on an expedition to civilization, such as it is. Chad wishes to speak to the sergeant, and I am in need of a diversion. Also, Chad has volunteered to host dinner, with some assistance from the chefs at a take-out establishment called Mario's. We shall return by six o'clock, bearing pizza. Convey the dinner invitation to Darrell, if you see him. G."

He made no reference to her furious departure, no comment, apology, or counterattack, nothing. Her anger had shaken her and left her trembling, and Gifford glided right past it without taking it seriously. He obliterated it from his awareness, and with it, her. Why had she ever tried to spare his feelings or hold back sharp words? She was a cipher, and her words did nothing to him. Any quantity of rage times zero is zero.

Below the large curling G that signed the note was a scribbled postscript in Chad's hand. "Finch, If you need the car, it's yours." An arrow pointed to a set of car keys beside the note. She stared at the paper, at Gifford's cold sculptured phrases, and then Chad's postscript, speaking concern and affection in half a dozen careless words. He had not called her Finch since his teens, when he had made up the name teasingly as part of their game with their mother and her birds.

She smiled a little, but still felt hollow. Her brother could not fill up the vacuum she felt, thinking of her husband. She could see Gifford's hand, long and slender, an elegant hand, holding the pen like a craftsman's tool, poised and waiting after each sentence as he phrased the next in his mind. He was writing a note to her, his wife Vincie, and yet he did not think of her as he wrote. His thoughts were absorbed by the beauty of words and the perfection of phrasing. She was the empty space inside a container waiting to receive his thoughts.

How had she come to this? It had not always been so. She had not always felt like a vacancy. She tried to recall how she had felt before, when she fell in love with him and he with her. She remembered the concert, a string quintet visiting the university. Afterwards she had stayed in her chair, dreamily, with the music still coursing through her. As the auditorium emptied, a man had paused in the row in front of her, leaned toward her and said, "Play on, indeed."

She looked up, startled and puzzled, and saw Professor Wainwright. He smiled and added, "'If music be the food of love,' that is. Not my period, but always a useful quote, provided it is taken out of context. Aren't you in my Late Victorian Poetry?"

"Yes, it's fabulous." Knowing who he was now, she became blushing and eager. "You make poetry come alive," she said. Her face was glowing, still warmed by the haunting melodies of Schubert and now taking on the added glow of her adoration for this teacher.

"Now that the soul has been fed, could I interest you in some food for the body?" he asked. "Perhaps dessert and coffee?"

She was amazed. "Yes, I'd love it." She felt she was repeating herself, gushing too much, but he did not seem to mind. He was looking at her with an expression that said her blush made her lovely and her awkwardness made her endearing.

"Do I know your name?" he asked.

"Vincie Nowle," she said. "Vernice on my papers."

"Ah. One of my few brilliant students. You should see the appalling things some people try to pass off as prose. But you, my dear, have a gift."

"Do you really think so?"

"I know so. I save your papers for the end, as a reward to get me through the others."

She had enrolled in his class as a coffee break from math and science, choosing him in particular because he was reputed to be the most entertaining teacher in the department. Now, in one moment, what had been a diversion became a vocation. She had a gift. This handsome, dark, sensitive man, whom she revered, said she had a gift, in a tone that told her the gift was priceless. All her other ambitions were swept under and she resolved that his was the field to pursue.

She did not remember what they ate for dessert. She remembered only how he had talked. With just his voice, he could hold a lecture hall in his spell, and now that voice was reserved for her alone, softened to fit the dimensions of a cafe table, but no less articulate. He revealed himself in ways men never did, telling her about his own adolescent anxieties, his difficulties with his family, his unsuccessful forays into romance. He analyzed his own failings with a frankness that disarmed her. It had been an amazing discovery, that a man so much older, so educated and successful, would willingly claim a share in so many of the weaknesses of humankind.

"I am too easily bored," he said. "It is a flaw I will never overcome, I fear, and it disqualifies me from many professions. Fortunately, I have found a field that offers some challenge. Most scholarship is drivel, of course, but I meet with just enough thinking that is original and provocative to keep me from sinking into despair."

For that evening, she had felt herself admitted to the small, charmed circle of minds that were original and provocative. She had not expected any sequel. It had seemed a moment separate from ordinary time, an enchantment that must end at midnight. But he had continued to seek her out, for long and intimate conversations, and after a time, to be taken to bed.

As a lover, he was adept and observant, but it was his talk that captivated her. From the moment she arrived at the university, she had been in love, not with a person, but with the life she found there, with striving, with conversation, with minds that wrestled out loud with issues that mattered. Gifford seemed the incarnation of the intellectual exhilaration she was feeling, and gradually all her newly roused passion, which had been diffused among a multitude of friends and ideas and fields of study, began to center on him.

She had been astonished at his need for her. He could have chosen any woman, and she was the one who gave him what he needed. If she could give him something he lacked, then she herself must be something definite, a woman who was strong and loving, who had thoughts worth hearing.

She remembered how she felt then, but she could not retrace the path of their failure since. Had she changed, or had Gifford, or was the change an evolution inherent in marriage?

She tried to recall how her parents had been after ten or twenty years together. Their life had not been perfect harmony. They had fought sometimes, wordlessly, as they did all one summer. Vernon had begun coming in later and later for lunch, because he was trying to squeeze in a bit more of the day's work before taking a break. Phoebe, fed up, stopped keeping his food aside and warm. She began to serve it up at the regular hour, one o'clock. She and the children and the hired man went ahead and ate, with Vernon's food sitting on a plate at his empty place. Vernon's response was to eat the food as he found it, cold, as if he did not notice or did not care. The stalemate went on for weeks and neither of them gave an inch. Finally, the days grew shorter, the hay and corn were in and stored, the pace of work slowed, and Vernon began coming in at one, acting as if the change had been dictated by the season and not by his wife. The following summer, though, he almost always came to the table on time, and when he did not, Phoebe kept his food warm on the stove.

Neither fights nor affection had ever been verbal. If he loved her, it showed by his taking time in spring when the soil was right to till her garden, leaving for a few hours the far more urgent need to get the cornfields plowed. If she loved him, it showed by her feeling his absence in the middle of the night, and dressing and going to the barn, offering her help, unasked, with whatever task had called him there, a difficult calving or a cow down with milk fever.

They were as different as two people could be, but neither cast a shadow large enough to obscure the other. Or rather, Vernon was too massive to be obscured, and Phoebe was too quick. She hovered and darted in his vicinity, a flock of cowbirds around the feet of a cow, looking tiny and audacious beside his bulk, but able to fly overhead while he stayed planted on the ground.

On winter evenings, when they had more leisure, she read stories to the children and Vernon sat at his desk in the alcove, doing farm paperwork or reading the newspaper. Phoebe read well. She could give each character its own distinct voice. She could wind suspense slowly tighter and tighter, or plunge forward breathless into battles and chases. Her children listened, rapt, hearing clash of swords and thunder of hooves, and the whining voice of the villain cut short by a sharp commanding bark from the hero.

Vernon always stayed apart, busy at his desk, but Vincie remembered once, looking over at him and discovering that he was no longer writing in his record books. He looked suspended. His elbow still rested on the desk, the pencil was still in his hand, but hand and pencil both hung forgotten in the air above the page. His head was turned sideways, so that his ear was toward the couch where Phoebe sat reading. His eyes were gazing at a piece of wall that held nothing but the thermostat. He was not smiling, exactly, but his face looked softened, as it did when he was teaching a newborn calf to take the rubber nipple. Absorbed in watching him, Vincie completely lost track of the story. It was one she had heard many times, anyway, and she was far more interested in watching her father listen to it. She wondered how long he could sit as he was, unmoving.

She watched him sideways, in quick glances, as he had taught her to do when watching deer, as if a steady stare would be felt by the creature and would alert it to her presence. She saw fleeting shadows of expression cross his face, in answer to the changing moods of the story and corresponding changes in Phoebe's tone of voice. The tableau lasted a long time, Vernon and her brothers aware only of Phoebe's reading, Vincie aware only of her father, and Phoebe aware of nothing except the dragons and knights she was conjuring off the page. As a child, Vincie had been surprised and delighted to think that her father liked the same stories she liked. Now, remembering that moment, she thought he had not been listening to the story at all. He had been listening to Phoebe's voice.

Absentmindedly, Vincie stuffed her husband's note into a pocket and walked into the living room. The couch had been re-upholstered in the years since, but mostly the room looked unchanged. The desk still stood in an alcove at one end, on the way to the kitchen. It was a plain oak office desk, dented and scarred. The files she had been examining yesterday still lay scattered across its surface. She sat down and picked up a file, telling herself it was a perfect opportunity to get on with the job, while the house was empty.

She held a financial statement in front of her eyes, but her mind would not focus. Vincie loved numbers, applied to any unit of measurement except dollars and cents. As soon as the dollar sign was attached, numbers lost their comforting objectivity and became charged with hope and despair. They ceased to be tools of understanding and became the messengers of envy, worry, hatred, generosity, compassion and fear.

She pushed aside the financial statements and picked up a different file, containing milk records. Unlike the financial records, these told a tale of triumph. Vernon's cows had been among the best in the state. His failure had not been a failure to keep up with the march of technological change. Probably Chad was right. His farm simply belonged to a species that evolution had slated for extinction.

She scanned the columns of pounds and percentages. They held no information she needed but at least they were harmless. She needed a pause. Everything she saw or touched called up images from her past, and her emotions felt pummeled and sore. So she stared at the columns of numbers and her mind graphed the seasonal rise and fall of butterfat percentage, and she felt momentarily soothed.

11

Boots stomped and scraped on the back porch. Vincie went into the kitchen and found Darrell just inside the door, taking off his coat. Except for hello, he didn't say anything immediately. He laid his boots in the tray, hung up his coat, wandered about the kitchen, and finally stopped and leaned against a counter with his hands in his pockets. Vincie could imagine him in the same posture in his classroom, leaned back against the edge of his desk, hands in pockets, staring vaguely at some spot on the floor as he gathered himself to speak.

She watched him in silence, waiting to see if he had some particular reason for coming. He was not handsome like Chad. His hair was an indeterminate brown. His face was rounder and less cleanly molded, as if he were a first try.

After a bit, he looked up and said, "So, are you getting along okay?"

"Okay, I suppose. It's not joyful times."

"No."

He was silent again, then said, "I thought we should have people in after the funeral."

"Here?"

"No, at our house. It's closer to the church. Georgeanne's arranged for some food."

She nodded.

"It may be kind of awkward," he said. "Some people feel awkward about...someone killing himself."

She smiled slightly. "It's harder to say the usual things. About his having lived a good life and so forth. Having died peacefully. Maybe we all feel an unquiet spirit still hovering nearby."

Was that why her mind wouldn't rest, being back in this place?

"It's different, isn't it? With Dad," Darrell said.

"In what way different?"

He paused for his two beats, then said, "It's more complicated. Mom was..." His voice caught and he stopped. When he had control of it again, he went on, "With Mom, there was nothing to feel except agony. With Dad..."

"With Dad, you're not as sorry?"

"I am sorry. I miss him a lot. But it's different. There's relief, too. As if a weight were gone. And I guess I feel some guilt, because I've been so angry with him ever since Mom...ever since the accident."

"You were angry?" she asked in astonishment. She had seen no trace of anger in him at the time. If anything, he had seemed unnaturally calm, as if he had some divine gift of acceptance after Phoebe's death.

"How could I not be?" he said. His body shuddered. He was looking right through her at some remembered sight. "It was his fault, you know. As much as it was anyone's." His voice was very low and controlled, but now, listening for it, she could hear the tremor of rage running through it.

"What do you mean, his fault? She was hauling a load of manure and the wheel of the tractor went into a hole. I thought she was alone, driving the tractor."

"She was alone. But she was going way too fast for that hill. She was in too high a gear. The load started pushing her down the hill, and the engine couldn't slow her down, and she skidded and hit that hole..."

"But why is that Dad's fault? Did he tell her what gear to use?"

"Of course he didn't. She knew how to drive. What I meant was that Dad made you feel such an urgency about things. Like the work was so deathly important and had to get done no matter what. Everything had to be done the right way, and the right way was getting every last bit of that manure spread quick while the fields weren't muddy. The tractor was in sixth gear when I found her. Sixth gear for God's sake. What was she doing in sixth with that load on that hill?"

"You found her?" Vincie interrupted him. "I always thought Dad was the one..."

"No, Dad was busy fixing the chopper. He got worried when she was taking too long and sent me off to look, in case the tractor might have quit on her or something. The damned tractor hadn't quit, that's for sure. It was still running when I got there. Turned over and halfway down the bank, but the motor hadn't quit. Those back wheels were just turning away, the way tractors do, like they're not in any hurry but nothing on earth is going to stop them. One of the hydraulic hoses had ripped loose and was dripping fluid. The thing looked like some kind of a wounded monster, lying tipped over, dripping fluids, with that bottom wheel grinding a hole in the bank and the top one spinning away as fast as it could go."

It seemed that some kind of load was pushing Darrell downhill now, and he couldn't stop. The words were pouring out of him, without a pause.

"I couldn't see Mom anywhere," he said. "At first I thought she must have jumped off before it went over and I'd missed seeing her somehow. But then I thought, she would have turned the motor off. I remember I just felt sick and couldn't move, and then I ran, down the bank and around the front of the tractor. I could just see her legs and part of her jacket, that blue one. She was so little and she was right underneath the thing, half of her right underneath that back wheel that was still grinding away. But she was still moving a little, and I thought maybe there's a chance. I was about to crawl underneath to pull the kill switch but then the motor stopped on its own and that damned wheel stopped turning, and I saw that she had stopped moving, too, that it was just the wheel that had been making her body move. I hadn't really noticed the sound of the motor, but once it stopped, and she stopped moving, I thought I'd never heard such a total silence. I think I knew she was dead. I couldn't even find an arm, to feel for a pulse, but I found her foot and pulled off the boot, to try and find an ankle pulse. It's funny, you have to do those things, even though you know. I couldn't feel any pulse at all, but I kept telling myself maybe I wasn't feeling the right spot, so I kept looking and looking and I think then I started seeing how much blood there was all over the ground.

"I went tearing off then, to get Dad, and the big tractor, and call the FAST squad. I knew it was no use, but you have to keep trying, keep doing whatever you can. Dad and I went back there with the big tractor and the truck and chains, to see if we could lift the thing off her. I remember we had to unhitch the spreader first. It was on its side and the hitch was all bent to hell. I remember pounding and pounding with the sledge and a bolt, trying to knock the hitch pin out, and I finally got it out, but then I couldn't get the PTO shaft unhooked. It was jammed on and I just pounded and pounded on it with the sledge, cursing and crying, and then Dad finished hooking up the chains and came to help, and he worked the collar and I hammered until we got it off. Dad got real calm then, and explained how we were going to try to tip the little tractor up enough to pull Mom out but we'd have to go slow and careful or the big tractor could go over backwards. It was like both of us were just blanking out what we knew was true, that everything we were doing was useless except that it kept us from thinking. We'd just gotten the tractor tipped back up a little when the FAST squad showed up. They pulled Mom out and after that there was nothing more for us to do. We both just stood there shaking, while the ambulance people did what they could. Once they had Mom clear, we did pull the tractor the rest of the way up onto its wheels and that was when I looked and noticed that it was in sixth gear. My mind got fixed on trying to figure out what happened. I didn't want to watch the rescue squad, so I started walking around, looking at the tracks she'd made. We'd driven over them a couple of times, but you could still see the marks, this long, long skid that started out straight and then started to slew off sideways, and then the right hand track went into a big dip and over the bank, while the left one just ended where the tractor tipped. I remember thinking the left one looked like those tracks you find in the snow sometimes, where a mouse or a rabbit is running along and then, poof, the tracks vanish, and the only trace left is a little brush mark from the wing of an owl."

He came to a halt finally. His face was wet with sweat.

"Did you ever tell Dad about what you found?" Vincie asked. "About her driving too fast?"

He shook his head. "What was the point? She was dead. No good would come of telling him. He'd only torment himself. He is the way he is...was...I guess there's a reason why, somewhere."

"Did you tell anyone at all?"

"Georgeanne. Later on, I told Chad a little, not the whole story. Just about her being in too high a gear. I haven't wanted to talk about it. I don't know why I did now."

Perhaps it was the unquiet spirit. Or perhaps, like her, he felt hemmed in by a crowd of memories all asking to be laid to rest.

"Dad's dead now," she said. "Your telling me can't make any difference to him."

"'Yuh. That's true." He sounded calmer, back to his more usual self.

"Did you hate him, ever?" Vincie asked.

"Hate?" He said the word almost as if it were unfamiliar and he had to search out its meaning. He shook his head. "No, I was in awe of him. I felt like something lesser than him. But hate...I was angry, but I never thought he was evil. You'd have to think he was evil to hate him. Wouldn't you? He was just...separate. Walled up in a tower. I grew up thinking he was a fortress, but now that I'm not a child, he seems more like a hermit, hidden away inside the walls. It's strange, once I stopped thinking I wanted to be just like him, it was easier to take him as he came."

"I've always thought you were like him," she said.

He smiled, a little grimly. "Only when I couldn't help it."

"You don't want to be like him at all?"

"I'd like to pick and choose. I'd like to be as honorable as he was. As steady and sure of what I believed. But I wouldn't want to be so alone inside myself."

"You are steady and sure. Or you seem so."

"No, I just keep the uncertainties out of sight. You should ask my students. Once one of them brought me a sheet of paper full of tally marks. He said he'd been counting up the number of times I said 'On the other hand…' in the space of one class. And I'm supposed to be teaching science. Sometimes I think I can see everyone's point of view clearly except my own."

The reflecting pool, she thought, its depths obscured by the image of whoever looked at it. Only rarely were the depths stirred up enough to blot the reflected image and remind the onlooker that the pool had substance of its own.

Through the whole time he was talking, Darrell had not moved from his place leaning against the counter. Vincie could not stay so still. She paced around the kitchen. It was time, she thought, to ask Darrell his opinion about her father and the dogs. She hesitated, though. His outpouring was over and he had returned to calm. She hated to stir up turmoil in a new place.

"Something has been bothering me," she said finally. It had to come sometime, so better now, while they were alone.

"What's that?"

"The dogs, being locked in the house with Dad."

Darrell was silent for a while, then said, "That bothered me, too. It wasn't something he would do."

"Why haven't you said anything?"

He shrugged. "I guess I didn't like thinking about it. What it meant. And I figured it would find its way into the open, if it was supposed to, without my dragging it there."

"It's been dragged there now, thanks to me," she said. She told him briefly about her conversation with the detective sergeant.

"So Bret's going to look into it?"

She nodded.

He was silent again, and after a minute she said, "What if we're all wrong about what it meant? Maybe Dad just thought someone would find them sooner."

Darrell shook his head. "What someone? He knew I wouldn't be out last Sunday, because Georgeanne and I were taking the kids up to Danville to help her brother with the sugaring."

"There's no one else who's said they meant to stop by and then didn't?"

He shook his head.

"What a mess," she said.

They didn't look at each other. If they had, their brother's name would have hung in the air between them, and they couldn't bear that.

"It could have been any of us," Darrell said, as if to counter the thought they were trying not to think. "Georgeanne was out with her friends, bowling all evening, but I don't know what time she came home. She could have gone out to the farm. And I was alone with the kids all evening. I could have gone out there, too, after they went to sleep. We're the most likely ones, really."

"Gifford was at a symposium in Philadelphia on Saturday. So I was alone, too."

"But when did he get back?"

"Not until Sunday morning."

To Darrell she spoke the truth she could not bring herself to confess to the police. She had told Sergeant Leroux ten o'clock and left him to assume she meant ten that same night. She had not been shielding Gifford. She had been shielding herself from the humiliating conclusion the police would undoubtedly draw, from the facts that her husband went off to a conference and fell into delightful dinner conversation with an attractive junior professor and did not come home until late the next morning.

To his wife, Gifford had said he was tired and decided to check into a motel rather than drive the three hours home. Vincie thought this was probably true. Probably he had done no more than talk with the young professor. Emotionally it made little difference. If he had taken the woman to his motel, it was only to stave off boredom for a few hours. If he had said good night and spent the night alone, it was only because she had proven more boring than solitude. But Vincie could never know which he had done, and that was what he wanted, as much as he wanted anything. He stayed the night to plant uncertainty, as if uncertainty might somehow strengthen his hold on her feelings.

"He could have come back Saturday night," she said. "The conference ended at four-thirty. He got talking to someone, and it got late, and he decided not to drive back. He doesn't like to drive when he's tired. He's not like Chad. He doesn't get a kick out of stopping at an all-night cafe and stoking himself with pie and coffee to keep going."

"He might not get real cream..." Darrell murmured.

"What?"

He shook his head. "Nothing."

"I suppose it is theoretically possible that he raced up here and woke Vernon up at midnight, but it's crazy even to think about. It's not his style. Can you see Gifford shooting someone with a revolver?"

"No. No more than I can see Georgeanne rushing off after bowling to do it. I woke up when she came to bed and she did exactly what she always does. She told me, almost frame by frame, the scores everyone bowled until we both dozed off. She fell asleep first, too, because I remember the scores would start to wander, and her voice would drift off into a mumble, and then she'd jerk and say very clearly, 'Marie hit an eight-two spare in the ninth frame...' and then she would drift off again. I've never for a moment thought she...but still, I try to see how things might look from the outside."

"I've never thought Gifford did it either. If nothing else, he'd have to have lied about going to dinner with the lovely Olivia Fanning, and that's easy for the police to check."

118

"Who is Olivia Fanning?" Darrell asked.

Vincie shrugged. "Someone he met at the symposium. They had dinner together. She was very attractive, according to Gifford, but she lacked the intellect necessary to sustain his interest." She retreated into her husband's language to keep her own thoughts at a distance.

"Mm." Darrell didn't say anything more, but for the first time he fixed his eyes on her, direct and unwavering, as if he were trying to see just her, unconnected to farm or parents or the possibility of murder. She couldn't stay still under his look, or meet it with equal steadiness, any more than she could have stared steadily into a mirror without needing to tidy a strand of hair or try out a new grimace or in some other way give herself an excuse for such intent self-scrutiny. She walked around the room, and Darrell's gaze followed her.

She felt compelled to explain. "Women like that aren't important. They don't matter. They liven him up for a few hours, that's all. He gets bored so easily. He doesn't even sleep with them. He just...plugs himself in for a while, recharges his batteries. He wouldn't ever fall in love with them. They're not a threat..."

She wound down, finally, thinking she protested too much, thinking he saw too much and drew conclusions she couldn't control.

"Are you happy?" he asked.

"We get along well. We don't have the hideous fights some of our friends do, where one person spends the night sulking in the spare room."

"I didn't mean you and Gifford. I meant you. Are you happy?"

"When have I ever been happy, really?" she said. "I think I'm as content as I can be. You have to know what you want to be truly happy. And I don't. So I get along the best I can. I can't blame Gifford for anything. He didn't make me this way. He's not doing anything to make me unhappy."

"You don't blame a pine tree for casting a shadow in the winter, but you can still step out of its shade into the sun."

"You think Gifford casts a shadow?"

He shrugged. "You're the one who knows that."

"I've lived with him my whole adult life. It's hard to measure the effect of something that's always there. Do you think I've changed? Do I seem less happy to you?"

"I can't tell that. From where I stand, you've just disappeared." He paused, looking for words. "Most of the time, what I see is Gifford, and Gifford's complement. I don't see my sister. I see Gifford's missing half. I don't know what it feels like to be molded around another person's shape and whether that can make you content. And then, every once in a while, you reappear and I think, 'There she is. That's my sister!'"

"How is she different?"

He smiled. "She's an ogre. She tells her little brothers what to do," he said. "One minute you'd be kidding us, and the next minute you'd lose your temper, because we were such brats. You were always so smart and so responsible. So much the oldest, trying to stop our arguments and acting as go-between with Mom and Dad. First you were a kid, taking the kids' case to Mom and Dad. Then you were a parent, coming back to present the parents' case to us."

"I sound like a busybody."

"Oh, you were. But you meant well. You were really nice to us, most of the time."

"Chad said I once threatened that Dad would fry up your livers and feed them to the dog."

"Yes, you did, and we deserved it. We were cutting up baby mice. I think you knew that no smaller threat would be enough."

"Did it stop you?"

"I don't remember. I only remember the threat. We both knew you didn't mean it."

"I remember the mice. I was very upset, and Chad just laughed. He didn't seem to be afraid of anything, not even Dad."

"He wasn't," Darrell said.

Both of them fell silent. Recalling Chad returned them to the present moment. It took six and a half hours to drive up from Chad's place. He lived alone, came and went erratically, and was often out of town. His neighbors were unlikely to notice if he drove off one Saturday afternoon and returned the next morning. They would assume he had a date, if they bothered to assume anything. He lived in an exclusive neighborhood of large houses screened from one another by shrubbery, long driveways, wrought iron, and a pointed lack of inquisitiveness. The houses cost in the high six figures, and part of what was bought was this indifference on the part of one's neighbors. As long as the grounds were kept tidy and the house painted, no one inquired further.

Chad lived in an architectural experiment, concocted from triangles, hexagons, expanses of glass, steel I-beams swooping overhead at strange angles and webs of painted ductwork and plumbing, snaking along the walls in bright primary colors. He always said, a little apologetically, that it had been designed by a four-year-old, but in truth he reveled in its absurdity. Perhaps he reveled, too, in its total departure from the style of his childhood.

Vincie thought the neighborhood an odd setting for him, too manicured and pretentious. He said, "I have to live somewhere and the alternatives are a lot worse. At least we don't have drive-by shootings."

He occasionally played tennis and swam at a health club in the neighborhood, and he bought groceries at the nearest mall supermarket. Apart from that, he treated the house as a kind of post office box for his body, a unit as self-contained and independent of its surroundings as a pod traveling through outer space. He could close it up and leave whenever he chose. He had no animals, and no plants except the landscaped grounds, which he left in the hands of a lawn-care company.

Of anyone in the family, he had the least need for money. He was a wunderkind in the field of marketing, a millionaire at thirty, with no visible limit to his future. Why would he care what his father did with the farm?

For Chad, making money was a sport and he played it with skill and relish. The digits after the dollar sign were the score in a game of pinball, given added zest because they had tangible value and because for most people a zero added to the score could transform their life, and a zero less could wreck it. He enjoyed the tangible rewards, as a cat enjoys eating the mouse it has caught, but the catching was the real object. Vincie couldn't see how securing an inheritance could have any of the enticement of sport.

"Chad told me he didn't do it," she said.

"Just like that, straight out?"

"He said, 'I didn't shoot him.' I guess that's straight out. I want to believe him. I can't bear the other…"

"Nor can I," Darrell said quietly.

"Are we imagining things? Maybe we're all wrong. Maybe Dad did forget…" She stopped. She was speaking what she wished were true, not what she believed.

He shook his head. "I don't think he'd forget."

"Neither do I," she said. "So someone else was here."

Darrell was silent for a bit, then said, "The police will see me as the logical person."

"Why should they?"

"I was here in Worthing. I was alone all evening, once the kids were asleep. Georgeanne and I aren't poor, but we aren't rich, either. A little extra money never hurts, especially with the kids coming along. And I helped on the farm. The police might assume I thought I had a claim. From their point of view, everything fits."

"How can you say that so calmly? How can you describe the situation as if you were talking about someone else?"

"That's how I think." He smiled. "Sometimes I almost convince myself I must have done it."

She wanted to say, "But you didn't, did you?" She couldn't say it. The question was too naked. If the answer was yes, it would send her reeling. If it was no, it would be meaningless, because it might be a lie. Darrell, seeming to understand her dread of the alternatives, did not volunteer an answer. His silence was in its way an answer, and one typical of him. She must judge for herself. He would not try to convince her of anything. As a child he might have suggested trading marbles, but he would not have offered any arguments to persuade her. Now he would not try to convince her he was innocent of murder. She hoped he would not end up in jail, simply because he could not bring himself to try to persuade a jury he was innocent.

12

As if to confirm Darrell's estimate of what the police would think, a patrol car pulled into the yard and Bret Leroux got out.

He greeted both of them, then said to Darrell, "I went by your house and talked with Georgeanne. She said you'd come here. Do you have a few minutes, or should I come another time?"

"Now is fine," Darrell said.

"It's a formality, really," Bret said. He felt awkward, having to be a policeman with someone he knew from his son's tee-ball team. He did not take off his overcoat or come more than a couple of steps into the kitchen.

"I don't mind, Bret. It's your job to find out what happened. Do you want to go into the living room?"

"Here is fine. It shouldn't take long."

His questions were routine, about where Darrell and Georgeanne had been on Saturday and at what time. Darrell repeated his summary, that Georgeanne had been out bowling and he had been alone with the children until she came home. He wasn't sure of the time. He'd only half woken up.

"Georgeanne said the children go to bed at eight. Is that right?"

"When she's there, they do. I lose track of time sometimes. It might have been eight-thirty or nine."

"Did you know where the gun was kept?"

"'Yuh. Up in that high cupboard." Darrell gestured with his head toward a cupboard near the door.

"Had your father told you about the agreement he was negotiating with the land trust?"

"'Yuh. He meant to sign away all the development rights, so the land would stay in farming."

"What did you think about that?"

Here Darrell paused. "I knew it was a lot of money to give away," he said slowly. "But it was his farm and he was the one to decide. And I agreed with him not wanting to see the land built up. Maybe, having kids, I wouldn't have been so quick to give away some of the options they might have had. But I could see his point, too, that once those houses get built, you've taken away any other option for that land and there's no going back. I guess maybe I was looking at the choices my own kids might have and he was looking at the choices the human race might have. He had kind of a large way of looking at things."

Now it was Bret who paused before asking, "Did you get along okay with your dad? Did you fight, ever?"

Darrell smiled. "Neither one of us was much for fighting. We got along, I guess. Dad wasn't someone you'd be pals with. And I'm not sure I turned out to be quite what he hoped."

"Do you think he was in a state of mind to kill himself?"

"I suppose anyone might do anything, but I wouldn't have said he was likely to. It would have been making too much of himself, somehow."

"Too much of himself?"

"He wouldn't have thought his own fate mattered very much. He'd have seen his death as part of a bigger pattern, to be accepted when it came. Not as a tool to end his own suffering."

"But he'd have put down an animal that was suffering, wouldn't he?" Bret asked.

Vincie had been only half listening, but now she looked at the detective with closer interest. It was the first question Bret had asked that did not sound as if it came off a standardized form, that

126

came instead from his own intuition.

"Yes, he would have," Darrell said. He too was looking at Bret more closely. "You may be right, that he might have thought of himself the same way. Although it still doesn't explain the dogs being in, or all the half-finished business he left with the land trust."

"Mm." Bret was silent for a few moments, leafing through his notepad. A little abruptly, he said, "I gather you think your father was partly to blame for your mother's accident."

A ripple of pain passed across Darrell's face and he didn't answer immediately. Vincie was wondering how the sergeant had "gathered" that piece of information. From Georgeanne? Not likely. From Chad, then?

"I guess I do," Darrell said. "Not directly. He didn't neglect the machinery or anything like that. It was just his way of being, and how it made people around him try to be. You didn't want to let him down. My mom…" He stopped.

"Chad said she was driving too fast."

Darrell nodded.

"What does that have to do with your father?"

"It's not that he did anything. He didn't tell her to hurry. He wasn't responsible, legally. But he acted in certain ways, and it made people around him act in certain ways, and the result was an accident. He didn't intend harm. It wasn't his fault in that sense." He seemed not to know how to explain further.

Vincie spoke up, trying to help. "He made you feel that you had to justify your existence. That humans come into the world as a burden, on their parents, on other living creatures. They have to pay back the debt. He didn't expect more of others than he expected of himself, but he expected so much of himself, it made everyone around him scramble to keep up. He felt we'd been given this extraordinary gift of creation and had to try to be worthy of it. It made him a rather daunting person to be around."

"He used to say that the human race did too many things that must make the whole universe weep," Darrell said. "He said it should be our quest in life to do what would make it smile. Do you remember that, Vincie?"

"Yes, and I remember wondering how we were supposed to know what would make the universe smile."

"Dad saw it the way a farmer would," Darrell said. "It was a matter of looking after all the things that had been put in our care. Mom was more lighthearted. Sometimes if she thought Dad was getting too serious about all our vast responsibilities, she'd say, 'God just wants applause. Humans came along so that there would be an audience with the mind to appreciate the beauty and ingenuity of the rest of creation. Someone to admire the skill and laugh at the jokes. First there came hawks and warblers. Then there came a species with the brains to invent binoculars.'"

"And yet she tried as hard as the rest of us to meet Dad's expectations," Vincie said. "We couldn't sit back and admire the beauty of a snowfall, not until every gate and path had been shoveled and plowed."

"And he was right, of course," Darrell said. "If you waited, it might rain and then freeze and make everything impassable."

"He usually was right. That was what was so overwhelming."

The detective sergeant shifted his feet, drawing their attention, and Vincie realized she had forgotten what question they were trying to answer. Bret Leroux seemed to have a knack for tossing out a topic and then stepping back and letting other people run with it. Perhaps it was because he seemed so cheerful and harmless. It was easy to forget he was a policeman, and that it was his business to track down a criminal, if there had indeed been a crime.

Vincie looked away from the wide blue eyes and ruddy cheeks, focusing instead on the sober dark suit and the notebook that went with his job. What was he thinking of them, as he wrote notes on his pad? He finished writing, shook hands and thanked them. His face was friendly but unrevealing. At least there was no sign of eagerness, no gleam of the hunter closing in on prey. He'll do his job, she thought, but he won't see it as sport.

13

Sport was remote from Bret Leroux's mind as he drove home. A number of thoughts were circling there, but the axis at the center was distaste and reluctance in the face of his present task. He was not normally squeamish about his work. Most violent criminals were people already known to be bad sorts, people he could see locked away and feel relief that they would not be troubling their families and neighbors for a while. This case was one of the occasional exceptions, where the criminal was someone departing from his normal behavior, someone otherwise likable, honest and ordinary whose motives were therefore doubly puzzling and disturbing.

Bret had joined the police force for some of the same reasons he had played football. He liked matching strength and brains against an opponent, he liked belonging to a team, and he liked to feel that he was one of the good guys. He thought, perhaps idealistically, that police work might be one of the few places left where heroism was still possible.

He had watched his own father, as a real estate salesman, hustling, calculating, massaging egos, and twisting words in ways that obscured the truth without being actual lies. His father lived in a world of paperwork, phone calls, appointments, and small talk. Speech was a tool of manipulation, not communication. With words as oily and malleable as warm butter, he made bogs into "pond sites," cramped, dark rooms into "cozy dens," and houses with wet basements and dry rot into places "rustic" or "historic." He earned a comfortable living, but there was no thrill of pride in his voice when he told people what he did for work.

Bret wanted to feel proud. For his first years as a policeman, he did feel proud, although the work was not entirely what he had imagined. He had not realized how many hours of tedium would separate the moments of drama. The bulk of his work was humdrum routine, punctuated by crises that could be shocking or sordid or pathetic, sometimes dangerous, occasionally comic. Over time, he learned to accept the routine and even to prefer it, because what was tedium for him was comfort and security for everyone else. He found he had escaped neither paperwork nor phone calls, but at least he did not have to hustle anyone.

He had been on the force four or five years when two incidents occurred that permanently changed his attitude toward his job. Neither incident was large, but coming so close together, they crystallized an accumulation of earlier incidents and observations into a suddenly coherent whole.

The first occurred when he was delivering a prisoner to the penitentiary after a conviction for breaking and entering. Scooter Larson was a shabby, hangdog young man, not very bright, who had been removed from an abusive household when he was nine, had proved unmanageable in foster care, and had wound up as a more or less permanent resident of correctional institutions. He never did anything seriously violent, but he was never out of jail for more than a month or two before being arrested again, for theft, vandalism, breaking and entering, or in one case, simple assault after an exchange of punches in a bar.

The prison guards had greeted Scooter with derisive familiarity, and then, as they were leading him away down the corridor, the one behind gave him a shove and the one beside stuck out a foot, casually, so that Scooter fell sprawling on his face. It was a crude schoolyard trick, pointless and bullying. It left Bret feeling sickened and angry, but helpless. He had no seniority, and the prison guards were in a separate chain of command, anyway. A bloody nose did not count as an "injury" and the guards would just say Scooter had tripped accidentally, if Bret did try to raise the issue.

Two days later, Bret and some other officers were sent to remove a group of demonstrators who were blocking the entrance to the state's only nuclear power plant. The protestors were sitting down in front of the gate and they greeted the police with hoots and taunts. This in itself was no disillusionment. As a teenager, Bret had watched anti-war demonstrations on television. He knew there were plenty of people who thought policemen were pigs.

The demonstrators did not resist arrest. They went limp, so that they had to be dragged to the van that was waiting to take them away. Bret did his share of dragging, until he came to a tiny, gray-haired woman, at least in her seventies. She was not a sweet old dear. Her eyes were fierce and she was hurling the same insults at him as the others, but even so, he could not bring himself to seize her under the armpits and drag her across the pavement. He bent down, put one arm around her back and the other behind her knees, and picked her up. She lay limp in his arms, and as he walked to the van, there flashed through his mind the other image of himself, the image he had dreamed of when he became a police-man, carrying a child or someone injured out of danger to safety.

Instead, he was carrying an old woman with political convictions to a police van, to be taken away for her hour in jail. When he put her down in the van, she looked straight at him and said, "You have a good heart. It must be hard for you, sometimes, to be a policeman."

It was that one word, "sometimes," that brought the whole of his work experience suddenly into focus. Without that one word, her statement would simply have been another sarcastic taunt, a dis-missal of him as misguided and his job as contemptible. Instead, it became an insight, perhaps even a sympathetic insight, into the reality his dream had become. In that moment, he acknowledged to himself the truth, that his colleagues were no more or less admi-rable than people in other lines of work, that heroism could not be planned or sought, but must come as a gift of fate, and that the identity of the "good guys" might sometimes be equivocal.

The loss of idealism did not leave him cynical. That was not his temperament. It left him only more cautious, and more detached in his view of his profession. It was work, like any other useful work. If he wanted a larger mission in life, he would have to make one for himself.

The present case was one of the reminders that came along at intervals, halting any drift back into the belief that his job was simple. The Nowles were in no way typical of the people he usually had to investigate. Before this morning, Bret had known most of them only by reputation. In one day, he had been drawn in close to their lives, and what he found was a family he liked very much.

He ran through them one by one in his mind, trying to fit them into the mold of a criminal. Logic and circumstance pointed to Darrell. He was the one closest by, the one most attached to the farm, the one who blamed his father for his mother's death. But Bret knew Darrell, and no matter how he turned the image, upside down, backwards or inside out, he could not make the man into a killer. Calm and matter of fact, Darrell had answered every question with no regard for how his answers might make him look. The man was a scientist to the core, so absorbed by the truths around him he had no awareness left for his own self. It took fear or hatred or arrogance to push someone to kill, and Bret could see no trace of any of these in Darrell.

Chad was a different story. He had the arrogance, at least. He also had charm, sensitivity and a liveliness that must pull people into his orbit irresistibly. Accompanied by Gifford, he had appeared that afternoon in Leroux's doorway, unannounced and without waiting for permission. He had looked serious, even sorrowful, and yet there was an underlying sparkle and vibrancy that shone through his mood, like a lamp whose shade only intensifies the light that escapes around the edges. He had come, he said, to find out the facts of the case, and to answer questions, if that was wanted.

He had answered as straightforwardly as Darrell, but his air was different, one of challenge and insouciance, as if he were fully aware how his answers made him look and did not care. He said quite simply that he had no proof he had not come to the farm on the evening in question. He had spent the afternoon in New York, gone to see a special exhibit at the Museum of Modern Art, bought some bagels for Sunday morning, shopped unsuccessfully for a scarf, driven home in time to warm up leftovers for a late supper, and spent the night alone. He had talked to no one except strangers between noon on Saturday and six on Sunday evening, when he had a date with his current girlfriend.

"Did you get along with your father?" Bret asked.

"We didn't not get along. We lived on opposite sides of a time warp. There was no meeting point, so there was no place for feelings, good or bad."

"What is your financial situation?"

Chad grinned. "I'm rich. Indecently rich, my dad would have thought."

"So you don't need money."

"No, I don't need money."

So Chad had the temperament, possibly, but no visible reason. Bret made a mental note to check that Chad was telling the truth about his finances and was not one of the legion of sleight-of-hand financiers whose apparent wealth was perched precariously atop an inverted pyramid of debt stacked on debt. Even without an obvious reason, he would not rule Chad out. There was something unsettling about Chad, a quality of elusiveness that probably led women on a spellbound chase and that might make a criminal hard to catch.

He put Chad's name at the top of his mental list and continued on to Vincie. Vincie and Gifford. Here Bret felt a guard come up, against a complex of feelings that could easily destroy objectivity.

On the one side was Vincie, who roused a flammable mixture of compassion and physical attraction. She was lovely, her beauty the female counterpart of Chad's, but she lacked his cockiness and overt charm. Rather she seemed uncertain, almost unformed, as if her growth had been halted at the age when most young people are just setting forth through the obstacle course of self-definition.

For a brief moment, when she first walked in and shook hands, she had appeared to be sophisticated and self-assured. Her clothing was fashionable; her manner was cultivated. Her beauty seemed too deliberate to be attractive. He thought he was going to dislike her.

Then she spoke, and his first impression evaporated. She said nothing remarkable and was hesitant to speak at all, as if she feared ridicule, but beneath the uncertainty and apology, he felt an intensity of suppressed emotion that overwhelmed any illusion of cool sophistication. It seemed some force had sent her will into paralysis, so that passion might burn fiercely inside but did not fuel action. She made him want to set her free and yet he did not even know what force it was that had paralyzed her.

On the other side was Gifford, who roused in Bret a revulsion almost as physical as his attraction to Vincie. He tried to pin down the source of his aversion. It did not lie in Gifford's self-importance, his condescension towards his wife, his snobbery. These were minor annoyances, traits Bret had met occasionally in wealthy absentee homeowners who came to the police headquarters to demand that a trooper drive by their shut-up vacation homes daily for the eight or ten months of their absence. In Gifford, the source was something deeper and more subtle, something Bret could only describe as a lack of manliness, although he didn't think it had much to do with gender. Gifford seemed to lack the best kind of strength, the kind that gives rise to generosity and care for others, and to fall instead into a sneering negativism and irritable over-refinement of taste.

Bret did not even know how he had come by this impression. He had seen Gifford only twice, first in the interview with Vincie, and then later, when he came in with Chad and sat to one side, interjecting an occasional remark. Yet his reaction had all the force of instinct. He felt an urge to pull Gifford away from Vincie, to yank him loose, as if he were a creeping tentacled organism that threatened to strangle her.

He did not entirely trust his own impressions. Perhaps he wanted to make Gifford into a dragon so that he would have a reason to slay him and come before his beautiful wife triumphant. Was he merely jealous? He could not think about either of them clearly, as he needed to if he was to do his job. He could not investigate a murder while wishing Vincie innocent and Gifford guilty.

Realistically, he doubted either one of them was guilty. If Vernon had died by slow poisoning, then he might put Gifford at the top of his list, but he could not picture Gifford seizing a gun on impulse and shooting someone. In any case, it would be easy enough to find out if he had had dinner with Olivia Fanning in Philadelphia on Saturday evening. Of the two of them, Vincie had had the better opportunity. She had been alone all day Saturday, not attending a public forum. Still, if she did come here, then they were lying about the time Gifford came home.

So what about Vincie? Was it possible? He could imagine her, if driven to extremity, flaring up in a rage that could end in violence. He felt strong emotion in her, not far beneath the skin, but had no clue to its nature, whether anger, passion, sorrow or terror, nor to its object, whether her husband, her family or something unknown to him. He knew only that she seemed reined in, taut with strain, and very unhappy.

To block his own response, the longing first to console and then to excite, he forced his mind back to plain facts, the proper material of police work. Could anyone verify her presence in Washington at a time that precluded her having driven to Worthing? He should ask again about Gifford's return, and watch for any wavering in their statements. What time had they said? Late, after ten. Had they said 10:00 P.M.? He was getting careless, diverted by brown eyes that should sparkle like Chad's, but instead seemed dark with sadness. Had she misled him without actually lying? He must ask again, specifically.

On the other hand, she was the one who had raised the question about the dogs. The case had been filed away, a suicide, and she had unfiled it. He could not conceive a motive convoluted enough to make a killer do such a thing. Finding himself smiling with relief, he warned himself again to avoid bias. He should make no assumptions about the convolutions in a killer's mind. He should stop trying to understand these people and concentrate on finding admissible evidence.

The trouble was, he had no evidence. He was fixated on the people because he had no facts. No witnesses had seen or heard anything that night. Any tire tracks had been washed away by the rain long since. The only fingerprints on the gun were Vernon's. Fingerprints in the kitchen would never have meant much, and would mean nothing now.

Everyone in the family had a motive of sorts. Except Gifford, any of them might have had an opportunity. Probably they knew where the gun was kept. Bret had neither witnesses nor physical evidence to make a distinction among them. Tomorrow he would begin the painstaking process of verifying people's whereabouts and re-examining what physical evidence there was. In the meantime, all he had were the people. He did not even know for certain that he had a murder.

It occurred to him that he had been leaving Georgeanne out of his considerations. She had the boldness to commit such an act, and there was no more evidence to exclude her than to exclude anyone else. So why hadn't he considered her? He had felt a certainty as instinctive as his reaction to Gifford. Now, thinking deliberately, he could trace it to its root. He was certain because Darrell was certain. Darrell had made no more attempt to protect her than he had to protect himself. With a lie, or even a half-lie, he could have protected her. He could have said, "I think she came home around eleven." But he had not. Darrell might leave himself undefended, but Bret did not believe that he would sacrifice someone he loved on the altar of literal truth. So he must have believed, absolutely, that Georgeanne did not need his protection.

Georgeanne herself had been exact, as she always was. "I left the bowling alley at ten-thirty. I got home at five minutes to eleven. Darrell woke up, but only part way. I recited bowling scores until I bored us both to sleep."

Damn this case anyway. Bret liked Georgeanne, as he liked the whole family. She said exactly what she meant. Her character was as emphatic and unmistakeable as a brass band. The only member of the family he didn't like, Gifford, was the one he must in honesty admit was the least likely criminal. The case was his job and he would do it, but if he did get a conviction in the end, his tally mark in the victory column, it was going to come at a high cost in pain to people he had begun to care about.

He turned into his driveway and parked beside his house, which was dark except for the porchlight beside the back door. It was only early dusk, not night, but the gloom of the season enveloped the house, preparing him even before he entered for the silence and emptiness inside. His son lived with his ex-wife, except on alternate weekends and eight weeks in the summer. The year since his divorce had not yet taught him to enjoy solitude. He turned on lights, turned on the radio, filled the woodstove and opened the draft wide to begin to drive off the chill of a house unattended since early morning.

Bret's nature was cheerful and even-tempered, but for this one hour of the day, before the house had warmed and he had cooked something for supper, he had to fight off melancholy. Tonight he had to tell himself, deliberately, that he must not grow too fond of the Nowles. He must not start attaching himself to someone else's family simply because he missed his own. Some small attachment was useful. It made his observations more acute. Too much attachment would make them unreliable, colored by his own desires.

He knew that his manner fooled people, and he did not scruple to use their misjudgment in his work. He looked like a fresh-faced farm boy. He talked like a hick. If people assumed he was a clod with neither intelligence nor intuition, and became careless in what they said, so much the better. But tonight, he had to quell a rebellion within, an impulse of masculine pride that wanted Vincie, at least, to recognize that he was smarter than he looked.

14

B RET NEED NOT have worried. In one sentence he had dispelled any illusion Vincie may have had that he was obtuse.

"Your dad would have put down an animal that was suffering, wouldn't he?" The sentence stayed in her mind, reverberating, because it echoed so many thoughts and images already there.

It was the kind of rapid, intuitive observation that Gifford might have made. Both men could grasp Vernon's affinity with animals and the possibility that he might regard his own suicide as identical to the euthanasia he would not deny an animal. But Gifford would have spoken with sarcasm, dismissing her father's attitude as a primitivism that could only be phony in the twentieth century. Bret's tone had conveyed empathy, not judgment, as if he did not so much observe and analyze as leap for an instant into another person's mind.

From the beginning, Vincie had admired her husband's insight into people. It was a quality she did not think was common in men. After living with him for years, she had come to assume that such insight was necessarily accompanied by obliqueness and irony, by fastidiousness, and by a bitingly critical power of judgment.

Now that assumption had been given a check. Bret Leroux appeared to have some of the same intuitive ability, but without any of those accompanying traits. Twice in one day, Vincie had forgotten his presence because she was absorbed in conversation, a conversation that he had provoked. When she did recall his presence, she could feel the intentness with which he had been listening and trying to understand the inner minds of the people talking. She had felt herself scrutinized with the simple goal of comprehension, and with no desire to publish the results of the scrutiny in a concise and cruelly honest portrait of her failings.

For a brief moment, she had felt herself relax and uncoil. For that moment, she had felt she could let herself be studied and not be afraid of what might be seen. She had wanted to be seen and understood, thoroughly.

The moment had gone as quickly as it came, as if she had passed through a sun-warmed patch of shallow water while swimming across a deep and icy lake. Bret had stepped forward to shake hands, had spoken a few ordinary words of thanks for their trouble and then had gone.

Almost as soon as he went, and before she could resume her talk with Darrell, Chad and Gifford returned, bringing the pizza they had promised for dinner. Close behind came Georgeanne and the children, and the house was engulfed in noise. The children ran from room to room and then dragged Chad away for a game that seemed to require more shouting and giggling than concentration. Gifford and Georgeanne sounded the bell for a second round of sparring and moved off into the living room where their combat would be unimpeded.

Vincie felt jarred by the change, and she thought Darrell did, too. Without talking, he made himself busy with dinner. He put the pizza in the oven to rewarm and collected plates and forks. He stood for a moment with the plates in his hand, puzzled by the problem of where to eat. Finally, he glanced at Vincie, gave a shrug and started laying the plates around the kitchen table. She shrugged in answer, took glasses from the cupboard and followed his lead setting the table.

When the food was hot, everyone sat down to eat. Unaware that the table had any special significance, the two children demanded seconds and squabbled with each other in voices just low enough to avoid a reprimand from their mother. The conversation among the adults began fitfully, but after a while, the sheer ordinariness of the event, a family bringing home take-out pizza for dinner, began to grow in over wounded memories. For minutes at a time, Vincie could join in the talk without the image of her dead father haunting her thoughts.

15

The funeral was well-attended, as funerals generally were in New England. Being occasions of painful duty, they tapped directly into the main artery of the New England temperament. Even the awkwardness of suicide did not appear to have kept anyone away.

Drawn by an assortment of reasons, mourners streamed into the church until most of the pews were full. Many of the people were unknown or barely known to Vernon's children. They came up afterwards to shake hands and introduce themselves, as members of the dairymen's association or the land trust, as people who hunted in Vernon's woods or snowmobiled in his fields, people from feed stores and equipment dealers, a man who kept beehives in the corner of his meadow, people who had bought calves from him or dipped raw milk from his bulk tank or helped re-roof his barn, a woman to whom he had given manure for her garden, and newcomers who enjoyed looking at his cows and meadows from the houses they had built on the hillside across the road.

Vincie took in the things they said about her father, but did not remember anyone's name. The service had left her too wrung out to do more than murmur her thanks.

Darrell had asked her to open the service, and she had read a poem by Robert Frost, one known to her since childhood. After she and her brothers outgrew fairy tales and adventure stories, their mother had read them poetry. Phoebe probably read it more for herself than for her husband and children, who were usually busy with something else. Still, some of the poems had stayed in Vincie's mind, imprinted there while she worked on homework or played games, like a tune barely noticed at the time, but always afterward holding the comfort of unconscious familiarity. For her father, Vincie had chosen "Birches." She loved its images of supple white trunks and ice shattering from the branches, and she could see her father as the swinger of birches, drawn towards the sky but always returning to touch the earth.

But the length of the poem had nearly sunk her. The images piled one onto another, and mingled with images of her own, of her mother's lilacs and rhododendrons bowed to the ground by a glittering, petrifying sheath of ice; of her father, in a rare moment of playfulness, scaling a maple tree to hang a bird feeder from one of its branches, when he could more easily have stayed on the ground and tossed a weighted rope up over the branch. Coming to the line "Earth's the right place for love; I don't know where it's likely to go better," she almost broke down, swallowed up by a rush of sorrow, not at something she had lost, but at something that had never been. She paused, made herself breathe slowly for a moment, then finished the last few lines, keeping her voice flat and emotionless just to get through them.

She sat down, and Reverend Graham followed. Doing as they had asked, he steered clear of sin and redemption, and talked only of god's love for humankind, the love which had taken Vernon's spirit back to itself. Vincie thought her father might have objected to having one species singled out from the rest of creation, but otherwise could have listened content.

For herself, the sermon was a moment of soothingly impersonal hopefulness and she tried to find comfort in it. She tried to rest in the thought that Vernon's spirit was now part of a larger and infinitely loving spirit. But everything inside her was crying out, "He missed his chance. There isn't any other chance and he missed the one he had here. It isn't enough to love trees and cows. You can't love god if you don't love people. He missed his chance. We missed our chance."

Then the minister finished, and Chad stepped forward to speak the eulogy for his father. That was where the strangeness began.

Chad spoke seemingly impromptu, just as he had for Phoebe, stringing together stories to construct an image of the man. He began with his own six-year-old memory of following his father out to the barn in winter darkness, when the snow was piled high in banks and drifts. Somehow he had wandered to the wrong side of a drift and could no longer see his father. He could no longer see anything over the vast banks of whiteness amid gray dusk. He had wandered and floundered for what seemed hours in snow up to his waist, unable to see anything but white, not knowing where the barn or the house or his father might be. Finally, he had sat down and curled himself up like a cocoon. He tried to pretend he was a hibernating bear, but he was shaking with fright. After a time, he didn't know how long, a huge figure loomed up beside him in the darkness.

"Chad, there you are. I thought you'd gone back to the house. How did you come here?"

"I'm a bear in my den for the winter," Chad said, trying to sound fierce through teeth that were chattering with cold. Even at the age of six, he had not wanted his father to think he had done something stupid, gotten lost. He was playing. It was all a game. He meant to be there.

Back in the house, Vernon had gone along with his game and had not humiliated him by telling the others that he had gotten lost and had been scared. "Chad got a little cold, playing in the snow. Maybe he should have some hot chocolate." That was all that was said. His terror was his own secret, safe from ridicule or disapproval.

The story was meant to show how Vernon had protected his son's pride, but it made Vincie feel like a six-year-old wandering alone through endless baffling cold whiteness, ashamed of feeling afraid and never able to tell anyone about the fear.

145

Chad went on to another story, about the day he discovered that the young bull calves and the old cows who were loaded onto trailers and hauled away were being taken somewhere to be killed and eaten. He had protested, why can't we keep them here? Why can't we let them all live? Vernon had explained to him, patiently, the same inescapable equation of life and death that Vincie remembered, that the pastures were only so big, and for each animal that was kept alive, there was another who could not be born, because there would be no room for it. Chad recalled how calm his father had been, how seemingly free from the futile rage that boiled in his son, whose every feeling of tenderness rebelled against harsh truth. He had wanted to cry out, it can't be so, there must be a way to change it, no creature should have to die, ever. His protest was stopped in his throat by his father's implacable "So it is." One did not rail against the beautiful and remorseless balance of the universe.

Chad was trying to portray his father's dignity and largeness of vision, but all Vincie could feel listening was the child's cry of grief for the gentle, large-bellied old cows, and the fine-boned, velvet-eyed calves, a cry that must be strangled down in the throat because it was of no use. And then she thought of her father, broken down in tears over a dead cow, and she wondered if Chad understood that his father, too, was strangling his howl of grief.

Chad continued on, talking about Vernon's skills as a farmer, his achievements with his herd, his awards, all the more conventional measures of his worth. But then this topic, too, somehow diverted itself, this time to an image of Vernon sitting at his desk, going over the accounts and pausing now and then to gaze ahead with a frown. Behind him, Chad and Darrell were wrestling, tumbling about on the couch, their teen-aged limbs threatening at any moment to knock over a lamp or sweep all the magazines off the coffee table. Vernon had seemed not to know they were there. His mind was fixed on a downward graph of numbers that could be extrapolated all the way to bankruptcy.

Phoebe had appeared in the doorway, just at the moment when a flying foot grazed a lamp and toppled it to the floor with a crash. At the noise, Vernon surfaced from his gloom and looked around. "Why didn't you stop them before this happened?" Phoebe asked, and he answered, quite sincerely, "Stop what?"

"I suppose you were thinking about something else," she said, and he answered, "I was thinking that at the rate we're going, we've got about nine more years."

As it turned out, he'd held on for fourteen, but the graph had never changed direction and in the end he had made the hard choice to give up his life's work before the choice was made for him.

When Chad finished speaking, Vincie sat numb. To her, it had seemed a chilling version of her father's life. Had other people heard it the same way? She turned to look at Darrell, but his face was, as always, still and unreadable. Beyond him, she could see Georgeanne. The grim fixity of her expression, too grim even for the relief of tears, told Vincie she was not the only one who had heard in Chad's words a tale that found as much or more sorrow in Vernon's life as it found in his death.

On the other side of her, Gifford fiddled with his program, then turned his head to scan the congregation. In his face she saw only the detachment of an uninvolved observer. He would shun the hypocrisy of looking grieved for a man he hadn't liked. He attended the service as a support to Vincie, nothing else.

The congregation rose to recite the twenty-third psalm. In that moment, coming after what Chad had said, the familiar words sounded bitterly ironic. Chad had seen no green pastures or still waters in his father's life, and the valley of the shadow of death looked like the only sheltered haven.

A final hymn was sung, a final prayer spoken, and Vincie, the oldest child, led the way up the aisle to the lobby. As people shook hands with her and murmured words of consolation, she was gradually drawn out of her trance and back to the more ordinary moods of a funeral, sorrow, solemnity, and gratitude for people's kindness, however fleeting it might be. Dozens of people filed past her, most

147

of them only distantly remembered, some never known at all. No one wailed, and few people appeared even to have wept. These were not weeping and wailing people. Like Vernon's, their feelings flowed silently, beneath the snow. They were there. They took the hours away from work. They drove over muddy roads to come. Their presence was witness to their respect. Greater display would be superfluity, even ostentation, as distasteful as the showy displays of wealth more and more to be seen on local hilltops, the grandiose new houses with walls of glass, built to look and be looked at from all directions.

The crowd began to thin, most returning home or to work, a few walking across the green in the direction of Darrell's house. Vincie noticed then that Bret Leroux had not come. Noticing his absence, she realized she must have expected him to come and felt a minor disappointment that he had not. She had thought he felt a personal as well as professional connection to the family. And even if he did not, might he not have come as part of his job, to watch who was there and how people behaved? With this thought came understanding of his absence. The death was now the object of a possible murder investigation. His presence would have put all of them into the role of suspects under observation.

In the same moment, she saw him come quietly into the church lobby. He stopped to talk for a while with Darrell, said a few words to Chad, then came towards her and Gifford.

"I wanted to pay my respects to your dad," he said. "I was afraid some of you might feel awkward, having me here for the service, but I wanted you to know I thought very highly of Vernon."

"Thank you. I'm glad you came. I hope Darrell mentioned we're having people in at his house. Will you come?"

He shook his head, apologetically. "I guess I won't. It's kind of the same thing, maybe more so."

She nodded and he said good-bye and left, as unobtrusively as he had come.

She and Gifford followed soon after, to walk to Darrell's. Out of anyone's hearing, Gifford was finally able to speak the observations that had been accumulating through two hours of enforced restraint.

"So how many of these people actually gave a damn about your father and how many are just carrying out a civic duty?" he said. "I think small town people attend funerals with an enthusiasm that's almost ghoulish. I suppose it's the best entertainment available. I only saw half a dozen people who looked seriously grieved. All the others were just making sure their presence was noted. Like the sergeant, not wanting to be thought remiss."

"I don't think Detective Sergeant Leroux gave a damn what we thought of him or his remissness. Nor many of the other people, either."

"You don't think they wanted their presence noted? It's just like signing in on the checklist at town meeting. It's proof of respectability."

"Of course they want their presence noted. It's how they show they thought well of Dad, that's all."

"How delightfully optimistic you are about human nature."

Vincie felt a chill spreading over her, a bleakness that had nothing to do either with the funeral or with the gray dampness of the day. Was he right? Were all these people merely totting up points in some account book of social status? Was everyone finally as small-minded and calculating as Gifford thought they were?

Her heart rebelled. She could not bear a human landscape as inert, cold and cheerless as April mud. She had to believe in the possibility of kindness, as she believed in the quickening roots and buds whose growth could not yet be seen. She remembered Roger Cobb, on her first morning back in Worthing, stopping to speak his admiration for her father. She clung to the memory, and to her first thought about Bret Leroux, that he had stayed away from the funeral out of concern for their feelings, and that he had come at the end, sincerely, to demonstrate his respect.

But Gifford was there, too, inside her own mind, like a television voice-over, disembodied, omniscient and mocking. Her every thought was accompanied by his commentary, and she could not keep her

149

hold on the thought itself. His voice said, with assurance, that the logic she saw in Bret's action was too simple to be real. Humans were not twelve inch rulers. The human brain never moved from one place to another in a straight line. She was naive to take the sergeant's words at face value. His speech was a form of politeness, unconnected to his true intentions. Probably it was a maneuver, designed to win their gratitude, lower their guard, make them more vulnerable to his future inquiries.

She felt her own thought start to soften and lose its form, ready to flow into the shape offered by her husband's certainty. She resisted. She sought her own reply to his pronouncements. She retraced impressions, of Bret's handshake, his hand square and firm, still cold from having been outdoors. "Cold hands, warm heart." The old saying flitted past, in the midst of other impressions. His eyes had looked at her steadily. His voice held no irony, no layering of meanings. "I was afraid some of you might feel awkward..." That was like Darrell, to look from another's point of view. But Bret did not strike her as a man who would fall into paralyzing ambivalence. She thought he would rather fail by acting mistakenly than fail by not acting at all. She thought, too, that he might not bother to devise snares because he thought it was simpler to wait and catch people in the snares they devised themselves.

Or was she deceived by wide blue eyes and pink cheeks and boyish diffidence? He seemed cheerful and uncomplicated, but perhaps she was still seeing the eighteen-year-old football player with his leg in a cast, borrowing a megaphone and pompoms from the cheerleaders to help rouse the crowd, hopping on crutches back and forth along the sideline, unable to stay still while his teammates played. Perhaps underneath he was as tangled and difficult as any other person.

She did not dare ask herself why it mattered, why it had become so deathly important that this man prove to be the straightforward, well-intentioned person she thought he was and not the devious, convoluted creature that Gifford saw. The question came too near the core of her existence. She sensed that if she answered it, something would disintegrate, her marriage and possibly herself, too, because often the two things seemed indistinguishable.

Instead she shied away, and made some remark to her husband about the choice of hymns, to force her thoughts onto topics neutral and public. Her remark launched Gifford into a dissection of the shield and fortress imagery in Christian hymns, and Vincie took shelter in listening, until they reached the wider shelter of a living room full of people.

16

THE GUESTS STAYED a suitable hour or so, then left. With relief, the family seized on the need to put away food, wash dishes and tidy the house. They were worn out from talk, and from all the forms of funerals that are designed to elicit sorrow. Their emotions were exhausted, and work offered rest.

Only Gifford still felt a desire to talk. Having no personal grief to be drawn out of him, he had spent the last hours observing other people. He was nearly bursting with the need for someone to hear about what he had seen. None of his relatives had the stamina to continue as his audience, so he stood near the door to the kitchen, offering his comments to the air as the others passed back and forth from kitchen to dining room and living room, carrying plates, glasses, dishcloths and trash baskets. He was answered by an occasional grunt, from whoever was nearest when a pause in the stream of commentary asked for a reply.

"I learned a lot about silage today. Old Mr. McClure had plenty to say about what cows like and don't like in their food. He ought to know. He was a walking emanation of cow aromas, even in his Sunday suit."

Chad murmured "Mm, hm," as he wiped the counter behind Gifford.

"Apparently, he's not as meticulous as Vernon was. The way he put it was that he likes to keep a few spare parts about, because he never knows what might come in handy. I can picture his place. If he lived in any other state, he'd need a junkyard permit."

"Probably would," said Georgeanne, with a shrug.

"He certainly had opinions about Vernon. Thought he was a fool, but an admirable fool. He said the only thing more stubborn and contrary-minded than a Jersey cow is a man who still raises Jerseys when Holsteins give more milk. He said you can go broke with either one, but if you go broke with Jerseys, people will say you're a fool, where if you go broke with Holsteins, they'll just say times are hard. I gather Mr. McClure raises Holsteins."

Darrell smiled a little. "No, he raises Jerseys."

"Does he?" Gifford paused, but only for a moment. He shifted to a new topic. "Maud Reynolds makes her presence felt. She's the principal where you teach, isn't she?"

Darrell nodded. He reached past Gifford to put a stack of just-dried plates into the cupboard behind him.

"I'd say she's every teenager's nightmare of a school principal. Two hundred years ago she'd either have been drowned as a witch, or else she'd have been the one supervising while everyone else was drowned. Probably the latter, given her size. She must be six foot two. I can imagine her towering over some quivering fifteen-year-old, fixing him with an X-ray glare that seems to search out every sin he's ever committed in his life. I felt impaled, the whole time we were talking. Is she as intimidating to work for as she is in a conversation?"

"Only if she doesn't like you," Georgeanne said.

"The kids don't mess with her, though," Darrell added, to dampen any spark Georgeanne might have struck.

"I'll bet not," Gifford said. "I gather her husband is on the board of the land trust. What a perfect Chamber of Commerce and Rotary Club type, slapping everyone on the back, best pals the moment he knows your name. I meet a lot of them in D.C. They've always got some angle in mind. They size you up in thirty seconds to see if you're a contact worth pursuing. The moment he decided I had no connections he could make use of, he was off across the room to chat up somebody else."

It seemed Gifford had traveled a good part of the room himself. He ran through a dozen or more sketches of people he had talked to in the course of the afternoon. By the time he wound down, all physical remnants of the occasion were cleaned up and put away. His listeners, who had only half-heard what he said, were inclined to sink back quietly into chairs and be left alone.

No one was hungry for dinner, and they agreed almost wordlessly to dispense with it. Georgeanne heated up hot dogs for the children while the others sat in the living room, in silence apart from a few desultory remarks about how well the service had come off and how well attended it had been. They agreed, as wordlessly as they had agreed about dinner, that the ragged wound in their midst was to be left untended for the moment. Their nerves needed to rest and recover before enduring the next bout of painful repair.

Vincie and Gifford did not stay late. Gifford was made restless by the impenetrability of everyone else's mood, and Vincie thought Georgeanne was probably exhausted after hosting the reception. Although Georgeanne had fed her children and put them to bed with her usual briskness, she made no reply when Gifford dropped a couple of baiting remarks that on other days would have been irresistible provocation. Her jaw looked set, the way it does when someone is kept functioning by will alone. Vincie roused her husband for departure, and he went along willingly.

The moment they were outside, he took a deep breath and said, "What a relief! The house was suffocating with the fumes of repression."

In the car, his restlessness found relief in more opinions. "That funeral service was certainly conventional enough to make all the neighbors approve. Couldn't you have found something a little more original to read than Robert Frost?"

"My parents liked Robert Frost."

"I know they did, and it's so predictable. Especially here in New England. With any thought at all, you could have found a poem that would have made the service distinctive. Or I could have suggested something, if you had asked me. Reading Frost is such a perfect cliché. It's exactly the sort of thing I would have expected Darrell to choose, but I thought you had more imagination."

For a moment his last remark took all the breath out of her. To be corrected herself was nothing new and would have prompted only a brief reflex protest. But the scornful swipes at her family landed like a physical blow to her diaphragm. She felt numb and sick, and then suddenly words began spewing out of her, coming without thought but with all the fluency and venom of fifteen years' training. "A funeral is not an off-Broadway play, Gifford. It's not a place to put on some virtuoso display of our own cleverness. The point is truth, not originality. The point is to connect my father to all the other people who have died and will die. I don't care if ten million other people like the same poem he liked. Dad wouldn't have cared either. He didn't have your colossal ego. He didn't have to have the whole world gazing at him in awe and amazement. He didn't have to make himself important by despising everyone and everything. You have such a gift of cleverness, and you use it in such petty, destructive ways. You're like someone who can't think of a better use for sunlight than to take a magnifying glass and torture beetles with it."

As quickly as her fury had come, it was spent, and she sat limp in reaction. She glanced at her husband, wondering if her words had made any impression, or if, as usual, he would appear not to have heard her. He did not say a word, and as she looked at him, he seemed visibly to shrink and sag, as if his bones had gone soft. She was reminded of a time in childhood, when a friend had showed her what happened if she poured salt on a slug. They had watched it writhe and shrivel as its fluids were sucked out by the salt. She felt now as she had then, a brief amazement at the success of the experiment, followed by horror at having been cruel, even to something as repellent as a slug.

It should not have surprised her, to discover that her opinion mattered. She had known before now that he was almost morbidly sensitive to how he was seen by others. He dreaded to be thought unsophisticated, ingenuous, or middle class. His professional life was spent among people who measured themselves by the acuity of their critical powers, and in a few cases those critical skills were honed to a razor sharpness that could shred an ego not defended by skills of equal sharpness. If a scholar was unusually confident, he might not care what his peers thought. If he was well-liked, his peers would direct their barbs elsewhere. If he was neither of those things, then he had better be well-guarded. Gifford's defenses were his sarcasm, his command of language, and most of all, the enveloping, squid's ink cloud of indifference with which he surrounded himself. He could not be attacked where it mattered, if he did not allow anything to matter.

But the one person who could see inside the cloud was Vincie. She lived inside the cloud. She could see how much he feared to look foolish and how much he wanted his work to be seen as "significant" in the field. She was the one person who knew exactly where he was vulnerable and had the power to strike at that spot, if she wished.

She felt no triumph in this discovery of power. It felt rather like a claim of dependency upon her, adding itself to all the other claims he made. If she had such power to hurt, then she must watch every word and deed. His vulnerability became one more means of governing her behavior.

In truth, she had always suspected her power, and had guarded her actions accordingly. She had been taught never to harm a living creature, and her husband was a living creature. Tonight, her guard had slipped. Tonight, he had stepped outside the deeply worn path of their marital quarrels, their long-practiced minuet of obliquely critical remarks from him and defensiveness in her, unvoiced until it flared in brief, directionless eruptions of anger. Tonight, his jab had been too direct, and aimed at a place in her less calloused by habit. Her reaction had been equally direct, and too quick for conscience to deflect her aim toward empty air. For a moment, her own actual pain had obscured the pain he might potentially feel, and she had replied to him in kind.

The moment was brief. Her conscience awoke and she felt a remorse that outweighed the satisfaction of having fought back.

Gifford recovered almost as quickly as she regretted. His posture straightened itself as a new thought formed in his mind and began to grow. By the time they reached the farm, his back was perfectly straight and the idea burst forth complete.

"You're right, of course, Vincie. Your father was not an original person. An original, creative funeral would not have expressed who he was at all. He belonged to some pastoral era of ancient times, an era that probably never existed except in myth. It's only fitting that he should be commemorated by all of the most conventional expressions of our culture's mythology. When I suggested otherwise, I neglected to take into account the sort of person he was. He truly was a simple man."

My father was not simple at all, Vincie thought, but this time she did not bother to answer. She was done with protest. She was too tired to argue, and not sure she cared who won.

17

GIFFORD WOKE UP peevish and announced that he would leave for Washington as soon as he had eaten breakfast.

"I'm not needed here," he said. "I've made my appearance at the funeral, so now I'll leave you to sort out the business matters with your brothers. I have to prepare my lectures for next week, and in any case I'm sure you'll do much better without me."

Again, Vincie did not contradict him, though perhaps he wanted her to. She did not care if he went or stayed, and could not muster even the token politeness of saying, "I'll miss your company." She made coffee and toast and set his breakfast in front of him, all the while wrapped in a silence as opaque as Darrell's. In the past, to be at outs with her husband would have been intolerable. She would have rushed to mend the breach, by saying whatever consoling or apologetic words were necessary to bring them back together. Today she was sunk in an apathy as stupefying as an anesthetic.

Gifford did not know how to reply to indifference. He had encountered her anger, her uncertainty, her fears and enthusiasms. He had never before encountered this utter absence of emotion. Their roles were reversed. Instead of Vincie trying to elicit some response from a man who viewed most of the world with boredom and contempt, Gifford found himself trying to provoke some reaction from a wife turned nearly catatonic. Nothing he said touched a sympathetic nerve, neither his complaints about the long drive home and the tedium of preparing lectures, nor his attempts to commiserate with her about the equal tedium she faced in sorting out her father's affairs.

Vincie's state of mind was not the product of calculation. It was as new to her as it was to him. She lacked even enough life in her nerves to feel amazement at the novelty. She stood near the stove and watched Gifford eat his breakfast, observing him as dispassionately as if she had happened to glance through the window of a restaurant while waiting at a stoplight, and found her gaze resting on one of the customers. He buttered his toast with precision, not missing a millimeter, then ate it neatly, crust first, in small bites that carved it into smaller and smaller rectangles until it was gone. He added cream to his coffee, lavishly, then added an exact rounded teaspoon of sugar. He continued to talk while he ate, and although his efforts to provoke her were growing more and more emphatic, his eating habits remained undisturbed. His remarks were alternately critical, sympathetic and pleading, but he did not gesticulate or raise his voice or alter the modulated tempo of bites and sips.

Vincie thought, with detachment, that he was as handsome now as when they met. His eyebrows were straight, black, elegantly drawn. His eyes were an arresting pale gray-green. The high baldness of his forehead only emphasized the distinction and fine shape of his other features. His appearance somehow managed to suggest that a thick head of hair would be superfluous and even slightly crude. At forty-three, his face was still unlined. He rarely scowled, grinned or raised his eyebrows. He had too much skill with words to need grimaces of expression to make his meaning understood.

She recalled the cool dismissiveness of his voice the night before, as he remarked on the triteness of her choice of reading. He had been too caught up in the insult to his sense of taste to consider what her feelings must have been, reading words so familiar to her and so intermingled with memories of her parents. She thought she should be angry with him, but she felt no anger. She felt simply nothing.

"You'll be on your own, then," he was saying. "I hope it won't be too dreary for you. I'm taking the car, of course, but I assume you can borrow one of Darrell's. Or perhaps your father still had one."

"I can use his truck," she said. "It's out in the shed."

"Fifteen years old and still runs perfectly, no doubt," he said. "I hope this process isn't going to take weeks. I don't function well without you. The microwave and dishwasher I have mastered, but your recipe file remains one of life's mysteries. I shall be condemned to eating out of plastic trays. I shall never understand the complexities of garlic and the magical properties of baking powder."

"I don't understand the properties of baking powder either. I can read English, that's all." Her voice was flat, devoid of sympathy.

"No, you have some divine female instinct that knows when all the ingredients are in balance. It is a gift of wizardry that men are rarely given and women take for granted."

She said nothing, but she thought of Bev and of many other women she knew who were very bad cooks. Gifford was not speaking serious thoughts. He was merely trying to find some statement that would rouse either pity or annoyance strong enough to make her react.

"I would stay with you, if I did not have obligations at home," he said. "There is no joy for me, I assure you, in a solitary apartment and the unrelieved company of anxious adolescents. And equally anxious faculty, all bickering and currying favor and stabbing one another in the back for the sake of some small scrap of power. At least you will be here in the quiet of the country, not bothered by anyone, surrounded by natural beauty…"

Surrounded by mud, Vincie thought.

"If you get bored, you can always amuse yourself with the rosy-cheeked young policeman, who so desperately wants you. He would bed you on the spot, if you were inclined."

"What are you talking about?" Vincie flashed out.

He smiled slightly. He had found a nerve.

"Isn't it obvious you've sparked his lust? He never takes his eyes off you. He looks like a big, dumb, panting Golden Retriever and you're the female he thinks is about to come into heat."

"That's ridiculous. If he's watching me so closely, it must mean he thinks I know something...or did something..."

"My sweet innocent wife. Men are cruder than you think. When they get that look in their eye, they have one thought and one thought only. I know you would like to credit him with noble motives, but I assure you, he's just making plans for a quick screw."

"That's what you'd be planning, anyway," she said. "You don't know a thing about Bret Leroux. Neither one of us knows a thing about him. He's just doing his job, and part of his job is to watch people."

"My, how she leaps to defend him. Should I be jealous? Is she indulging a secret infatuation of her own? And for a state trooper, of all things. Perhaps it's the badge, and the intoxicating aura of power."

Her nerves were awake now, and aflame. "I don't give a damn about Bret Leroux. If he's feeling lustful, that's his worry. But there's no reason for you to take a perfectly ordinary man with ordinary feelings and transform him into something sordid and calculating."

"No transformation is necessary, alas. That is what men are, sordid and calculating. That is what humans are, I should say. Heaven forbid that I should be sexist."

"No, you're not sexist. You despise everyone equally, male or female. So very egalitarian."

"Just realistic. Neither sex is any better than the other."

"Or any worse."

"True. For what it's worth." He stood up and brought his dishes to the sink. "I must be on my way. I don't want to drive late at night."

The argument had reassured him. He was back on familiar ground, meeting Vincie's anger with his own unshakeable composure. Apathy had unnerved him. Apathy offered no holds for a countermove. Anger could be diverted into the channel he chose, its energy harnessed for his purposes.

"You needn't worry that I'm jealous," he said. "I know some men might be, but I trust you. I trust your powers of discrimination. The sergeant may entice you into a superficial sexual fling, but he can't touch the deeper feelings, the passions that really matter. You and I are two halves of one soul. He can't change that, even if he gets what he's after."

"What he's after is a murderer," Vincie murmured, but Gifford was already headed upstairs to pack and did not hear her.

When he had left for Washington, she made her own breakfast and sat at the table to eat. It seemed the pizza had exorcised the memories of horror from the room. She thought of her father as she sat down, but felt no superstitious shudder in response.

Her thoughts dwelt on her husband, not her father. Was he right that they were two halves of the same whole, inseparable? She often felt her mind pulled into line behind his, seeing things as he saw them.

It frightened her, this sensation. She seemed to have lost her own ability to judge reality. It was almost as if she had ceased to exist. She had become a subset of Gifford, fully encompassed by him. The world came to her through his senses. His eyes saw creeping mildew. His ears heard the silken hiss of insinuations. His nose smelled the nauseating sweetness of decay. He took it all in with a shrug, and said it was only to be expected.

Vincie could not shrug. Her mind recoiled. Such a vision was unendurable. She thought she saw another side as well, a happier side, and she longed to believe it was not illusion. But she did not trust her own senses. She saw hopes, not truth. It was Gifford who forced her to face reality, unembellished. Without him, she might retreat into a dreamworld, a sunny bubble of wishful thinking, because her own senses could no longer distinguish between truth and invention.

Her head had begun to throb, as if her brain were performing painful contortions in its effort to observe its own workings. She stared at her coffee cup, fixing on a tangible object to halt the inward spiral. Like a scientist testing an instrument of doubtful reliability, she tried out her eyes on the round, smooth surface, measuring shape and size and color.

She saw a thick white stoneware mug with straight sides, unadorned and impossible to break, unless it were hurled against concrete. It was one of a set, part of her family's kitchenware since her childhood. In an instant, she recalled her child's feel of it, clumsy and heavy in her hands. She could hold it only by wrapping both hands around the sides. She felt the thick rim against her lips, so thick and round that she must concentrate and press her mouth tightly against its contours to stop milk from leaking out the corners. The cup was solid and real. She could feel its weight, the smoothness of the glaze. Its shape had nothing to do with Gifford. She had known its shape long before she knew her husband. The cup existed and she existed, both apart from him.

She raised her eyes to look around the kitchen. The walls were pale yellow. The counters were sage green linoleum with metal trim around the edges. The cupboards were white. Without moving from where she sat, she could feel how each cupboard opened, how hard a pull was needed, some doors stiff and reluctant, others barely held shut at all. She could open each drawer as well, feel the weight of its contents, and hear the clink of shifting spoons or the thump of the rolling pin. She knew everything in this room. She did not need Gifford's help to experience it. She had known it before him, and she could know it again now, without him.

Was this how a baby felt, laboring through its first walking steps, or a stroke victim, relearning everything once known?

She ran water in the sink to wash dishes, hers and Gifford's. Gifford had eaten from the plate, but her hands felt nothing of him as she washed it. She felt the same plate she had always known, thick and heavy like the mug. She heard the same sound she had always known, the underwater thump of dishware against the enameled cast iron of the sink.

She emptied the sink, wiped the table, and put away the coffee and bread. She was intensely aware of each small action, her hand on the sponge, her arm stretching to reach the cupboard, herself inhabiting this body. Each movement reminded her that she existed.

And if she existed, then she had a point of view. She could see Gifford as a man entirely separate from herself. She could form her own estimate of Bret Leroux, entirely separate from Gifford's estimate. She almost laughed, these actions were so elementary, so taken for granted by most people. How absurd, to be taking baby steps at the age of thirty-five, but so it was. She stood the two men up in her mind, like two dairy heifers at a cattle show, with her the judge. She could point out strengths and weaknesses, the development of the udder, the straightness of the back, the spring of the ribs and the set of the feet. The two could not be less alike, a Holstein and a Jersey. But which was which? She smiled. Gifford had to be the Jersey, fine-boned, self-absorbed, eccentric and, if you had the patience, captivating. Bret was unquestionably the Holstein, solid, practical, unglamorous and easy-going, the cheery black and white creature made faddish by mugs and T-shirts.

She put the comparison aside. It would fall apart if pursued. Gifford was like a Jersey only in being unlike either Bret Leroux or a Holstein.

She remembered her first impression of him, seen from a middle row of a lecture hall. He had strolled into the room, leaned casually against the lectern, and smiled out over the heads of his audience as he waited for the last stragglers to find seats. Even when the room was quiet, he waited a moment longer. Then he said, "Hello, I am Professor James Gifford Wainwright, Gifford to those who know me. This class is Late Victorian and Early Modern Poetry. You do not need a calculator for this course, but you do need a brain. The poetry we will discuss is as challenging and complex as anything the human mind has ever produced. If you think you are in the wrong classroom, this might be a good moment for you to leave and find the course you meant to attend."

He paused and waited, but no one moved. Even if someone truly had come to the wrong classroom, the person would not get up and leave at that moment, not when it would look like a humiliating flight from challenge.

After a minute, Gifford began to speak, weaving words into a lecture that was mesmerizing. Vincie and everyone in the room were drawn in, enthralled. After every lecture he was rushed by groups of students eager to ask questions. Vincie had never been one of them, but even so, she often felt his gaze pick her out from among the rows of students and rest on her while he spun his luxuriant sentences. His voice felt almost as intimate as a caress, and she fell in love, with Yeats, Hopkins, the Rossettis, Eliot, all of them, because their voices came to her through Gifford's.

Or had she loved him, in part, because of them? The question pulled her up short.

Years later, after she had struggled through her time in graduate school and finally given up, she began to think her worship of the poets must have been a momentary hallucination, brought on by her worship of Gifford. Once marriage made him mortal, and often difficult, the glow of the poets, too, had faded.

But perhaps it was the poetry that had made him so mesmerizing to begin with. Perhaps she would have fallen in love with anyone who could bring that strange, intricate, gorgeous language to life. Perhaps it was because he had stopped speaking the voice of the poets and started speaking his own that his stature had shrunk. Perhaps the accumulation of day-to-day disappointment in him had finally spread its tarnish onto the poetry and dulled her early passion into a muddy indifference.

The question now became, if he was not the dazzling being she had first loved, could she still find love with the actual man she had married?

And who was that man? In their early years, she had thought him a man full of fire and feeling, and gifted with the power to put that feeling into words. Now she thought the fire had all been secondhand, candlelight reflecting off an exquisite crystal goblet. He still had the words, in abundance, but it seemed that the flame that gave them life had burned in Gerard Manley Hopkins and Christina Rossetti, and not in him.

The phone rang and she jumped. She looked around to see where the sound had come from. Without dishwater and plates to keep her connected, she had forgotten where she was. Seeing cupboards, she remembered, and remembered, also, Chad's story about her father, so deep in thought he had no awareness of two teenaged boys roughhousing on the furniture.

18

THE VOICE ON the phone identified itself as Bret Leroux.

"I've got another couple of questions," he said. "Is there a time I could talk with you and your husband?"

"Gifford has left for D.C. I will answer anything I can."

"Could you come here, or should I stop by the farm?"

"I'll come there. I'm not doing anything in particular, and I imagine you are."

"I'm not doing all that much in particular, but it would be a help if you came here. I'm waiting for a couple of calls."

"I'll come over now," she said.

She fetched her purse and coat and went out to the machinery shed, where she had seen her father's truck parked. It was a GMC, ten or fifteen years old, and probably Gifford's remark was accurate, that it still ran perfectly. She reached for the ignition and found it empty. She felt the same cold shock she had felt hearing the silence on the farm, and finding the kitchen door locked. Vernon had never taken the key out of the truck. He had a place for everything, and the place for that key was in the ignition. If it wasn't there, then Vincie had no idea where it might be. She searched the cab, then returned to the house and looked through drawers, in the kitchen and in Vernon's desk, but without luck. Perhaps Darrell had taken it. She was about to call him and ask when she noticed Chad's car keys lying on the counter.

She ran upstairs, knocked on his door, and received a drowsy, "What is it?" in reply.

She opened the door and stuck her head in. "May I borrow your car to go to town?"

He sat halfway up and grinned. "Help yourself. She's only happy at speeds over sixty, though, so don't drive like an old lady." He flopped back down and pulled the covers up around his neck to doze some more.

At the police headquarters, Bret stood up to shake hands and invited her to sit down, but then did not sit down himself. He seemed ill at ease, almost jumpy.

"I was going over my notes and realized I wasn't quite clear about the times," he said. He picked up his pad, as if he needed to consult it, but his eyes did not focus on what was written there.

"You said your husband came home late, after ten, maybe eleven. Did you mean ten that evening or ten the next morning?"

Vincie flushed. Strictly speaking, she had not lied, but the effect had been that of a lie. "It was ten the next morning. He was tired and stayed in a motel instead of driving back."

"That makes more sense, then. I should have asked the first time, instead of leaping to conclusions. But this backs up what Professor Fanning said."

"So you already knew he didn't come home Saturday night."

Bret looked embarrassed and reluctant. "Not entirely. We knew he couldn't have gotten to Washington by eleven, anyhow, but you might have misjudged the time. If he stayed the night, then everything fits."

"What did Professor Fanning say?"

Again he hesitated. "She was a little vague about times. But she did say it had to be at least ten before he left, probably later. She said she was so caught up in the conversation, she didn't pay attention to the time. I guess you could say she was awestruck by your husband. And a little flighty by nature. Sort of a free spirit." He paused, then added, "What she actually said was, 'I don't wear a watch, because time is the slavemaster of modern civilization and I refuse to be its prisoner.' She said she really couldn't swear to anything about the time, except that it must have been later than ten. So we knew he couldn't have been in Washington by eleven."

Bret was looking more and more uncomfortable. The implications of Olivia Fanning's statement were too evident for him to pretend they hadn't occurred to him. Every word he spoke might be a painful embarrassment to Vincie. He was doing what little he could to temper the hurt, and avert his gaze so that he would not compound her humiliation.

His concern for her was palpable, and in the moment when she should have been mortified by his knowledge of her husband's possible infidelity, she found her thoughts singing with relief, "He's not all what Gifford thinks. I'm not just daydreaming."

She hurried to free him from a concern that was needless. "Gifford often has people like Olivia Fanning hovering around him, awestruck," she said. "It's a hazard of his profession. He's a hero to young people, but he makes sure to stay detached. Even if... He stays detached, even if the time was a lot later than ten o'clock. Even if the time was midnight, or breakfast time the next morning."

She looked straight at him, trying to convey that nothing he had said had distressed her, and that she recognized his concern and was grateful for it. "Gifford and I may have a problem, but it's not Olivia Fanning," she said.

He nodded, and the worry cleared from his face. The departure of one expression left another exposed, for just an instant, as they faced each other. Then his eyes ducked away toward his notepad, drawing a curtain over private emotions that did not belong in his institutional green office.

For one split second, she had felt herself looked at as a woman and beautiful.

So Gifford did see half the truth, she thought. He saw half the truth, but not all of it. So it was with him always. He had piercing insight into the half of everything. He had eyes that saw the infra-red and penetrated the deepest darkness, but he was blind to the ordinary spectrum. His understanding stripped away all the disguises with which people hid their failings and uncertainties, but denied the reality of actions carried out in full view. To Gifford, actions were all part of the disguise. They were too simple, too obvious, and not to be trusted.

She knew he was right, that the eye could not see truth without looking into the shadows. But she was right, too, that the eye needed light as well as shadow to see the truth in all its dimensions. At night all cats are gray, she thought. Another old saying. Bret Leroux's presence seemed to call forth old sayings, perhaps because he seemed like the embodiment of everything simple and open. No doubt he had depths, if one knew him, but he also had a surface. She watched him leafing through his notepad and for a moment enjoyed the restfulness of floating there, on the surface.

When Bret had steadied himself, he looked up from his notes. "Professor Fanning's statement puts your husband completely in the clear. I expect that's a relief to you."

"It is, although I've never doubted he was in the clear. His mood on Sunday was what it would be after a flirtation, not after a murder. Anyway, I couldn't imagine him shooting someone."

"No, I guess not. It does leave another question, though."

He paused, and she asked it for him. "What was I doing all that time, now that it's twenty-four hours and not twelve?"

"You're quick."

"Sometimes. The answer is that I was doing what I usually do, this and that but not much of anything to the purpose. I suffer from a lack of direction, even in something as simple as what to do on a Saturday afternoon with Gifford out of town."

"You were in Washington the whole time?"

"Yes. Sometime on Saturday I called our friends Raoul and Sophie to invite them for dinner this week. Damn, they were coming last night and I forgot to call and cancel. Oh, well. Anyway, I don't know what time that was. I don't think I talked to anyone else. I

went to the bakery on Sunday morning to get some almond croissants to have with the *Post*. Other than that, I read and ironed
some shirts and in the evening I watched an Ingrid Bergman movie
on television. Earlier in the afternoon, I went for a walk. The
blossoms are coming out down there and it's quite beautiful. No
mud, just asphalt."

"That's all?"

"That's all I remember. It was a perfectly ordinary day, at the
time. There was no reason to take note of what I did. It wasn't until
Darrell called that I thought back over the day, or saw it as anything significant. Then I went back and thought, this is what I was
doing on the day my dad died. I thought, probably he died while I
was watching Ingrid Bergman and Cary Grant. I thought, maybe
while I was out walking and looking at the buds opening, my father
was alone in his house, falling deeper and deeper into despair. When
I went to buy croissants, he was dead and nobody knew. That was
how I thought back over the day. Maybe that's how life always is,
that you don't know at the time what events are significant, and it's
only later that you can look back and understand what they meant.

"And then later still, I found out about the dogs, and suddenly
everything that happened meant something different again. The
fact that Gifford had dinner with Olivia Fanning meant he hadn't
killed my father, and not just that he was having a little dalliance.
The fact that I spent the day alone meant that someone might
wonder if I did kill my dad, because there was no one who could say
I didn't."

"But you didn't, did you?"

"Kill my dad? No."

She looked away from him and fixed her eyes on the only adorn-
ment on his wall, a wilderness calendar whose April photograph
showed a desert with cactus in bloom. "The worst thing is imagining anyone else doing it. I can't conceive of my brothers that way.
I've been trying not to think about it because I didn't want to
picture either one of them..."

"Don't picture it," he said. "There's no point. The reality is bad enough. You don't have to put yourself through every possible version of it when you don't know which one is right. If we do find an answer, it's not going to come by psychoanalysis. It will come by plodding through all the facts there are to be found. If we're lucky, all the little details will come together in the end to make a whole picture."

"I'm not sure I want a whole picture."

"I know. But at least if you know, then you won't have to doubt everyone."

She smiled a little. "That's making the best of it."

"When winter lasts six months, you have to make the best of things or go crazy."

"Not everyone thinks that way."

He shrugged and smiled.

"Did you have some other questions?" she asked.

"A couple, maybe. Do you know how to shoot?"

"Yes. Dad taught me. He taught all of us. We did target shooting now and then."

"Do you know if he kept ammunition with the gun?"

"He always did in the past. The gun wasn't loaded but the ammunition was right with it."

He slid a photograph across the desk. "Did this belong to your father or to someone else?"

She winced, looking at it. Darrell and Chad were laughing, elbowing each other for position on the seat of a brand new red International tractor. From the ground, Phoebe was watching them. Her short blond hair was mussed by the wind, and she looked tiny beside the huge lugged wheel of the machine. She was only in her early forties then, and Vincie was reminded, with something of a start, how much she and her mother and Chad all looked like one another. In the photo, Vincie was turned away from the camera, bent over to peer at something inside the engine. The bottom half of the photo was stained a rusty brown and the surface had wrinkled.

"The camera was my mom's, but Dad must have taken the picture," she said. "Any of us might have had a copy. Or it might have

174

come from one of Mom's albums. Did you look through them to see if any pictures were missing?"

"We didn't find any obvious gaps, but not every page was full, either. Could your Dad have kept it around loose somewhere?"

"My dad seldom kept anything around loose. He hated chaos."

Bret was silent for a while, then asked, "Did you get along with your dad? I asked your brothers that, but I never asked you."

She answered slowly. "There was no dislike," she said. "I admired him. And loved him, too, I suppose. But I never felt that I was of enough consequence for it to matter whether I loved him. It's hard to explain. My brothers both talk about how small they felt next to him. I felt that way, too, insubstantial. As if I made no impression on him, so there must not be much to me. When Gifford took an interest in me, it seemed a sort of miracle. I must be someone, if this amazing man picked me out of the crowd. That feeling didn't last, obviously. Things turn everyday and the shine goes off, but for a while I had a feeling that I was somebody definite.

"I've thought a lot about my dad this week. Maybe I've detached a little and looked at him less as my father and more as a man. I can react less personally, because I can see that no one else made much impression on him either. Except maybe my mother. I think he must have been very lonely. I think the place he felt most at home was out by himself on the tractor late in the evening, chopping corn."

As a child, she had lain in bed on autumn nights, listening to the buzzing whine of the chopper, like the sound of a giant devouring insect. It grew louder and louder as it crawled toward the near end of the field, and then it turned to go back the other way and slowly faded into the distance. Sometimes, if she couldn't fall asleep, she climbed out of bed and went to the window to look out into the darkness at the small patch of light inching its way across the field, the machines a dark silhouette against the light of the headlights shining on the ranks of cornstalks. In high school, she had taken her turn running the chopper, if it wasn't a school night. From the closeness of the tractor seat, the chopper's whine was too deafeningly loud to have any mood. Heard from her bed, though, and again now, in memory, the sound was monotonous and mournful and doggedly persistent.

19

BRET WATCHED a shadow pass over Vincie's face. Her expression registered every mood visibly, even the mood of some fleeting, unspoken thought. Was she right, that her father had not wanted human companionship? And what would it be like, to believe that about one's father?

While Vernon Nowle was still alive, Bret had known him only distantly, by reputation. That was how most people had known him. Distantly, by reputation. He was considered aloof, solitary, a fanatically hard worker, a skilled farmer, but not someone who would lean against a fence rail and swap yarns. It was not only his children who were a bit awed by him.

Most farmers in the area were downright garrulous, if a person caught them in an idle moment and worked through the first minute or two of reserve. The reserve was a habit, born of long hours of solitary work. It was not an expression of personality. Once a person broke through it, there would likely come a flood of pent-up conversation that had simply been waiting for an audience. Vernon was different. He was not taciturn, exactly, but most of the time he gave people the impression that he was lost in thought. When he did start talking, the words did not burst forth in a rush. They came out clearly and deliberately, as if speech were a tool to be used with the same care as any other tool.

Bret thought back to a time, just a year ago, when he had heard

177

Vernon speak at the school district meeting. Times were hard and the town was sharply divided over how much money must be cut from the schools to give people relief from property taxes. A good part of the town attended the meeting, and many people spoke on both sides, often with anger. Near the end of the debate, Vernon had stood up to speak. It was the first time Bret had heard him say anything at a town meeting. He had sounded neither angry nor eloquently persuasive. He had sounded merely grieved.

"I'm not sure your dad cared as little about people as it might have seemed," Bret said to Vincie. "Did Darrell ever tell you about him speaking at town meeting last year?"

Vincie started a little, as if she, too, had been lost in thought. She shook her head. "He's never mentioned it."

"People were arguing about whether to cut money from the schools, and saying ordinary folks couldn't afford to own a house because of the taxes. There was a lot of bitterness and some nasty things said, but I still remember how your dad talked. He said he was about as broke as anyone in town, and for sure he paid as many taxes as anyone, but even so he'd give up just about anything else before he'd give up the things that would make the future better for the kids growing up. He said nothing else mattered to him, compared to his daughter and his two sons, and the kind of world they'd be living in."

A look of disbelief spread across Vincie's face. "My dad said that?"

Bret nodded. "It wasn't like he made a big speech about it. It was more as if he'd been listening to what people said, and feeling more and more saddened, and finally the feeling had to come out. He only talked for about half a minute."

"Did it make any difference at the meeting?"

"No. People were pretty well set in their minds before they came. No one turned any tides. I only mention it because it seems so different from the way you saw him."

"You could say that." She seemed to have difficulty assimilating this information. She looked young and confused, and perhaps wistful.

He remembered the little he had known of her when they were

in high school. When he was a junior, she had arrived at the high school as a freshman, one of the group who came to Huntsbury High each year from the tiny elementary schools in the outlying villages. She was immediately noticed by almost every male in the school. With her hair bleached pale and her skin tanned from a summer of haying, she looked as if she had walked in off a California beach, except that her hair was chopped short, probably to make sure it would not get tangled in spinning machinery. As far as Bret could tell, she was entirely unaware that she was pretty.

He and his friends had schemed together about how to attract her notice, but none of them had been brave enough to put any of their schemes into action. She seemed unapproachable, not because she was shy or unfriendly, but because she was too beautiful, too smart, and something else as well, something that lay deeper. They felt a nervous tension in her, a volatility that was daunting. They could not slide her comfortably into a niche in their usual daydreams, about inviting a girl to a movie and making out with her in the back row, and if they were lucky, persuading her to go somewhere in their car later. Something about Vincie generated static in the picture. She was someone in whom no emotion could be casual or experimental.

His orbit and hers did not intersect, but he remembered the one time they made a near approach. In the cafeteria, he always sat with the other football players at a center table. They were a rowdy, jocular group, all showing off a little in front of the rest of the school. On that particular day, the team captain, Kevin Tyler, who was handsome and popular, the definition of cool, was talking loudly and crudely about a girl from Worthing. He referred to the girl as a woodchuck, because her family lived in a shack on one of the more remote dirt roads and scraped out a living cutting firewood, sugaring, bushhogging fields and plowing driveways. Vincie happened to be walking past with her tray just as Kevin made some remark about the girl having head lice and being willing to put out for any guy who could offer her a bath in kerosene.

From his seat at the other end of the table, Bret had watched

Vincie stop still, and start to tremble, and then, almost in a trance, pick up her plate of hamburger stroganoff and turn it upside down on Kevin's head. "I'd rather have lice in my hair than in my brain," she said and walked on. Her hands were shaking so much that the silverware rattled on her tray. The whole room had gone silent in shock, at the sight of a freshman girl dumping food on the most popular senior boy in the school, not in flirtatious horseplay, but in dead earnest anger.

Later, Bret passed by in the hall as Vincie was taking books out of her locker. On an impulse, he stopped and said, "That hamburger slop is poisonous. I guess if Kevin had any head lice, you've gotten rid of them." She jumped about a foot when he spoke.

He smiled then, awkwardly, and added, "Probably didn't get the ones in his brain, though."

"I can't believe I did that," she said. "Sometimes I think I'm possessed." She was flushed and nervous. "You can tell him I'm sorry."

"I guess he had it coming."

He hesitated, trying out sentences in his mind—did she want to go to a movie, could he give her a ride home, did she like pizza—but before he could choose one and try it out, her eyes blazed up again and she said, "He's got everything everyone else wants. Why does he have to beat up on someone with nothing?"

Bret was halted before he began. Her question was too serious, and unanswerable. He couldn't reply by inviting her to a movie. He just shrugged in apology for his teammate and backed away.

He thought probably she still remembered the incident, but did not remember who had spoken to her. She had been too upset to register who he was. He was just someone on the team.

By the end of the year, she had begun to blend in. She dressed and talked more like the other girls, and was less intimidating. She also had begun going steady with a boy in Bret's class, a boy almost universally regarded as a drip. Eddie Trescott came from the town's tiny professional class. His father was a lawyer. Like Vincie, he was a good student, but unlike her, he was conceited, prissy and snide. Looking back from his present perspective, Bret thought Eddie Trescott looked very much like a larval stage of Vincie's husband.

Bret's reaction then had been the same as it was now. He felt that his male imagination had just met some insurmountable barrier in its effort to comprehend a female's point of view. He tried to understand. He told himself, the man is intelligent, he is not bad looking, he makes good money. But just when the reasons had begun to gather momentum, they slammed head on into that barrier, "But what a creep!"

After he finished high school, he lost sight of her. Perhaps he had seen her here or there, in a store or at a basketball game, but only for a passing moment. He had seen her wedding announcement in the paper and then had hardly thought of her again, until her father died and she appeared in his office to ask questions. Her demeanor that day held an odd mixture of tenacity with uncertainty and apology. Gifford had hovered in her vicinity, interjecting comments but otherwise looking conspicuously bored so as to dissociate himself from his wife's momentary fit of irrationality. He looked like a professor, with an intelligent, refined face and an air of being someone to whom people listened. Every few seconds, Vincie darted a look at him, as if seeking reassurance that he was not disgusted with her.

Every trace of teenaged roundness was gone from her face. Her bones stood forth clearly defined, but it did not seem to Bret that her character had firmed up correspondingly. She had changed, but not in the way he might have predicted, if he had thought to make predictions when he was seventeen. Her quickness of mind and intensity of feeling might have been expected to combine in dedication to some difficult endeavor. Instead, they had remained fragmented and unfocused, and she acted in fits and spurts and hesitations. The current of emotion he had felt as a boy was now scattered into dribbles and rivulets, and was no longer frightening. He wondered if it would ever be brought back into a single channel.

At the moment, she was lost in a revery and he could watch her without her noticing. They sat, both of them silent, for quite a long time. Then, abruptly, she turned towards him and her eyes came into focus, as she remembered she wasn't alone. With an inward smile, he acknowledged a small bruise to his ego, that she could so entirely forget him when he was so acutely conscious of her.

"Thank you for telling me that story about my dad," she said. Her eyes, when they did focus, focused intently. Did she look at everyone that way, as if she wanted to bore through the facade of manners?

"It helps, to hear those things," she added. "I sometimes think children know less than anyone about their own parents."

"They have the most information, but all of it is unreliable," he said.

She laughed, and he smiled in return. He had not heard her laugh before. The sound rippled out of her and disappeared, a pebble disappearing into a bottomless lake.

"I should go, unless you have more questions," she said. "I borrowed Chad's car and he may want it."

As they shook hands good-bye, he noticed how soft her palm was. The calluses of childhood were long gone. Her skin was pale, and her hair, elegantly styled, had none of the sun-bleached home-haircut abandon he remembered from his first young man's sight of her twenty years ago.

If only he had had more courage when he was seventeen. Could he imagine that other potential existence that never happened? If he had tried to tackle her impossible question, could he have found things to say? If he had talked with her then, if he had looked for her after classes, if he had dared to approach her at a dance, might she have come to see his face as well as his blue and gold letterman's jacket? Could he have made her like him, face and jacket both? Could he have stepped into place ahead of Eddie Trescott? And even if he did not marry her himself, could he have been the precursor to a different sort of man than Gifford?

He did not dwell long on all the possible existences that never were. He was already picking up his notes to resume work when his intercom buzzed and the dispatcher said he had a call from the police in New Jersey. Could he take it?

Yes, he could. He made some quick notes to check telephone and credit card records, then picked up the phone.

20

THOUGH SHE HAD SAID she must return Chad's car, Vincie lingered in the parking lot. The car was the sort that encased the driver like a cocoon, with deep contoured black bucket seats, a roof that brushed the top of her hair, and its steering wheel, gearshift and controls all located to be reached with a bare twitch of the muscles. Once she had folded herself inside, it seemed like a place she should stay for a while.

She sat without starting the engine, trying to imagine her father saying the things Bret Leroux had heard him say. Nothing mattered to him as much as his kids? Then why had he planned to give away half their inheritance?

His kids and the kind of world they would live in, that was the kicker. He cared about kids and the world in the abstract, not about Chad, Darrell and Vincie. His land was to be saved for future generations, even if it was lost to his own three children. The general he could handle. The particular he avoided.

Yet it was not so simple. She had felt something else there, in Bret's story. Bret had no burden of childhood history, as he listened to her father, and his nature seemed generous. What he had heard was that Vernon cared about his kids and all kids, and that everything he did was done with an eye to their lives. But Bret had heard, also, a sadness that wove itself through the care, and the sadness had echoed in his voice as he repeated Vernon's words.

She thought again of the monotonous droning whine of the chopper, out in the dark autumn evening. She would fall asleep to the sound, and when she awoke in the morning, her father would already be out in the barn milking.

She thought again about the cry that had leapt up in her at the funeral, as she listened to the minister's reassurances that death was not final. Vernon had his chance here, and he missed it. Even at Phoebe's funeral, his face had been impassive, keeping whatever he felt to himself.

Vincie felt herself swallowed up by a loneliness as unfathomable as the empty depths of outer space. She was wrung by an urge to weep, but all tears were locked up in ice. She longed to reach out a hand in search of human touch, but her limbs were numb and paralyzed. All around her, voices were talking and laughing. She wanted to join her voice to theirs, but her throat was closed up and rigid, and no breath could pass through it any more.

Was she even alive, or was she in a coffin, airless, with cold April mud falling in thumps on the lid?

She yanked open the door of the car and stumbled out into the air. Rain had begun to fall, thudding on the hood and roof. She drew in gasping breaths of wet air and felt cold drops landing on the skin of her face. She was alive. The cold trickle of rain met warm stinging tears. Her body shuddered and she leaned against the car as wave upon wave of sobs swept over her, convulsing her body and wrenching cries from her throat. Vernon was dead, but she was alive.

For a moment she had crossed over with him, and the terrible thing had been, not that he was dead, as everyone must be, but how short his crossing had been, as if he had begun the journey years before and the stopping of his heartbeat was one last small step, almost a formality.

And had she ever tried to reach a hand after him? As his figure receded into mist, had she ever called after him, "Stay a while longer. Tell us a story, or let us tell you one." She had not dared. She saw him as huge and inevitable and frightening, and had never wondered what it felt like to flow unseen in a narrow space between frozen earth and depths of snow. She had not believed in a sunlight strong enough to melt the snow and shatter the ice and loose the floods of springtime. She had remained a child before him. She had not attained the power of the full grown, who say now I can give more than I take.

When finally the sobs passed, she straightened and looked around her. What a place to choose for mourning her father, she thought, an asphalt parking lot with two police cruisers for company, with embankments of dirty slush on three sides and a flat-roofed concrete box on the fourth. Short of a shopping mall, no place could have been more alien to Vernon's spirit.

That thought was followed almost instantly by another, "Welcome to the modern world, Dad."

She climbed back into Chad's car, started the engine and said, aloud, "I guess we're your eyes and ears now. Where we go, you go. So hold onto your hat, we're going for a ride."

With a feeling that was almost relish, she roared out of the parking lot and onto the highway.

21

SHE KEPT THE CAR at its happy speed all the way back to Worthing, despite the sheets of water on the pavement. The road hugged every curve in the Owens River and the car, cocky, hugged every curve in the road. At each bend, she could see the foaming muddy rush of the river, swollen by spring run-off from the hills.

In Worthing she stopped at Norwood's to buy gas, as repayment for the loan of the car. She pulled in beside the pumps, which were now sheltered by a huge fluorescent canopy overhead. Norwood's Texaco had been in Worthing since she was a child, but two years ago it had undergone a complete makeover. It added the canopy, and a store full of videos and snack foods, and became Norwood's Mini-Mart, clean, modern and ablaze with lights, rescuing the village from the dark stillness of nighttime.

The car took more gas than she expected. All that power needed nourishment, she supposed. She fished inside the glove compartment to see if Chad kept a gas book, as Vernon always did, and as she still did herself, from habit. She found only maps and a wad of charge slips, which she inadvertently dumped on the floor.

As she collected the scattered bits of paper back into a stack, a single word caught her eye, and then a date, and then she felt as if in one instant the whole flood rush of the Owens River had been locked up in midwinter ice.

Brattleboro. April 5. Brattleboro, Vermont, one week ago, last

Saturday, the day Vernon died. The day Chad said he had idled away visiting the Museum of Modern Art and buying bagels. She closed her eyes and opened them again, as if perhaps the thin slip of paper in her hand might now read something different. Her hand had begun to shake, but there was no mistaking the fuzzy carbon imprint.

Chad was here that day. If he had stopped in Brattleboro to buy gas, he could only have been coming to Worthing. Her whole body began to shake and she pressed her head back against the headrest, trying to make it stop.

She had not known how it would feel.

She had been the one to start asking questions. She and Gifford had discussed, hypothetically, what might have happened that night. But now, staring at a printed slip of fact, objective and undeniable, she felt physically sick. Her body was racked by the spasmodic trembling of a person with a deadly fever.

Behind her, a horn blared and she jumped. She was blocking the pumps. With a concentrated effort, she started the engine and drove fifty feet to the edge of the parking lot, then turned off the engine and sat. She saw, now, that she had never quite believed in the possibility of murder. Her imagination had not been able to make the leap, unaided, to feeling what she felt now.

Bret Leroux had known. He had so clearly dreaded the possibility she had suggested, not for his own sake, but for hers and her family's. He had known what it meant.

She had not known. She had launched her quest for truth like a scientist, who wants to know all that is knowable and does not fully consider the consequences of knowledge until she is faced with a nuclear bomb or a mailbox filled with an exponentially multiplying collection of mail order catalogs. She had set out after knowledge and now she had it.

So what should she do with it? And did it even matter what she did with it? Once it came into being, knowledge had a life of its own. It became part of what exists, impossible either to contain or to will back to nonexistence. She could burn the incriminating charge slip. She could eat it, like a secret agent. The knowledge would be there nevertheless, in her mind, and also in some vast computer network that could undoubtedly be searched by the police. Probably the search was going forward at this moment. Probably the power of electronic technology had already been harnessed to ferret out the tiny scrap of truth she held in her hand.

It was such a tiny piece of truth, just a city and a date, but it was the first creeping root that might end by splitting open a concrete foundation. Chad had been in the state the day her father died. He had lied about it as well. He had invented a whole day's events to reinforce the lie. Why would he cover tracks, if the tracks led somewhere innocent?

She could no longer dodge or ignore her conclusions. She could not blunt the impact of one dreaded possibility by imagining several others. But what should she do? Should she take the charge slip to the police? Should she confront Chad with it? Should she leave it where it was, and let events follow their own course?

Or should she destroy it? Should she try to protect her brother, whom she loved?

But did she love him? She felt no love at this moment, only a horror that spread through her body like sickness, in wave after wave of uncontrollable shaking. She gripped the steering wheel, trying to bring her body back under control, trying to think clearly. She must do something. She could not just stay in this parking lot. She must decide, somehow. Whatever she did or didn't do was a choice.

Quite suddenly, her mind cleared. The trembling of shock gave way to anger, pure and searing. Her muscles stopped shaking and grew taut. Her decision was made, then, almost without deliberate thought. There was only one thing she could possibly do.

Once again, she started Chad's car. She pulled out onto the highway without a trace of relish, or even any awareness of the magnificent machine she was driving. She drove at a strict thirty-five and ignored the discontented mutterings of the engine. By the time she reached the farm, her reluctance had slowed her to less than twenty.

"I didn't know my car went that slow," Chad greeted her cheerfully. "I could hear you half a mile away, practically idling. Were you reading the newspaper?"

"No." She laid the keys on the counter. It was after twelve, but Chad was still finishing his breakfast. He sat perched on the kitchen stool next to the counter. She noticed that detail, that he still avoided the kitchen table.

"There's more coffee left. I made a big pot." He gestured toward the stove.

She considered whether she wanted some to brace her nerves, but then could not imagine mixing what she had to say with sips from a cup of coffee.

"No, I've had enough."

Chad went to pour himself another cup, and she waited while he added sugar, stirred it and returned to his stool.

"Is something wrong?" he asked. "It's not like you, to pass up coffee that's already made, and to stand there like a sphinx. A soaking wet sphinx. How did you get so wet?"

"Chad, what happened last Saturday?"

"What do you mean, what happened...?" he said, then stopped. Her eyes were fixed on him, with silent, relentless insistence on her question.

When they were children, she had often asserted her authority as the older sister, but there had been hesitancy mixed with her tone of command. She knew she should be the boss, but was not always sure what orders to give. There was no hesitancy in her look now. It said simply, "I asked a question. I expect an answer." He looked away and fiddled with his coffee cup.

She waited, without moving, and barely blinking. She almost could be a sphinx, to whom the difference between an hour and a year, or a year and a century, is insignificant. She was not recognizable as Vincie, but neither was she entirely strange. That patient, persistent, slow-moving but far-seeing person was one they both knew.

He shivered suddenly, then said, "I didn't shoot him, you know. I may have killed him, in a way, but I didn't shoot him. He pulled the trigger himself."

"But you were here."

"Yes, I was here. Not while…not when he actually did it, but before. And after…" His gaze was pulled toward the table, irresistibly, but once there, it recoiled.

"I suppose you could say I talked him into it." He laughed, not happily. "You know I can sell anything to anybody. So, I sold my dad the idea of death. Not in so many words, maybe. Not deliberately. But that was the effect. And it wasn't very hard. He was most of the way there all by himself. I just took advantage of what was already in his own mind. That's what marketing is anyway. Figuring out what's in the other person's mind and using it to make him want what you're selling.

"Dad knew he didn't belong any more. Civilization had moved on and left him behind. You know how he looked at things, from such a distance, with his own self one little microbe among the billions. Well, he could see all the other microbes zooming around faster and faster, faxing papers back and forth, cooking dinner in thirty seconds, eating it in twenty-nine, hooked into computers that send mail to Argentina at the speed of light, watching T.V. ads that show twenty different images in a fifteen second slot. He wasn't stupid. He knew these things were happening on all sides of him.

"And then he looked at himself and thought, here is a maladapted specimen that is bound for extinction. His pulse is still sixty-four beats a minute. He still puts a seed in the ground and waits five months for a harvest. He still feeds a calf for two years before she returns him any milk. What a fool! So he decides he has to speed up. He can't make a cow give milk before her time. He can't stop the sun overhead, to make the corn grow faster. But he can buy more fertilizer. He can buy bigger tractors, plow more land, work more hours, breed better cows who give more milk. Everyone else is moving faster, and he'd better, too, or he'll be out of business. So he starts racing faster and faster, keeping up with every new chemical, every genetic improvement, every new machine. And then one day, he looks down from his vantage point out in space and says, who is that busy little microbe, racing in circles? He can't even recognize himself any more, and all of a sudden his whole life just comes to a halt.

"We talked a long time that evening. I pointed all this stuff out, but I wasn't telling him anything he wasn't already thinking. I think it was a relief when he realized he could let go of it all. He could stay where he was, be the man he had always been, and let the rest of the world go on without him. By the time he sold his cows, he was already halfway out of this world. All I had to do was give him a reason for the one last step. I'm a good salesman, but I couldn't have sold death on a cold call. He was just waiting for someone to sell it to him."

Chad's tale had come out in one long rush, sounding like thoughts that had been fermenting and building up heat and pressure for a long time. Now he stopped, the pressure spent for the moment.

"Just how did you close this particular deal?" Vincie asked, with a bite in her voice.

Chad did not seem to notice her tone. "It wasn't hard," he said. "It never is, when the other person wants what you're selling. All I did was tell him what Darrell had told me about Mom's accident. That she flipped the tractor because she was driving too fast, and she was driving too fast because she was trying to keep up with the pace Dad set for himself. I wanted him to know that it wasn't just him who paid the cost of his failure. We all paid, you, me, Darrell, Mom…

"He didn't take it all in right away. Once he did, I felt like I was watching a man who's had a vision and sees every last piece of the divine mystery fall into place. His face had no expression at all, and his eyes were looking at something farther away than I'm ever likely to see. He was quiet for a long time before he remembered I was there. Then he looked at me as if he couldn't figure out who I was. As if he had left life behind and wondered how I could still be there with him.

"He said to me, 'You should go now. I have something to do and

194

I don't want you here.' I knew what he was thinking. I could tell by the way he said it. So I went outside."

"And the dogs were still there..." Vincie murmured.

"That's right, the damned dogs. He asked me to take them to Darrell's. So I took them and put them in the car, but I didn't leave. I stayed outside and waited. It felt a little the way it did when Dad and Darrell took Sparky outside to shoot him and you and Mom and I stayed behind in the house, waiting and listening. The silence went on and on, and finally, when the shot did come, I jumped, because I'd almost started to think it wasn't going to. I waited a while longer, and then I went inside to see. He was lying just the way they found him later, fallen forward onto the table. There was a lot of blood. I didn't touch him, because there was no way he could still be alive. I was about to call Darrell to tell him, and then it dawned on me how it might look to other people, that I was here. I realized they might not believe what happened, if they knew, and I began to feel really scared. So I found that photo in one of the albums and put it in Dad's hand, as a way of saying what happened. And I left and drove home. That is, I put the dogs back in the house, and then I left."

Vincie was shaking her head, like a creature given a blow out of nowhere, trying with movement to shake off the pain and bring her mind back into focus.

"But why, Chad? Why did you want him dead? What difference did it make to you? If he was headed that way, why didn't you try to stop him instead of pushing him over the edge?"

"No one stops Dad from anything. He does what he's going to do, regardless of other people. Maybe god could have changed his mind, but I'm not god. All I could do was make his path a little smoother so he would travel down it a little faster. I didn't come up here with that idea in mind, you know. I came up here to talk to him about the land trust. I couldn't believe he was just going to give half the place away, and without even asking us what we thought. Maybe he asked Darrell, but he never asked me. So I came up here to tell him what I thought. I wanted to point out to him that he might get some money out of those development rights. He could still pre-serve the land, without throwing away the value of it. Organiza-tions will pay to preserve a place like this. But you know what he said? He said, 'If they pay to preserve this land, then there is some other land somewhere that won't get preserved because they spent the money on mine.' So typical of Dad, looking at things from his spot in outer space. He saw the big picture and didn't consider at all what it might mean to you or me, his own kids. That almighty detachment of his."

"But you don't need the money, do you?" she said.

"That's exactly what he said. Christ, are you ever your father's daughter! It isn't the point, whether I need the money. The point is, any normal parent would look after his own kids before anything else. Ahead of a bunch of stupid cows, for god's sake. Ahead of whatever slobs might someday drive by the farm and think how pretty it is and how nice that it's been preserved for them to enjoy. He had no normal feelings at all. All he had were his damned principles. And his principles were about as relevant to modern life as a wooden wheeled oxcart. He did not belong on earth. Can't you see that? I don't know where he did belong, but not on planet earth with the twentieth century almost history. I did him a favor. I gave him a chance to find some realm where he'll feel at home, where the pace of life doesn't make him dizzy. And the rest of us can get on with our lives without him looming over us, accusing us of frittering away our three score and ten on trivia."

Vincie stared at him in silence, and he met her look, defiant. His face was flushed and his jaw set. His physical beauty looked very fragile, as if one small turn of events might twist it into an image of cruelty or madness. She thought of her mother. Chad looked re-markably like her just then, perhaps because he looked so in danger of shattering.

She wanted to understand what Chad had felt, and to make sense of what he had done, but the wish was overwhelmed by the thought of her father finally knowing the whole story of how Phoebe had died. She felt Vernon's grief and agonizing remorse drowning her, engulfing any other feeling either of them might have felt. She felt his horror, too, at the sight of hatred in his son's eyes, the son he loved passionately and must somehow have failed. The two people he loved most were there before him in one body, heartbreakingly beautiful to see. Yet behind the beauty lay fear and hatred and a genuine wish for his death. How utterly he had failed, that his wife should fear his disapproval and his son should want him dead. Inside the flood was swelling, pressing against the encasing ice and frozen earth, but it was too late. The winter had been too long, the frost had gone too deep, and the flood, when it came, could not gently melt the ice away but must split it wide open.

"What are you going to do?" Chad asked. "Now that I've told you."

Vincie brought her eyes into focus on her brother.

"I don't know."

"You do believe me, don't you?"

"I don't know."

Which was worse? To think that her father had been driven to an agony that could make him take his own life? Or to recall the picture she had first imagined, of her father distracted by a photo of happier times while Chad slipped close beside him and put him to death? Which death would leave the more unquiet spirit? Which killer was the more unnatural?

"You say you can sell anything," she said. "How do I know I'm not being sold a story now?"

He had invented an entire day in New York. He could easily invent an hour with his father.

"I suppose you don't know," he said. "All you have is my word."

"It doesn't much matter what I believe, in the end. It matters what the police believe. And a jury, if it comes to that."

"It doesn't have to come to that," he said. His voice had grown soft and strange to her. His eyes were velvety, the eyes of the child who knew his winsomeness could not be resisted. "The police wouldn't have come into it in the first place, if you hadn't been so insistent about the dogs. It can stop with that."

"The police will find the same information I found."

"Not if they don't think to look." His voice had dropped to a tone still quieter, and suddenly some animal instinct in her awoke, telling her to choose every word with caution. She was finally, forcibly aware that she did not know this man completely, though they had grown up together. He had wished his father dead, possibly had killed him. "You are your father's daughter." She could die, too, for a reason no more comprehensible than the reason that had killed her father.

"You may think the police are slow and stupid," she said, "but one skill they do have is thoroughness. Especially about something as routine as a credit card record. I expect it is the first thing they check."

"Possibly. Or possibly not. But they will certainly check if you go to them and tell them to."

"I do not intend to go to them. They can find what they find on their own."

"And why should I believe that? You were quick to take them your idea about the dogs."

"I didn't think enough about what it meant, until after I had told them. And then it was too late."

"Too late, for damn sure." His laugh was bitter. He moved toward the window and looked out. "I think you and I should get away from here for a while."

"Get away where?"

"Someplace safe. Until I can figure out what to do. I can't think straight here. And I'm not ready to bet my life that you will lie to the police. Somehow that doesn't look like a good bet. We could be at Kennedy in five hours and onto a plane before anyone knew we were gone. It won't be for long. Once we're out of the country, you can do as you please. You can come back and tell the police whatever you want. Just come with me now, like the obedient creature you are."

He opened the door and held it for her, signaling "After you," the gesture of chivalry turned into a gesture of command.

For a moment, she wavered, debating. How much of his story did she believe? Were his intentions what he said they were?

At the airport, there would be people all around. She could easily find help and get away from him.

But if she could think of that, then so could Chad. If he seriously intended to flee the country, then he must not intend to let her come anywhere near any people who might stop him.

What was he really planning? Had he in fact killed his father, and was he now desperate enough to kill her, too? And if so, how? Did he have a gun of his own? A knife? Did he mean to use his bare hands?

Or was her imagination out of control, dreaming up possibilities that had not entered his mind? Was he truly that desperate? Or did he merely intend what he said, to keep her with him until he was out of the country and then let her go?

She could agree to his plan. She could get in the car and wait to see what developed. If her worst fears proved true, she could hope her wits would find a way to save her.

Or she could refuse. She could force him to action right here, in this kitchen where they both had been children and where she knew the sound and feel of every cupboard door.

"My passport is in Washington. I can't go with you anywhere," she said. "I think I'd rather wait here and see what happens."

They faced each other, and Vincie looked at him steadily, not moving, barely breathing. She must show neither fear nor doubt. She must show nothing at all, except the calm that comes from absolute determination, from having made a choice and agreed to accept the result. If her worst hallucination turned out to be truth, if he indeed meant to kill her, then it must happen here where all the ties of blood and memory could witness her spirit's flight. If her best hope turned out to be truth, if he was merely frightened and baffled and seeking some refuge, then perhaps they could still talk to one another. Perhaps they could still, inch by inch, work their way back down the treacherous path that had led them to a precipice.

She waited, not moving.

"Suppose I don't agree with you," he said. "Suppose I don't want to wait here for the police, like some moronic bovine waiting to be slaughtered."

His voice still held bitterness, but it held, also, a tremor of uncertainty that had not been there before.

"You can go if you like. I won't stop you."

"You can get on the phone the moment I'm gone."

"Unplug it and take it with you."

"You could take Dad's truck."

"The keys aren't in it, remember?"

"Then you could walk next door. It's only five minutes."

"So I could. Listen, Chad, the police are going to come after you whether I tell them to or not. If you flee, they will assume you are guilty. But if what you told me is true, then you have no reason to flee."

"Do you think anyone besides my loving sister is going to believe what I told you?"

"I don't know. Is it true?"

"Yes, it's true, but what difference does that make?"

"People will believe you, then."

"And you are so naive. As if truth had anything to do with what people believe. They believe whoever pitches them the most persuasive line at any given moment."

"Then you are safer still. Who on earth could pitch a more persuasive line than you? You're the master."

"And yet you aren't sure you believe me."

"I wasn't sure before. I believe you now."

"Why now?"

"Because you're still here. You're still talking to me. You could be long gone and you're still here talking."

"You're family. You're predisposed to take my side. Other people won't be so easy to convince."

"You'll convince them in the end."

She didn't speak her whole thought, that other people would be horrified enough at what he admitted having done, even though it stopped short of a legally punishable crime. Instead, she added, "It will be the ultimate test of your powers of persuasion."

"And if I fail, I go to prison."

"You won't fail. When has there ever been a tight spot you couldn't get out of? Anyway, if you're telling the truth, there can't be evidence to prove...the other. If it didn't happen, there can't be proof that it did."

"But how can you believe me, when you say yourself I'm the master of persuasion?"

"Maybe because I want to believe you. Maybe because I knew you before you even learned to talk and I can't bear not to believe you. Maybe because I'd rather be an ingenuous dupe than a clever, soul-destroying cynic. The world has sorrows enough that are real. I don't want to create new ones out of my own mistrust. So I believe you. If you tell me something different tomorrow, I will believe that. Until there is a good reason not to, I will go on believing you. You're my brother. You're half myself. If you tell me now that you did kill him, I will believe that, too, but it will tear me apart. I think I understand now why Dad took a gun and killed himself. It wasn't because of the farm, and it wasn't because of Mom. It was knowing you wanted him dead. He loved you more than anything on earth, and you wanted him dead. What was there left to hold him here? I'm surprised he even needed a bullet. He could have freed himself of that last spider thread of connection with a brush of his hand."

She felt weak, suddenly. She pulled out a chair and sat down, trembling. Tears welled up in her eyes and overflowed, because she had no will left to contain them. She did not sob. She sat in a chair and felt the drops well up one by one and trickle down her cheeks.

Chad did not speak or move from where he stood, but his hand let go of the doorknob. He was staring out through the storm door, at his magnificent red car, parked in the rain and mud, and the red barn beyond, empty of life.

"Do you really think that was the reason...?" he said slowly.

"That I wanted him to do it?"

"I didn't mean it was to please you," she said. "I meant that knowing you wanted it must have been the one last terrible thing that was too much."

"It's funny. If I'd thought that was true before..." His voice trailed off.

"Then what?"

He shrugged. "I don't know. Probably nothing. I can't change anything now. It all seemed so clear at the time, and now it all seems a little crazy. I think now, how could I have felt that? How could I have wanted that? But I did. I wanted him to suffer. I wanted to read his mind and find every single thing that would cause him pain. And the only way I could be sure he'd really felt it was if he died. That was proof that I had power over him and was free of his control. I remember, when I heard the shot I felt triumphant, as if I'd won a contest. And then I went back in the house to make sure and it wasn't..." He stopped. "It didn't feel the way I thought it would. I've never seen someone dead like that. He was so still. So inert. Just a lump of meat with the spirit gone. There was a lot of blood and mess, but that wasn't what bothered me. It was the total stillness. You don't realize how much a living thing moves, even when it's asleep, until you see..." He stopped again.

"It didn't feel like a victory at all. It just felt like an emptiness. You can't gloat over beating someone if they aren't there. I didn't hang around. I found the photo and put it on the table and then I got out."

They stayed still in silence, both of them drained, listening to the hum of the refrigerator, the cawing of a crow outside the window, the never-ending drip of rain from the eaves.

"How much longer is it going to rain?" she would ask, when she was still small.

Her father would shrug and reply, "Can't say. But no one's ever picked a fight with the weather and won, that I know of."

202

Seeing Vincie's face fall, her mother would add, "It's bound to clear soon, but just in case it rains forever, maybe we should build a raft."

They would gather scraps of wood and a hammer and nails, but then, before the raft could materialize, Phoebe would be pulled away to chores or supper or Chad wandering into harm's way.

As she got older, Vincie took her father's answer as the given, and didn't ask any more. When she was older still, she learned she could turn on the radio and hear a voice attach a number to the probability of continued dreariness. She saw that Vernon listened to the weatherman's numbers, also, but with the mixed doubt and hope of someone listening to the incantations of a witch doctor. His faith was strictly qualified. He would use the numbers to plan his plowing and mowing, because he had to use something, but he would not rely on them to the point of making promises to a child. He regarded truth too highly and did not consider that what the child wanted was hope and reassurance, not truth.

In time, Vincie came to understand his passivity, his unwillingness ever to say, absolutely, it won't rain tomorrow. Too much depended on it. His livelihood depended on it, and yet he was powerless. The weather governed him absolutely, and with absolute indifference to his wishes. For a farmer, arguing with the weather was a short route to madness.

But today, the rain did not matter. She could rail at it if she liked, because it had no consequences beyond her mood. There was no one here to worry that the fields would be too wet for planting later, or to rejoice that the moisture would give a good start to the grass. The farm was empty, and rain was merely an annoyance.

22

THE CRUISER PULLED IN at a sober pace, no siren or flash-
ing lights. It was late afternoon. The sun had dropped behind the
hills long since, but the change could be seen only in a dimming of
light that was already flat gray.

"We have to ask a few more questions, I guess." Bret Leroux
sounded almost apologetic as he spoke to Chad.

"You work fast," Chad said. "Or had Vincie already talked to you?"

Bret glanced toward Vincie, then said, "Maybe it would be better
if you came down to my office."

Chad shrugged. "If you like. What did she tell you to make you
come poking around again?" Facing a policeman, his air of defiance
had returned.

"She didn't tell me anything," Bret said. "One of your wealthy
neighbors hires a night watchman on the weekends, and that night
watchman is paid to notice who drives down your street at four in
the morning. That's all. For him it was reassuring to recognize your
car last Sunday morning, but I can't say it's reassuring to me. Also,
your credit card company has just processed a charge slip from last
Saturday, from a gas station in Brattleboro. So I thought maybe you
should come down and tell me again how you spent the day."

"Am I under arrest?"

"No, not yet. I'd just as soon hear what you have to say and then
decide."

"Should I have a lawyer?"

"If you want one. We can talk that over when you get to my office."

"You're so polite. I thought you'd have me spread-eagled against the wall, reading me my rights."

"Do I need to do that?"

"No, I suppose not." His body shivered and he said, "I think I want my coat today." He went to the front hall closet to retrieve the coat. It was a dark wool overcoat that looked Parisian, far too elegant to be hung on a hook beside the back door.

As he followed the policeman to the door, he stopped for a moment and turned back toward Vincie. "Will he believe me, do you think?" he asked.

"If you tell him the truth, the odds are better," she said.

"On the contrary, if I lie and say I shot my father, he will believe me immediately."

"In that case, don't lie," she said, with a ghost of a smile.

He managed a small smile in return, but there was no sparkle in his eyes. "You haven't changed, anyhow," he said. "You're still my very upright big sister. Right now, that's a comfort."

Oh, but I have changed, she thought.

She watched through the window as the two men walked to the car, the policeman solid and methodical in his tan raincoat, and beside him Chad, straw-blond and slight, a wisp of physical presence who looked as if he might whirl away on a breeze. The car door closed and her brother disappeared behind reflections off the glass. Before getting in after him, Bret stood for a moment and looked around at the farm.

Would he believe Chad's story, she wondered. She could not make herself into a stranger to hear it as Bret would, uncolored by affection. Perhaps it would sound preposterous, once it was distilled down to pure fact. She muttered a vague prayer, more like a child's wish on a star, that the pure facts not be anything worse than what she already knew.

23

BRET WANTED to believe Chad's story. He probed for detail upon detail. The more minute the detail, the greater the likelihood that the whole was true.

Where was he standing when he heard the shot?

In the doorway of the milkroom.

Why there?

Because sleet had begun to fall and he went under cover. He went first to the wide doors of the main barn, but the drumming of sleet on the metal roof was too loud. He couldn't hear anything else. So he went to the small attached milkroom, which had an asphalt shingle roof that was less noisy.

Could he see his father through the kitchen window?

He saw his father pass by the window once and then back again. He did not see him sit down at the table. The table couldn't be seen from the milkroom door.

"What things could you see?" Bret asked.

"The door into the living room. Part of the refrigerator, I think. I wasn't peering through the window. I was just looking out at the darkness, and the patches of light from the kitchen window falling on what was left of the snowbanks under the eaves. I wasn't really watching anything. I was listening."

"Why were you so sure what he intended to do?"

"I just knew. Not the way you do after the fact, seeing it with your eyes. Sometimes there are things you just know, without any proof that anyone else would recognize."

"Why didn't you try to stop him?"

"Because at that moment, I wanted him dead."

"You say, 'At that moment.' Do you wish now you had done something different?"

Chad paused, and considered. "I'm not tortured by remorse, if that's what you mean. But..."

Bret stayed silent, waiting.

"It hasn't made the difference I thought it would," Chad said. "I thought it would make me free of him. When he was alive, I always felt that he was watching me, from some distant, detached vantage point. Now he's dead, and I still feel him watching. He's a little further away, maybe, but still there. So maybe there was another way. I'm not sure what. Talking to Vincie today, I got little glimpses, but I couldn't see the whole. And anyway, what good would it do now, to see what I could have done instead. You can't battle something out with a dead man."

"Is that why you came to see him, to battle something out?"

"I came to discuss the land trust. I was angry about it, but I hoped I might persuade him to change his mind. But instead he acted just the way he always has in the past. Nothing I said made a dent in his thinking. I could just as well have turned my chair around and talked to the stove and the cupboards. Something took hold of me then. I was going to get a reaction out of him, whatever it took. It wasn't a calculated plan. I never thought to myself, I'm going to make him commit suicide. I just wanted him to react, and the only thing that would make him react was pain, so I started pulling every string in his mind that might cause pain. When I saw that I was succeeding, I felt a kind of intoxication. I knew then that I could get inside his mind, just the way I did with everyone else. I could see what made him tick, and what would make him stop ticking. And once I saw it, it was as if I had to go ahead and do it. Can you understand that feeling? Once you know you can do something, you start to feel a compulsion to go ahead and do it. That's what drives the human race, isn't it? We keep discovering new powers and new capabilities, and once we discover them, there's an irresistible urge to use them. Just because we can. Not because they are good or right or will make us happy, but just because we can. So now I can look back and say, well, nothing good came of that, but at the time, I just had to find out if I really did have the power I thought I did. And I did. For what it was worth."

He stopped. He was not looking at Bret. His gaze moved about restlessly, from one object on the desk to another. The movement did not seem like avoidance. It seemed like seeking, as if he wished he could find something that would catch and hold his gaze.

Bret was still silent, leaving a pause before asking more questions. He watched Chad and thought how much he was like Vincie, wistful, appealing, and somehow in need of care. Then he reminded himself that he was looking at a man who cast spells on people, and might cast one doubly on Bret, precisely because of his likeness to his sister.

Bret returned to details. "You say your father asked you to take the dogs. What did you do with them when you went outside?"

"I put them in the car."

"In the front seat or the back?"

"In the front. The back seat of my car barely has room for a briefcase."

"Have you cleaned the car since then?"

"Thoroughly. Muddy pawprints do not fit into my lifestyle very well."

"Have you had dogs in the car since then?"

"God forbid. I must have been very determined to help my father out of this world if I agreed to take his dogs in my car."

"What time did you leave the farm?"

"A little before ten, I think. I don't know exactly."

"And what time did you get home?"

"Quarter to four. That I do know."

"So, six hours."

"Five hours. We lost an hour to daylight savings that night."

"You're right." Bret paused and made a quick calculation in his head. "So you drove more than three hundred miles, including New York City, in five hours?"

Chad smiled a little. "It's a fast car. I have a radar detector, obviously, and not even New York has traffic at three in the morning. The only real hazards are the potholes on some of the highways. And other pieces of our crumbling infrastructure. I figure if I go fast enough, I'll be across the bridges before they can collapse under me."

It seemed that he had regained his composure. He no longer looked in any way vulnerable.

"I want to back up a minute," Bret said. "After you heard the shot, you took the dogs back to the house and found your father dead?"

Chad hesitated, then said, "No, I went back to the house first. Without the dogs. Once I saw him there, I started to think about the situation differently. You must understand, I didn't visualize details beforehand. It was an abstraction, my father dead. But seeing his body, seeing what looked like my father but with the life gone out of it, and blood everywhere...It stunned me, physically. I hadn't expected that. I think it shocked me back to reality, and then I started to see how the whole thing might look to other people. Maybe I panicked a little, when I realized. All I could think of was getting away before anyone found out I'd been there. And if I had taken the dogs, people would know I had been there and might assume I killed him."

"I try not to assume things," Bret said. "So you went out and brought the dogs back to the house?"

"Yes."

"What did they do?"

"The dogs?"

"Yes. When you put them back in the kitchen with your father's body."

Chad stopped and thought. "Stubbs didn't do anything. He's as inert as a houseplant and not much smarter. He just went and lay down on his bed. Caramel was upset. She kept sniffing Dad's hand and whining and nudging him. I didn't stay around to watch."

"Did you leave them any food or water?"

"They had some water. I didn't think about it much. I assumed someone would find them in the morning. I didn't realize it would take two days."

"You thought Darrell would come by?"

"I didn't think that specifically. It was a reflex assumption, from how the place was when we were kids. There were always people around. The milk truck came every other day. The hired man came most days. My parents were always there. We were always there. Friends came to play. My mother was on committees. People stopped in to buy raw milk. The A.I. man came to breed the cows. Something would never have gone unnoticed for two days. So I just didn't stop to think, that everything was different now."

"Was there blood on the floor?"

"Some. Mostly on the table."

"Were the dogs interested in it?"

"No. But I didn't stay around long." Chad's gaze suddenly focused. "Did they...Was the blood gone when he was found?"

"There wasn't any on the floor."

Chad winced, but didn't say anything more.

"Did you see where his wound was?" Bret asked.

"The side of his head. I didn't look closely."

"Which side?"

Chad stopped to think, seeming to look at a picture in his mind. "The right, I think. I couldn't swear. Dad was right-handed, so it would make sense."

"Are you right-handed, also?"

"Yes."

"Was the gun still in his hand?"

Chad shook his head. "It had fallen on the floor."

"Did you touch it?"

"No."

"Was it the same gun he'd always had?"

"I assumed so. I didn't look at it, though. I suppose it could have been a different one."

"Did you eat dinner with him?"

"No, he'd already finished when I came."

"Do you know what he had?"

"We didn't talk about that."

"Did you have anything at all? Coffee? A drink?"

"Ginger snaps."

"Ginger snaps?"

"He had a box of them out. He was eating some for dessert when I got there. So I ate some ginger snaps while we talked. At some point he put the box away in the cupboard. I didn't have anything else. Some tea would have been nice, but he didn't keep any in the house."

"Did the conversation turn into an argument? Did either of you yell or get angry?"

"My father never yelled. I once saw him throw a wrench against a cinder block wall when he was frustrated, but he wouldn't have done it if he had known I was there."

"What about you?"

"I probably raised my voice."

"So you were angry with him."

"Of course I was angry with him. I've already said I was. He was being stubborn and stupid and completely unreachable. I told you, I wanted him dead. I tried to make him want to be dead, and I succeeded. He did exactly what I wanted him to do. My dad always could make a cow do anything he wanted. It was as if he could get inside her head and know what she was thinking, and then shape her thoughts until she decided to do what he wanted her to. It's a useful skill, when you are handling animals that weigh a thousand pounds. Well, that was what I did to him. I have that same skill, only I have it for people. It's my job and I'm very good at it. Maybe it seems even more despicable than if I had shot him myself, but that's how it was."

"And that day in New York that you told me about? You gave

every detail, the bagels, the scarf, the long catalog of paintings. You must have invented all of that. So why should anyone believe you didn't make up all the details you've just told me?"

"I didn't invent my day in New York. I really did do all those things. It's just that I did them a week earlier than I said I did. If you'd checked what I told you, you'd have found that the exhibit I described with such brilliant critical insight had closed and left town on the thirty-first of March. I forgot that detail myself until I was too far along to go back. After that, I had to hope you didn't know much about art and would forget the names of the painters."

"It's not my field, but that's why I take notes. We'd have gotten to it after a while."

"But now it's moot."

"Yes." Bret stood up. "That's all I need for now. This was taped, as you know, and will be transcribed. Are you still willing to consider the transcription your statement, and sign it?"

"Yes, I said I would. Are you going to arrest me?"

Bret shook his head. "Not unless something contradicts what you've told me."

"Insufficient evidence…" Chad murmured. "Do you expect to find what would be sufficient, before you're done?"

"You should know the answer better than me. I can't find something that isn't there."

Bret escorted Chad out to the lobby. The dispatcher was busy on the radio, making notes as crackling voices reported a couple of drunk drivers, a suspicious black van parked near a closed-up summer house, an arrest involving unruly customers at a bar. When the radio quieted, Bret said he was going home for the day but would drop Chad off at the farm first. He was taking the case file with him to look through later that night.

"Can we stop some place where I can pick up some food?" Chad asked. "I'm ravenous, and I expect Vincie has already eaten."

"I'm hungry myself," Bret said. "The Pit Stop has take-out sandwiches, but I doubt they're up to New York deli standards."

"I was raised on Velveeta cheese and Wonder bread. There is

nothing I won't eat," Chad said.

Bret smiled. He was thinking, here is a man who says he persuaded his father to commit suicide, and yet a person can't help liking him. To steady himself, Bret made a mental note to check Chad's car for any trace of the dogs having been inside it, and also to stand in the milkroom door to find out if he indeed saw the refrigerator and not the table.

24

LEFT ALONE, Vincie walked into the living room to lie down on the couch. Weariness had descended the moment Chad was gone, and she wanted nothing except to fall into a deep sleep.

She thought, I can't absorb anything more right now. I need rest.

Even lying down, she could not banish thought. She ought to call Darrell and tell him what had happened. The thought flitted past but her body ignored it and stayed still. What was Chad telling the police? Had he told her the truth, this time? Was it possible to push a man over the edge into suicide?

She could hear Chad's sales pitch, going on and on, pulling every string of regret and doubt and sorrow in her father's mind. You have failed the land, failed your children, failed your wife. The human race is evolving into something you do not want to live to see. Humans are becoming a multiplying, rushing, devouring swarm that is crowding out every other species except the ones that serve the needs of the swarm. The swarm does not care about the things you care about. Your beliefs are outmoded. Your children would be happier with you dead. You can say good-bye. You can abandon a struggle that is fruitless and let yourself be carried away. You can merge your soul with god and give your body to feed the soil, the worms, the grass, the clover and the cows.

Vincie's mind protested, weakly, that the existence of god was not certain and that her body would be made indigestible with embalming fluid, and then she drifted off to sleep.

She woke, jarringly, to darkness and the telephone ringing. She stumbled into the kitchen, following the sound until she reached the phone.

"Where were you? I almost gave up." It was Gifford.

"I fell asleep."

"I thought you would be hard at work, organizing files of papers, and instead you've been sleeping. You'll never be finished and come home, at this rate."

"How was the drive?" Her head was still fuzzy and that was all the conversation she could muster.

"Tedious, as it always is. I came through New York on the parkways. The bridge was jammed up, as usual." He retraced the drive for her, route number by route number, and toll booth by toll booth, until at last he reached the Beltway, their exit, their neighborhood, their street, their doorway. By the time his recital reached the cup of tea he had brewed for himself before sitting down to call her, she was awake.

"So you made it," she said.

"Yes. But I'm bone tired. I feel no inspiration whatsoever for this lecture on Monday. Fortunately, it is material I have covered many times, but there is always reworking to be done." He went on talking, barely pausing for her one-syllable replies. Her replies were just the signal light on an appliance, indicating that the machine is plugged in and functioning, but nothing more. He outlined for her some new critical articles he meant to include and some new ideas of his own that had sprouted in recent months. The revised lecture took shape as she listened.

"The apartment is very quiet without you," he said. "It almost makes me wish we had a cat. If cats weren't such an encroachment on one's freedom, I might be down at the pet store tomorrow. Perhaps a white Persian, elegant and strokable, just like you. But lacking in conversation. You really must get on with the job. I am quite desolate without you."

"It's only been eleven hours, Gifford."

"But such a trying eleven hours. Seriously, how long do you think you will be away?"

"I have no idea. I haven't thought about it."

"How could you not think about it? Do you forget me completely the moment I drive off?"

"I had some other things on my mind today."

"Are you still obsessing about those dogs? I thought about that, among other things, during the many hours I had for meditation on my drive. I think that theory was a product of your imagination. I think you greatly exaggerate your father's concern for his animals. If you weren't such a worshipful little girl, you could see..."

"Chad was here that night," she said abruptly, cutting him off.

"What?"

"Chad was here that night," she repeated.

"What do you mean? How do you know?"

"I found a charge slip in his car from last Saturday. When I asked him about it, he admitted he was here."

There was a pause, and then he said, musingly, "So it was your charming baby brother Chad. I've always thought he was a little too good to be true. No one could be quite that wonderful. If it weren't so dreadful, it would almost be a comfort. Has he been arrested?"

Vincie almost flung the receiver away, as if it were writhing and coiling and oozing venom in her hand. "I don't believe you, Gifford. For you this is just another specimen of human loathsomeness to be picked apart and chuckled over. No, he hasn't been arrested. He didn't shoot my father. And even if he did, he's my brother and there is no comfort in it whatsoever."

"I didn't mean that it was a comfort to find out it was murder. I only meant..."

"I know what you meant. That it's a comfort to think that Chad is human, meaning vile, and not someone sweet and clever and loving and therefore too good to be true. Your whole spirit is furred over with gray mold and the only way you feel any kinship with other people is by spreading your mold onto them. You don't even

217

think about what all this feels like, for me, for Chad, for Darrell when he finds out. You just gloat because someone's image got tarnished and now you won't look so ugly in comparison."

There was silence, and then he said, "I'm sorry, Vincie. I didn't realize how it sounded. I was making a joke. Of course I'm not pleased to hear bad news about your brother. But what did happen, if he was up there that night?"

"They had a conversation, and afterwards my father shot himself. He asked Chad to take the dogs and go, and then he shot himself."

"That's what Chad says happened?"

"Yes, obviously. There isn't anyone else to say what happened."

"And you believe him? It's an awfully thin story and he has every reason to lie. Why would he take the dogs and leave your father to shoot himself, instead of trying to stop him? And if he's innocent, why didn't he tell the truth right away? It makes no sense, Vincie."

It had made sense until it got caught up in Gifford's relentlessly grinding skepticism, which could turn granite into quicksand.

"All I know is what Chad says. The police are talking to him right now. I guess it's up to them to find out if he's lying. In any case, it doesn't make much difference which way it happened."

"How can you say it doesn't make a difference whether he's a murderer or not? It changes everything."

"It changes everything for him. He might go to prison for life. For me, it doesn't change things that much. He's still Chad."

"What a high-minded platitude! And hypocritical to boot. It's pure myth, that 'love endureth all things.' People fall into the most grotesque posturings, trying to pretend that it's true. Love is just a mating call, or a baby's howl for milk, dressed up in a lot of high-flown rhetoric. So spare me your saintliness."

Spare you. Gladly will I spare you, she thought. They had diverged at last, and there was no meeting point left. If she had once loved him, then that love had not endured all. He was receding into the distance, and she felt barely a wrench. She had nothing more to say to him. They used words that appeared to belong to the same language, but conveyed no meaning to each other.

Her grief was crying out for someone who could understand it. She had not known before, what blood meant, but now she knew. Chad was her blood. If he had done the unspeakable, he was still her blood. If love and horror could not be compelled to occupy the same small space, then she herself must fly into pieces. This love was not a quickening of the pulse; it was the heartbeat itself. This horror was not a chill contracting the bowels; it was a rending of all the vital organs. She needed every ounce of strength to overcome the repulsion between the two things.

But to Gifford, the struggle was all hypocritical posturing. So what on earth did she have left to say to him?

"Never mind, Gifford," she said. "It doesn't matter, so let's not discuss it any more. Perhaps a cat would be a good idea. I've never known a cat to be guilty of saintliness."

She was ready to end the conversation but Gifford was not. He ignored her weary sarcasm and went on talking, his mind busily running through possible scenarios of her father's death, analyses of her brothers, analysis of her. It seemed simpler to listen than to try to stop him. She sat on the kitchen stool in the darkness, hearing his crafted phrases describe filial hatreds, sociopathic absence of guilt, wilful self-delusion. Only occasionally did she interject a syllable or two, enough to indicate that she had not put down the phone.

Her back grew tired and she shifted her stool so that she could lean an arm on the counter. She felt the sharp corner of the countertop, its metal facing one of the many details from her past that called forth Gifford's scorn. Yet hadn't she married him, in part, because he noticed such details?

The metal edge pressed into the muscle of her forearm and she was pierced by a sudden memory, of her mother in much the same posture, perched on a stool near the counter, not this polished wooden stool, which Vincie and Gifford had given as a Christmas present, but its predecessor of metal and vinyl, ugly, indestructible and easy to clean. The counters were too high for Phoebe's small stature and she had used the stool constantly, perching on it to cut vegetables for canning, to stir a bubbling pot of molasses candy, to quarter a chicken with fast, practiced strokes of a kitchen knife. She had called it the queen's throne and laughingly declared that anyone who sat upon it and wielded the sceptre, meaning the knife or spoon for the task at hand, could issue decrees at will and everyone within her domain, the kitchen, must obey. Vincie had always been eager to be the queen, and it wasn't until she was much older that she realized how her mother, Tom Sawyerish, had induced her to carry out a multitude of kitchen tasks without thinking of them as work.

"Chad is the classic charming manipulator," Gifford's voice broke in on her. "People with that sort of charm have no deep feelings. They can manipulate other people because they have nothing at risk themselves..."

In the midst of work, Phoebe's eye would be caught by something outside the window and she would bolt from the kitchen, screeching in protective fury, perhaps at a cowbird about to lay its parasitical eggs in the nest of a finch, perhaps at a bluejay murderously pecking some smaller bird, perhaps at a deer bending its graceful neck to devour the blossoms on the delphiniums.

Vincie's ear caught another sentence, "...almost a symbol for human existence, the facade of virtue and beauty masking the reality of calculated self-interest..."

She felt herself uncoil and leap, a spring compressed beyond its limit.

"Speak for yourself, Gifford," she said sharply, distinctly. "You don't have any idea what's inside Chad or me or any of us. I don't know everything about Chad either, but I know he feels plenty. He may be confused, he may be messed up, he may even be spoiled and thoughtless and cruel, but he's not cold and ruthlessly calculating. He's not dead inside, any more than I am. And he's part of me. I helped take care of him. Your attack on him is an attack on me, and I've had enough."

"I'm sorry, Vincie." Gifford was retreating, as always, once she had reacted. "It wasn't meant as an attack. I was simply trying to look at the situation and understand it."

Nothing personal. Just trying to be objective. As ever. His mind was a scalpel, its function dissection, whether the body was living or dead.

"Sorry comes too late," she said. "One thing I said back there is a lie. Part of me is dead and has been for a long time. I can see now, I've just gotten in the habit of being your wife. Habits can be kind of like snapping turtles—their body keeps on moving for days even after their head has been chopped off. This particular body may be slow but it has finally gotten the message that its head is gone. I'm not your wife any more. We can deal with formalities later, but I am no longer your wife."

He immediately protested, that she was overwrought from the events of the past week, that she didn't know her own mind, that his life would be barren without her. She sat in the darkness and listened to his protests. She thought it only fair to hear him out, after so many years, but for herself, her mind had never felt so clear. I do not love you. I am not your wife.

She knew they were not entirely done with each other. He would be in her life a while longer, tangibly, as furniture, lawyers, car titles, mortgage papers, books, friends, all to be sorted out and divided up. She had watched enough endings to know what lay ahead. He would stay in her inwardly, too, as regret and relief, as memory, as someone who had had a part in shaping her being. But she was not his wife.

She saw headlights flash across the side of the barn, then turn so they were shining in the kitchen window, then go out.

The door opened. "Chad? Vincie? What's going on?"

The overhead light was switched on, blinding after so long with her eyes wide open in darkness.

Darrell saw her and said, "Why were you sitting in the dark? Oops, sorry. Didn't see you were on the phone."

She took his arrival as an excuse finally to cut off the conversation. "Darrell's here. I have to go. I'll call you sometime this week."

She hung up.

"Why were all the lights off? And where's Chad? His car's still here."

She paused a moment, pulling in her breath, then said, "Chad is talking to the police. He was up here last Saturday."

Darrell looked at her for a long minute in silence, as what she had said made its way, step by step, through the structures in his mind.

"What does he say happened?" he asked.

.She told him, briefly, Chad's story.

Again, the long silence. He was shaking his head slowly back and forth. "This is going to be hard," he said finally. "Was he okay?"

"Chad?"

He nodded.

"I'm not sure. He's so volatile. You don't know which part of him will come out uppermost."

"No." He was silent again, then said, "He and Dad were...they were like a dog and a cat tied together with a rope. They each thought the other was an alien species, but neither one of them could make a move that didn't tug on the other. I wish they could have found a way to stop fighting the rope. I guess that was too much to hope for."

He paused and this time looked intently at Vincie. "And what about you?" he said. "Are you okay?"

"What's okay in this situation? I'm miserable. How else could I feel right now? How else could you feel...? Gifford thinks I should be scornful of Chad. He says its hypocritical to act as if I love him the same way I always have, and that I'm just striking a pose of nobility and forgiveness. But it's not something I decided. I'm not even sure I do forgive him. But he's Chad. I can remember helping him walk, and teaching him to say, 'Chad is an ooey-gooey earthworm,' before he knew what the words meant. I can't just wipe that out of existence. Gifford doesn't seem to know what it's like to love someone because they're part of yourself. He mocks the whole idea. He thinks love and kindness are romantic fictions that people use to dress up ugly reality. He's so brilliant and analytical, but he turns everything he looks at into something gray and rotting."

"Gifford is the one who's the damned earthworm," Darrell said abruptly. He began to pace around the kitchen, with a restlessness that was unusual in him. "I'm sorry, Vincie. I shouldn't have said that. He's your husband, and I guess you must love him." He paced some more, and then couldn't contain himself. "But I don't like him. I didn't like him even when he made you happy, and I really don't like him now, when he's making you miserable."

Vincie stared at her brother. In her whole life, she could not remember hearing Darrell say he disliked someone. It was not just that he kept his opinions to himself. He simply did not dislike people very often, and when he did, the dislike probably caused him more pain than it would ever cause the person who was its object. At this moment, he looked acutely uncomfortable about what he had said.

"It's all right, Darrell. I don't like him either," she said. She spoke half-facetiously, and yet the moment the words were out, she almost laughed, because she realized they were true. She had once loved her husband, she had once enjoyed sex with him, she had once been in awe of his brilliance. But she didn't like him.

"You don't?" Darrell said.

"No, I don't." The laughter burst out of her, then, laced with hysteria. "He doesn't know it yet. One of these days, I'll have to tell him. He's big on honesty. He should take it very well. Thank me, even, for giving a genuine opinion."

She laughed harder, and her body began to tremble uncontrollably.

Darrell watched her for a minute, then rather deliberately pulled out a chair and told her to sit in it. He did not offer a hug of comfort. Such a gesture was not his habit. Instead, he asked if she had eaten any supper. She shook her head. What about lunch? She shook her head again.

"I'm going to make you tea," he said. "And something to eat."

He turned on the burner under the kettle, then opened the refrigerator to see what food there was. "How about a grilled cheese sandwich?"

She nodded. Her laughter had stopped, and the trembling subsided to an occasional brief spasm. She did not feel hungry. Her body had no circuits left for a sensation like hunger to use. But her weakness told her she must need food.

She watched as Darrell searched the cupboard to find the tea Georgeanne had supplied, and a saucepan to use as a teapot. He brewed the tea, sliced cheese and laid it between two pieces of bread, and melted butter in a frying pan to toast the sandwich. He set the mug of tea in front of her, and then the sandwich, once the cheese had melted. He poured tea for himself, also, and sat down across from her.

The first bite of food awoke her hunger and she wolfed the sandwich.

"Want another?" he asked.

"Not yet." She clasped her hands around the mug and sipped the tea, which Darrell had made milky and very sweet, as if she were a sick calf who needed every calorie of nourishment she could be induced to swallow. He was silent, watching her eat and drink and sipping his own tea.

With quiet and food came calm, and clearer thought.

"It's all out of our hands now, isn't it?" she said.

He nodded.

"Except what we do ourselves. What do you think we should do?"

"Nothing."

"Nothing at all?" she asked.

"Nothing different, I meant. As you say, most of it is out of our hands." He smiled a little. "Anyway, isn't that why we have a god and a criminal justice system? So that you and I can still have a brother?"

She smiled, too. "I suppose it is."

She had been wondering what lay behind his stillness, which only the thought of Gifford had visibly disturbed. He had given her a glimpse of understanding, that he loved Chad, that he loved her, that neither grief nor love could be measured by speech, that truth could be obscured by talk as much as by silence.

On an impulse, she said, "Bret Leroux told me about something Dad said at town meeting. That his kids were more important to him than anything else in his life."

"Yes."

"Yes? Is that all? It didn't surprise you that he said that?" she asked.

"Maybe that he would say it. But what else did you think he considered more important?"

"I don't know. The land. His cows, maybe."

"His cows! The cows were a duty. Maybe even a sacred duty. But his family was his life, his soul."

"Then why did he always put the care of the animals first?" she asked.

"Because he grew up in New England. Duty first, and then the things you love. Four months of winter, and then a month of sleet and slush and mud, and then finally, a day when the sun bursts through, and wisps of fog are hanging over the fields but the sky is blue, and the blackbirds are singing in every tree, and your heart wants to swell up and explode with joy."

For just an instant, his eyes sparkled and danced, and then he was still again.

"And we were the things he loved..." she said.

"Yes."

"How is it you understood these things, when Chad and I couldn't?"

"I haven't always," he said. "Only now that I'm older. And have kids. Maybe I am just what Chad likes to say I am, Dad's yokemate, hearing the same calls of gee and haw, and just as bemused by all the traffic racing past. Except that he was the willing puller of the two. I'm the one who would get distracted by a patch of clover and have to be urged. Now that he's not here any more, everything seems out of balance. Sometime I'll find my footing, but right now it's sort of the way it is when the wind suddenly dies down and you almost fall over because you've been pushing against it without knowing that you were. I've spent a lot of effort trying not to be too

225

much like him, but I never figured out what I wanted to be instead. My only clear goal was negation, and that's not much of a goal. Especially when the thing you're trying to negate is half your own DNA."

"Chad wanted to bet me you'd come back and farm this place, if we agreed to keep it."

"You should have bet against him. You would have won."

"You'd never come back, then?"

He shook his head.

"Why not?"

He smiled a little. "No money in it. Georgeanne would have to support us all." Then, more seriously, he added, "I guess Dad paid all the dues that were owing. I'm not a businessman any more than he was, and you have to be, nowadays, to make a go of it. He spent his life trying to learn how to become one. I don't want to make the same mistake he did. I don't want to be a willing puller who's being driven down the wrong road."

Yet Vincie could easily see him becoming that, in spite of himself, and perhaps Vernon had seen it, too.

"I wonder if he was trying to make sure you didn't," she said.

"What do you mean?"

"By giving away the development rights. Without that equity, you'd have a much tougher time borrowing the money to get started farming again. You might still be able to, if you were really determined, but you couldn't just slide into doing it because it was there. Maybe he wanted the land farmed, but only by someone who would go into it from scratch because it was their dream."

A car door slammed, and she paused. Neither of them had noticed the car driving in.

"That must be Chad," Vincie said, and then in a reflex of caution, corrected herself, "I hope that's Chad."

The door opened and their brother came in, followed by Bret Leroux. Chad looked pale and weary, and drained of all talk for once. The sergeant said hello, and then seemed not to have anything more to say either. Vincie wondered why he had bothered to come into the house. He shuffled his feet a little, and glanced first at Darrell, then at Vincie, with the look of someone checking a pulse, a brief studying look that made an assessment and moved on.

"I'll leave you, then," he said. "I'll just check on a couple of things outside. If that's okay."

"Of course," said Vincie.

When he had gone, Chad sat down. He slouched in a chair beside the table, unaware, finally, of the associations with the spot. "Well, they haven't arrested me yet," he said. He managed a faint smile.

"Do they plan to?" Darrell asked.

"He says not, unless some new evidence turns up."

"But that's good, Chad," Vincie cried. "He must think you are telling the truth."

"No, he just doesn't have any proof that I'm not. And I don't have any proof that I am, so we're even. But a tie goes to the runner, and it seems I'm the runner. Is there any alcohol in this house, do you suppose?"

"There's beer in the refrigerator," Darrell said. "And maybe a couple of very old bottles of bourbon and rum in that bottom cupboard." He pointed, and Chad stirred himself to open the cupboard and look. He found the bourbon, poured a couple of fingers into a glass, and cut it with water. He took one swallow and sat down again, holding the glass almost absentmindedly. It seemed he was looking for a token of solace, and not to drug himself unconscious.

Vincie stood up and put on her coat. "I want to ask the sergeant something before he goes," she said, and slipped out the door. She did have a question, but she also thought her brothers might like a minute to talk without her there.

25

SHE FOUND Bret Leroux standing in the door of the milkroom, gazing back toward the house and the lighted kitchen window.

"What are you looking at?" she asked.

"A refrigerator and a doorway. No table and no people," he said, and she thought he sounded pleased.

"Is it important?"

"Not very. But I like it better when some little detail turns out to be true. It tips the scale of probabilities a hair towards the good."

"How far is it from probability to certainty?"

"Quite a ways, still. But we don't often make it all the way to certainty," he said and smiled.

"Do you believe Chad's story?"

"It doesn't matter much what I believe. It only matters what I can prove."

"I'd still like to hear your opinion, inconsequential though it may be."

"All right, then," he said. "I think that what Chad says happened is a lot less likely than a simple murder. So, I'm inclined to believe him."

"Can you explain that piece of illogic to me?"

"Okay, here's my illogic. I think Chad's native habitat is improbability. So if his story was something ordinary and everyday, then I would think he made it up to sound believable. But his story, on the face of it, sounds crazy. So I think, that's exactly the kind of thing that would happen to Chad. Or do you think he predicted my illogic, and made up something crazy to outmaneuver me?"

"I would be afraid of getting tangled up in my own tactics, if they became that convoluted."

"That's what I'm hoping. So far I haven't found anything to put a hole in his story."

"You don't sound entirely objective about this. I thought police-men were supposed to be bloodhounds on the track of wrongdoing, and you seem to be searching for signs of innocence."

"We don't go looking for crimes. We just try to find the criminal when a crime has been done. If no crime was done, so much the better. Anyway, we've been talking about what story I believe, and that doesn't have much to do with my job. I can have my own opinions, as long as they don't run my investigation."

"But you must like Chad, if you are hoping he's innocent."

"I like Chad well enough, but he's not the only one who would be hurt if he's guilty."

Vincie heard a slight softening in his voice and turned swiftly to look at him. He was staring straight ahead at the lighted windows of the house, but his stare was much too intent when there was nothing to be seen except a doorway and part of a refrigerator.

She became abruptly aware of her own physical existence, and of where she was standing, barely three feet from him. Until that moment she had been aware of nothing except her own questions and his answers and what they meant for Chad. Now, suddenly, she noticed sensations in every nerve. She felt the coolness of the air on her skin. She saw the darkness around them, and his face only faintly lit by the distant house lights. She smelled the wetness of the soil, and felt the wool of her coat around her neck and arms.

She knew he was aware of her, physically, sexually. She felt she had become a charged particle in a magnetic field, all senses alive and reactive, not only to him but to everything else that touched them. She felt the tiny currents of movement in the night air. She smelled the damp concrete of the milkroom behind her. She heard his breathing. She was immersed in sensations, and the minuteness of the sensations only intensified her awareness of them. She noticed her own weight on the soles of her feet, and a pellet of fabric between the fingers that were curled in her pockets for warmth. She saw that the rain had stopped, and that the wet ground had begun to exhale wisps of fog as the air cooled. An air current brought a moment's scent of decayed leaves down from the wooded hillsides, and a few stars were appearing through gaps in the clouds overhead.

Bret had not moved or spoken or looked at her. The silence between them, their total stillness, the charged gap of air that separated their bodies, all were turning into an act of seduction. Her skin was aflame, and she barely breathed. If he moved to touch her, she would answer instantly. If she moved to touch him, she knew he would answer likewise. Yet they both stayed still, separated by nothing but air, for minute after minute. Slowly, sensation abated and thought returned. Her body felt strangely relaxed, almost as if they had seduced each other in fact and not in imagination.

"I should go in," she said.

"Yes."

She hesitated, wishing to make a gesture that acknowledged the unspoken, but not one that would seem merely flirtatious or teasing. No gesture matched her wish. She simply looked at him, and this time he met her look. He shrugged and smiled a little, then put out his hand for her to shake. As they shook hands, he kept hers in his grasp for an extra beat or two past the number of seconds that defined polite leave-taking. And that was all. They walked across the muddy yard together, he said good-bye and stepped into his car, and she returned to the house.

26

THE REASON FOR Bret's restraint was not complicated. Vincie was married. If she made no move, then he would make none. He would not have scrupled to respond, if invited, but he would not intrude where the welcome was uncertain.

He had felt the difference in that moment, the change from previous moments when he had noticed every move she made while she had noticed him hardly at all. He had felt her eyes on him. He had felt the tension in how she stood, across a space that was wide enough to be safe but narrow enough to arouse every nerve in their bodies. He had not looked at her. He knew if he did, restraint would fail and his body would try to follow where his thoughts had already been, many times. He had waited and kept his eyes fixed on the lighted window, though he did not see it.

He thought possibly the tension he felt in her was a struggle to stay loyal to her husband. That was her own struggle, and he was determined not to try to undermine her. He would simply await the outcome. His principles were not overfine, but they did dictate that much.

Gradually, he felt the tension in her ease and her posture relax. It seemed that loyalty had won. His own nerves quieted, too, but without any accompanying relaxation. She might have conquered her attraction, but he had not conquered his. It had only retreated, out of discouragement.

Driving home, he felt inclined to curse his own honorableness. When they shook hands, he had held hers for an extra moment, and she had not drawn it away. He felt her return his gesture, acknowledging what had passed, and he became certain of what had been in doubt before. She would not have drawn away. If he had seized the moment when desire was in the ascendant, if he had looked at her and allowed restraint to fall away, if he had pulled her body to touch his, she would not have drawn away.

So why had he waited? Why hadn't he acted, boldly? It was high school all over again. Then it was shyness, now it was scruples, but either way, it was a chance he had let pass, and another man would win her love while Bret looked on. Or was it some barrier of inevitability, a decree of fate that they were not meant for each other?

Damn fate or damn himself, what did it matter? The result was the same.

At home, he sat down with a beer and opened the case file he had brought with him. He wanted to think about something besides his own futility. He doubted he would find anything overlooked, but he thought the information might fall together differently.

What he wanted was a single irrevocable fact that would clinch the case, one way or the other, murder or suicide. His intuition was telling him that the fact did not exist, and that this case was destined to remain a summation of probabilities, just as Vincie was destined to remain in the infinite parallel existence of all that might have been.

He reread the autopsy report, which provided much of the basis for their original belief that the death was suicide. "A single bullet entered the right temple and exited the upper left side of the skull...The muzzle of the gun was touching the skin...The angle was precisely consistent with a right-handed man holding a gun to his own head. A second person could hypothetically duplicate that angle, but it would not be the most natural angle, assuming that the second person approached from behind and was standing up while the victim was sitting."

Another fact was noted. There were no other bullets in the gun. Whoever loaded it had put in a single bullet, presumably from the open box of cartridges that was found in the cupboard.

Bret chalked up two points for suicide. Then he came to the items that had been sources of doubt. There was the absence of a note. There were the business affairs that Vernon Nowle had left unfinished. If Chad's story was true, these two difficulties vanished. The suicide became a more impulsive act. Vernon might have forgotten about the business matters, or even changed his mind. And his intention, though not written, was implied by what he had said to Chad. These items were now neutral. They were still consistent with murder, but they were no longer inconsistent with suicide, as Chad portrayed it.

The probabilities looked better, but he still had no irrevocable fact. Short of an eyewitness, what fact could there be that would make an absolute distinction between Chad's account and murder? With one or two small changes in detail, the event could change from one to the other.

If only dogs could talk, he thought. There had been two witnesses, but they could not say what they had seen and heard. Were they in the car, as Chad said, listening to a suicide? Or were they in the kitchen, watching a murder? It was such a simple question, but the ones who could answer were voiceless.

He continued through the file, coming next to the photographs of the body and the room. He barely glanced at the ones of the body. The medical examiner had told him all there was to be learned. The photos of the room he studied closely. All the chairs were pushed in under the table, except the one in which Vernon was found. The drainer held dishes for one place setting, and a couple of saucepans. Every inch of the room had been photographed—the dog mess on the floor, the cupboards all neatly shut, the jackets on hooks by the door, both Vernon's. The exiting bullet had shattered the side of the skull and spattered blood and tissue onto the wall and floor beside where Vernon was sitting. Bret paused over the photographs of this blood. He saw a detail that had not seemed important before. At the base of the wall, below the streaks of blood, lay a folded gray blanket, the dog's bed.

He studied the wall and the bed, and saw something quite clearly that had not been seen before, because it had not mattered before. Like the wall, the blanket was stained with blood, a spray of distinct dark splotches. But not the whole blanket. In the center, there was a large oblong patch with no splotches. There were a couple of small smears, as if blood had rubbed off a dog's coat, but no splotches from drops soaking directly into the material. He stared at the oblong absence of blood, the silhouette of his voiceless witness.

He sat a moment, thinking, then picked up the phone and dialed the number for Darrell and Georgeanne.

"What's this about?" Georgeanne asked as she met him at the door. "Darrell is still over at the farm."

"I expect you can tell me what I need to know," said Bret. "I'm sorry to bother you so late."

"I was awake," she said. "This hasn't been a week for lounging in bed. Does this have to do with Darrell? Are you investigating him?"

"No, I'm not investigating him. But it does have to do with his father."

He saw her quills relax a fraction and hurried to ask his question before her worries could move on from Darrell to other possibilities.

"You and Darrell have been taking care of his father's dogs. Is that right?"

"Yes."

"You brought them home with you last Monday evening, after he was found?"

"Yes."

"Do you happen to remember if either of the dogs had any blood on their coat when you first picked them up?"

"Yes, I remember. Stubbs did. It was not pleasant. I gave him a bath immediately, before the kids could touch him."

"Only Stubbs?"

"Only Stubbs. Caramel was clean. Stubbs is sort of a lump. If you dropped a bowl of oatmeal on his head, it would probably still be there a week later."

"Can you describe the blood? How much there was, and where?"

"There was quite a lot. Mostly on his back. At first I thought he must have rolled in it. You know how dogs love almost anything that people think is revolting. But when I started washing it off and looked more closely, it didn't look like something he had rolled in. It wasn't smeared into his coat. It was more like little dried blobs here and there, stuck to the hair. Some of it wasn't just blood. There were some bits of stuff like what you pull out when you're gutting a chicken. I was just glad I got it cleaned up before the kids saw it. As I said, it wasn't pleasant."

"I expect not," Bret murmured. "Can you swear to all of this? You're sure you have all the details right?"

"Imagination is not one of my gifts. If I didn't remember, I would say so. I would not make something up."

"I don't know why I bothered to ask that. Your accuracy is legendary."

"Thank you, for what it's worth. Your blarney is equally legendary. Is that all you wanted to know?"

"Yes."

"Would you mind telling me why it matters? What exactly are you trying to prove?"

"That particular information proves that Stubbs was in the kitchen when your father-in-law was shot. Nothing more."

"Is that important?" she asked.

"Possibly."

"Did someone else shoot him?"

"Possibly."

"But not Darrell."

"No."

"Do you know who?"

"Yes, but I probably can't prove it beyond a reasonable doubt in court."

Not unless Chad feels a need to confess, he thought as he drove away. He could prove Chad had lied, but that by itself would not prove guilt, not in court.

Bret had his one irrevocable fact. In his own mind, he was close to certainty. But his own mind did not count. As a murder case, it was still just a shifting balance of probabilities.

Another detail floated past, Chad's statement about what the wound had looked like when he came back into the kitchen. "It was on the right side, I'm fairly sure. That would make sense. He was right-handed." In fact, the exit wound on the left was much more conspicuous. Someone who came upon the body would probably mention that wound first. But someone who knew Vernon had been shot from the right would probably say he saw the wound on the right. It was not a fact, just another probability that shifted the balance a few degrees more.

As it stood, the case could not be proved without a confession. Did Chad have the need to relieve his mind? Not many people could go through a deeply shocking experience without wanting to tell someone, anyone, what had happened. But Chad was different. He was inventive, unpredictable, and as far as Bret could see, only partly repentant. As casually as a boy pulling plums off a tree, he could pluck nonexistent events out of the air and then make them look real enough to taste.

For a moment Bret recalled listening to his own father, on the phone with a potential house buyer. He was not as imaginative as Chad, but he used words the same way, not to describe or explain, but to mold other people's actions. He was adept at creating false impressions without actually lying, so adept that he sometimes lost track of the truth he was concealing and did not even have to fake his tone of sincerity. The deception was not really calculated. He was simply intent on a goal, to nail down a sale, and speech was the tool he used to attain that goal.

Chad had a goal, too, to keep himself out of jail. Probably he would say anything he thought would help him toward that goal. The question was, did he also feel an urge to unburden himself? If he was arrested, which way would he jump? Would it strengthen his determination to resist? Or would it plant doubt and fear, and ultimately drive him to the relief of confession? Who could guess. Chad was volatile and he liked to talk, which were reasons to hope. He also enjoyed a duel of wits, which was a reason not to hope too much.

At the very least, he must be questioned again, and Bret must try to make it look like there was a case against him.

Bret radioed the dispatcher and asked for a second cruiser to meet him in Worthing. Then he looked at his watch. It was almost eleven o'clock.

27

Vᴵɴᴄɪᴇ ᴡᴀꜱ ᴜᴘꜱᴛᴀɪʀꜱ getting ready for bed when the two patrol cars pulled into the yard. Through the window, she watched Bret and a uniformed officer walk toward the house, leaving a third trooper waiting beside the cars.

What had they found out? With three of them there, they must intend to arrest Chad. She ran down the stairs and into the kitchen, just as the policemen knocked on the door. Chad and Darrell were still sitting at the table, where she had left them. The table was scattered with crumbs from a package of cookies, nearly empty.

The business took only a few swift minutes. Chad was told he was wanted for further questioning, informed of his rights and led out the door. Bret turned for a moment to look at her with an expression of apology and regret. Then they were gone, and she and Darrell were alone, staring at each other. The room seemed very large and empty now that Chad had been forcibly removed from it. She felt only the vacancy, and not the presence of what was left behind.

"I don't understand," Vincie said. "Two hours ago, Bret said he was inclined to believe Chad's story. So why are they hauling him in again? Did Chad tell you anything, when I wasn't with you?"

"No. He mostly talked about his car," Darrell said. "Although at one point, he did comment that you are a trusting soul."

"Meaning that I shouldn't be?"

241

Darrell shrugged. "Maybe. But he didn't seem to want to talk about Dad any more, and I didn't push him."

Vincie could hardly think about her father, either. Every time she thought she understood what had happened, something changed and she was left in confusion again. By now, her ability to think had been reduced to one word, why?

"But why did he do it?" she said. "I don't understand."

It hardly mattered, whether the police were right about the details. He had killed his father, one way or another. The police could concern themselves with laws and proof and punishment. In her mind, there was only an overwhelming "Why?" Perhaps even Chad himself did not know the answer. She remembered his eulogy, which was not a eulogy, but a child's cry of longing and loneliness, and the rage of helplessness.

"Do you think he considered it a small thing? Do you think he really believed Dad would welcome death, so it wasn't such a big action, to push him over the edge?"

Darrell was silent for a while, before saying slowly, "I think Dad scared him. Not in the common way, by being stern or angry. It was something else…" He stopped again, to form his thoughts. Then he went on, in the tentative tone of a scientist who is putting together and testing a theory. "Dad wouldn't have thought of death that way, like a cliff you fall over. He saw death so much, having animals and plants and all of them dying in the end, that it wasn't something separate. Not that he didn't grieve. I think he mourned every single thing that died, even a mouse that drowned in the water tank or a shrub that got winter killed. But when you see things die every day, maybe you lose some of the fear. Not the grief, but the fear. So he didn't try to keep it at a distance. He let it be part of him. It was a sign of being alive, that he was going to die. The only things that didn't die were things that had never been alive.

"But Chad…For him death is something terrible and unjust that you either fight against or flee. It's a kind of tin can tied to his tail, that he keeps trying to outrun. He always has to stay

242

light on his feet. If he were to settle into something, like getting married, it might be the first step in the slowing down that ends in death. So he keeps moving and moving, ready to dodge at any moment. But then there would be Dad, like a wall in his way, forcing him to think about things he didn't want to think about. He'd go faster and faster, and just when he thought he was about to get ahead of the tin can for good, there would be Dad, watching him and seeming to ask why he was running so fast when death was in front as well as behind, and inside as well as outside. I think something in Chad had to strike out and try to fight back. I think he felt that accepting death was next door to being dead. A person who could accept death must not have any feelings at all, and he already thought that about Dad anyway. As far as he could see, Dad was completely indifferent, about dying, about his children, about everything, and Chad couldn't stand it."

"But why now? Dad hadn't changed. He'd always been the way he was. So why would it suddenly get to Chad?"

"I guess it might have been the money," Darrell said. "Not for itself, but because it made things tangible. Two hundred thousand dollars might look like a lot of indifference."

"I suppose it might. If that's how you lay out the equation," Vincie said. "But you said you didn't think Dad was indifferent at all."

"No, I'm sure he wasn't." Darrell smiled a little. "But then Dad and I were yokemates, remember? I know what it's like to feel that my insides are roaring and burning and shaking, while my outside looks as placid as a potato. When I met Georgeanne, at the university, I thought my heart and stomach and bladder had jumped on three sides of a merry-go-round, and she told me later that she thought I was absorbed in some biochemistry problem and hadn't noticed her at all. Luckily, she is the sort of person who can look at a brick wall and envision rubble. She was damn well not going to go unnoticed. She said we had been out on four dates before she was sure I wasn't just agreeing to go out of politeness."

"She's sure now, I hope," Vincie said.

He smiled again. "Yes." He fell silent and stared dreamily into space. Vincie hoped he was still thinking about his first dates with Georgeanne.

For herself, she could not put the present out of her mind. Looking across the table at him, listening to the hum of the electric clock and the silence beyond it, she felt like one of a dwindling band of survivors, as if her family had been picked off one by one, until only she and Darrell and Georgeanne were left. Her parents were dead, her brother might go to prison, her husband was an object of apathy at best. But Darrell was there, still, and she felt grateful for his calm and solidity, though he might dismiss them as potato-like.

"This would be a lot harder, if you weren't here," she said. "I would be adrift."

"That goes both ways," he said. "You're kind of an anchor right now."

"Me?" she said in amazement. "I'd have said I was more like a soap bubble. Someone like Georgeanne is an anchor."

"Not always. Some things she could never understand the way you do. Do you remember the time we spotted a pileated woodpecker up along the brook? You let me be the one to tell Mom about it, because you could see how desperate I was to be the one who scored that coup. And it wasn't Georgeanne who threatened to peel my skin off in strips and braid them into a jump rope if I ever snooped in her diary."

"Was I really that vicious?"

"Oh, much worse. That was mild. But then you'd turn around and spend an afternoon with a bulldozer and a dumptruck helping me build a four-lane highway across the vegetable garden. I was sure you were going to be an engineer someday. You were going to be an engineer, I was going to be a scientist, and Chad was going to be the ringmaster for a circus."

"You're the only one who came close," she said. "Look where

Chad and I have ended up."

"You haven't 'ended up' anywhere. Not yet, anyhow. You could do whatever you chose. You could still be an engineer. You've got Dad's brain, and he was an engineer, until…" He stopped.

"Until duty called."

"'Yuh."

"I'm so out of the habit of thinking that way. Do you really think I could do it?" she asked.

He smiled and said, "It will be May before long. Everything is possible in May." Then he added, more seriously, "Yes, I know you could."

"Maybe."

"No, not maybe. 'Maybe' is one of my words and you can't have it. Try 'absolutely, definitely, without a doubt.' A hundred times before bed, every night."

She laughed. "I'll work on it."

He stood up and said, "I should get home." He dampened a sponge and began wiping up the cookie crumbs still scattered across the table, recalling them both to more immediate concerns.

"Do you think he'll go to prison?" she asked.

"I don't know. But I've never seen him get in a mess he couldn't talk his way out of."

"What I meant was, do you think he did it?"

Darrell didn't answer for a moment. The sponge paused mid-swipe and he stood still thinking. "I guess I won't ever know, for certain."

"Does that bother you?"

"Yes, some. I wish I could know. But then it's one of a long list of things I don't know for sure." He shrugged and went back to wiping the table. "Anyway, whether he did it or not, he's still got that tin can tied to his tail." He smiled a little. "I guess that's why some people like the idea of a hell. They want to believe they go somewhere nice when they die, but it would be too galling to think that all the unpunished sinners go there, too."

He rinsed the sponge, put the remnant of cookies back into the cupboard, and went to put on his jacket and boots. At the door, he paused for a moment.

"Don't forget, a hundred times before bed, every night," he said, and then startled her by stepping forward to sweep her into a hug, one armed and awkward, but still his idea rather than hers.

28

BRET WAS stalemated and knew it. He had made his move and Chad had countered it, without hesitation. If Chad was struggling against an urge to confess, he showed no sign.

"You're right," he said. "I made that bit up, about him asking me to take the dogs. The truth is, Dad never said a word about the dogs. He never gave them a thought. But the only reason you ever started asking questions was because of what Vincie and Darrell said about the dogs. So I was afraid you'd never believe they were wrong. The truth is, he just told me to go, and then he shot himself. It was stupid of me to make that up, but I didn't have any proof of what happened and I thought that extra detail might help convince you. I should have just stuck to the truth."

"That would have been nice," Bret murmured. In his official voice, he added, "But everything else you told me is true? That you stayed around and waited in the milkroom. That you went to the house afterwards and planted the photograph."

"Yes."

They went over it again, detail by detail, and Chad's account didn't vary. Bret had caught him in one direct lie, and he had answered with an explanation no less plausible than the rest of his very implausible tale.

So he let Chad go. Bret was thinking the same thing a jury would probably think. Chad was guilty of something, but not something

247

proven and punishable within the boundaries of the law.

What a tiny little fragment of fact it was, that still remained unknown. Whose hand actually held the gun? About one hundred feet separated truth from falsehood, the distance from milkroom to kitchen. This particular truth was locked away in the one unbreakable vault that existed, a single human mind. In Chad's memory, the image of that truth might be as distinct and vivid as the blooming cactus on the wall calendar right in front of Bret's eyes. Yet Bret could, if he chose, imagine the cactus bare of blossoms and half buried in a drift of snow. If asked what he saw, he might describe either one, the flaming red cluster of flowers, or the plain green spiny lobes protruding from a swirl of snow. And the flowers, so improbable against their backdrop of rocks and sand, were the truth, and the bleak dormancy of winter, so easily believed, was the moment's invention.

Bret's province was the law, and the law did not reach inside the mind, not yet. If the truth could only be found there and nowhere else, then the law must give way. He had only to think about the alternative to know that this was good. If the cost was that some guilty people escaped punishment, it was still good. He told himself this several times, to counter an urge to start swearing.

He could still see the way Chad looked, as he told his revised story. At one moment his eyes were melting with sincerity. In the next they were sparkling with eagerness to match wits against all comers. Police, lawyers, judge and jury, he would take all of them on and win.

Seeing that look, Bret knew he was stalemated. A man who could see sport in this situation would play it out to the last point. Bret had been hoping for a failure of nerve, but Chad appeared to have disengaged his nerves. He seemed to have decided that being investigated for murder was as exciting and absorbing as any other pastime.

Bret asked one of the other officers to drive Chad home. He did not want to spend any more time in Chad's company, because it was starting to make him doubt his own eyesight. He was looking at the world through a kaleidoscope, with colors and shapes that shifted with every turn, and as his brain grew more and more dizzy, Chad stood by laughing and said, "Isn't this fun?"

Now Chad was gone, and Bret sat at his desk, staring at the flowering cactus and restraining the impulse to swear or break something.

He needed to think about something besides this case for a few hours. Tomorrow was Sunday. Would his wife let him take Jason for the day, even though it wasn't his weekend? The weather was clearing. Perhaps they could drive to Boston for the afternoon ball game. Ever since Jason started playing tee-ball, he had been wild to go to a real game. There would still be tickets, so early in the season.

Did Vincie like baseball? He could invite her to go, just casually, no big significance.

Hah. Who was he trying to fool? She wouldn't be interested anyway. A woman who liked Gifford would never like baseball. Damn this family, anyway. They were turning his brain into a Nerf ball. He put on his coat, turned out the light, and walked out to his car.

Still, there wasn't any harm in asking. The worst she could do was say no. He'd looked like a fool before and was still here to tell about it.

Hah, again. He'd never dare.

In the morning, he would ask his wife about Jason. That was enough. He would find out if Jason could go.

After that, after he knew his son could go, he might think about the other.

29

WHAT HAD STOPPED HER?

Vincie lay in the darkness, trying to answer that question. If she had not held back, if she had bedded the policeman, to use Gifford's blunt phrase, might Chad's fate have been different? Instead of returning to the investigation, and discovering whatever fact had led him to question Chad again, Bret might have been occupied with her.

But she had said good night and he had returned to his work on the case and now he had dredged up some new bit of information that must have been vital. If he had waited until morning to think about the case, perhaps the significant detail would not have caught his attention. Perhaps the information would have fallen together in a different pattern, and some detail would have leapt out that seemed to prove Chad's innocence.

More likely, it made no difference. More likely the information would have looked the same in the morning as it had tonight, and Chad's interrogation would only have been postponed a few hours.

But what had stopped her? It was not fidelity. During the minutes when she contemplated seduction and then let it pass by, Gifford had not once come into her thoughts. If not Gifford, then what had barred the way to acting out a desire she clearly had felt?

She tried to call up an image of Bret Leroux, the man who had attracted her, but what came to mind was damp night air and the smell of leaves, and the memory of a cheerful boy in a cast, waving pompoms. She hardly knew the actual man. Her attraction was a creature of her own need, and her need, at that moment, was for a direction and a shape. She had changed state, an apparent solid turned suddenly fluid and seeking a channel in which to flow or a mold into which to pour itself. The structure that had seemed to give her life a shape had dissolved, and she found herself mobile and formless, a compound of possibility and uncertainty, exhilaration and fear. She felt as she had at eighteen, that she might become anything, or nothing.

It was frightening, to leave behind a state of being without knowing what was to take its place. She could see clearly only what she did not want. Bret drew her because he looked like the opposite of one of the things she did not want. He was everything Gifford was not. How easy it would be to rush toward everything that looked like the opposite of what she was leaving behind. She could become something other than office help living in some place other than D.C. married to some person other than Gifford.

But she had already tried that. Fifteen years ago, she had fled Jello salad and chicken pie suppers, grease guns and conversations about chain saws and mastitis. She had fled the solitude and everpresence of farm work. Most of all, she had fled from Vernon, the silent, unbending figure in whose presence she had felt so small and inconsequential.

In Gifford and his professional world, she saw a vision of the perfect opposite. She saw culture, sophistication and brilliant conversation. She saw a clean, modern and convenient lifestyle. She saw a man who loved to talk, who loved to delve into the deepest recesses of the psyche, especially his own, and to share with her what he found there. She saw a man whose hard-won approval had been won by her. She saw all the things she believed she lacked, and leapt to seize them when they were offered.

Now, fifteen years later, she could recognize exactly what she had gained. Her lack of purpose was more elegantly dressed. She moved more quickly in no particular direction. Her small talk used a larger vocabulary. The tedium in her life was free of grease and dirt. But she had not found what her spirit still craved, a reason why she, Vincie, walked on the earth. She had looked to Gifford for something neither he nor any other person could give her.

This time, feeling herself fluid and longing for form, she had not leapt to seize the first new shape that offered itself. Some instinct had made her pause.

It was not a conscious thought that had stopped her. In the moment when her body was pulled by desire, she had not analyzed Bret Leroux's character, or told herself that he was merely a reaction against Gifford and her present existence. She had not thought, as she was thinking now, that no sensible engineer would design any fluid system, whether a turbine or a hydraulic piston, a pipeline or a pump, until she understood the properties of the fluid itself. In that moment in the darkness when she had to choose, she had not thought anything at all. Yet her choice was the one she would make again now, after reflection.

So what had stopped her? Was it chance? Was it her subconscious mind? Or was some benevolent spirit passing by, perhaps on its way to a séance, perhaps on its way home from church, perhaps just strolling out from its home in an elm tree to watch the mist rising over the fields? Did it see her dilemma and pause from its own business long enough to give her a gentle guiding push? Who could say?

She heard a car drive into the yard and climbed out of bed, almost gladly. She was no closer to sleep than when she first lay down. The back door opened and someone came into the kitchen.

"Darrell?" she called down the stairs, questioningly.

"No, not Darrell. Have you lost faith in my powers of persuasion?"

"Chad!" She ran down the stairs, still in just a nightgown. "What on earth happened? I thought they were going to arrest you."

"I talked them out of it. For the moment."

He explained to her what the police had found, and how he had responded.

"Nothing has changed, actually," he said. "They still think I'm guilty, and they still don't think they can prove it."

"But why did you make that up, about him wanting you to take the dogs?"

"I didn't think anyone would believe me otherwise. You and Darrell were both so sure he wouldn't forget them. I didn't think you would believe the truth."

"How could you think that something you invented could be more believable than the plain truth? If what you say now is the plain truth."

"You see? You're not sure now."

"How can I be sure when you've said so many different things?"

"What if I said one more different thing now? What if I said, yes, I shot him? Would you believe that, when it's just one of five different stories? The police would. If I wrote down five different versions of what happened, and signed all five, they would pick out that one and say it must be the true one and send me to prison. I learned a long time ago that what is true and what people believe wouldn't always recognize each other if they met on the street."

"Yet you know the truth about what happened."

"Yes, but I can't make anyone else know it the same way. They have to decide for themselves what they believe. Some things people can agree on and say are fact, like the law of gravity. But then there are all the other things that have to be guessed at or taken on faith. For instance, what Dad was thinking when he died. Even if a dozen witnesses had seen Dad kill himself, none of us would know what was passing in his mind. We'd all make guesses, according to what we have in our own minds."

Was he right, that the most important truths came down to what a person chose to believe?

She thought about his story, the newest one, which might be true. He said his father really had forgotten the dogs. In the moment of final crisis, pain had obliterated duty. Chad had battered

254

him with terrible facts and urged him on toward death until all thought of duty was lost in the vision of his dead wife and his living son, together before him, filled with hatred and accusation. Grief had finally shattered the ice and loosed a flood that would wash away the channel in which his whole life had run.

It was true, she thought. This was what happened. She did not have to choose to believe it. She believed in spite of choice. That was what he felt, what I would have felt...

But why? Why had Chad hated his father so much? Why had he lied so many times? Why had he done what he did? And how many more times would she be faced with another why?

"Are they right?" she asked.

"Which they?"

"The police. Are you guilty?"

"I didn't shoot him, if that's what you mean."

What did she mean? "But you did kill him," she said. "You destroyed his will to live."

"That's not the same as killing him."

"You sound like a land developer, saying he's not killing frogs when he drains the marsh they live in."

"And you sound like Dad!" Chad burst out furiously. "You don't see what's right in front of you. You just see some big pattern in the universe. And it's not even a real pattern. It's some ideal you have in your heads. I feel like I'm talking to a big institutional building with granite pillars in front. That's what it felt like that night. Like he was impervious. I didn't make any impression at all. I hardly existed. I was just some insect crawling around down in the squalid world of money, that he couldn't be bothered with. Nothing I've ever done had any value in his eyes. I could make a billion dollars and still be worthless, as far as he was concerned. Two hundred thousand is a fortune to most people and he was just throwing it away like it was nothing. And nothing I could say made any difference. I didn't want the damned money, but that's what he thought I wanted. He thought I was being greedy and shallow, like the rest of the human race, and all of us so far below him. But it wasn't that.

I didn't want his money. I just wanted..."

Chad's voice broke and he stopped.

After a moment, Vincie said quietly, "You wanted him to think well of you."

"Yes, I guess so." Then he flashed out, "But he didn't and you don't either. You think I'm wasting my life. Probably Darrell thinks so, too, though he'd never say it."

"What about you?"

"What do you mean?"

"What do you think about yourself?"

"How can I think well of myself when no one else does? You all despise me. You think I'm crass and frivolous."

"I don't think that at all. I don't know what to think, because I don't know what standard you use to measure yourself. What standard do you want me to use?"

Chad didn't answer right away. His eyes roved the room, searching.

"I don't know," he said finally. His eyes continued to wander about the room, not fixing on anything, just avoiding the table.

"Chad, tell me what happened. Exactly."

"I have told you. That was the truth."

"Yes, but how did it come about? What did he say? Why did you want him dead?"

"I don't even know any more." He closed his eyes and his face was lined with pain. After a while, he said, "He never asked me anything. Not one single question. I said all the things I had to say and he listened, but he never asked one question, about me, about anything. There was just that statement, 'You don't need the money, do you?' Like he was summing me up and dismissing me. Like there was nothing about me that could interest him. If he had just put it differently, if he had just asked a question, 'Do you need the money?,' I would have felt like I was a person and he was a person and we were talking to each other. As it was, I hardly existed.

"I couldn't stand it. I just started to rage inside. You remember how Mom used to tear outside and shriek with rage at the cowbirds, even though she knew it wouldn't do any good. She knew they'd be back, doing what cowbirds do, the moment her back was turned, but she just had to rage at them. That's how I felt with Dad. I knew it wouldn't make any difference. I knew he'd go back to being the way he was, but for that one moment I was going to make him know I was there. He was going to know I existed, right down to his bone marrow, because I was going to make him suffer, right down to his bone marrow. If I couldn't make him happy and proud, I could at least make him suffer. I think I wanted him to die, just to prove to myself that he was human. I think half of me didn't think he really could die, any more than a block of marble inscribed with proverbs could die."

"But he was human and he did die," Vincie said abruptly. "Does that make you happy?"

"No, it doesn't make me happy. What good is someone who's dead? Except he'd just as well have been dead when he was still alive. We have exactly the same connection we did before, none."

"He loved you, Chad. Maybe he couldn't say so, but he did."

"Oh, sure, he loved me. He loved the universe and I was part of the universe. He loved everyone and everything, just the way people say god does, from way off there where you can't see him. But I wasn't somebody in particular. He didn't even register who I was or hear a word I said, and there was nothing short of a bullet that could have penetrated his awareness."

Vincie stared. "Did you use the bullet, Chad?"

"Not a real one. What would that have proved? I wanted him to feel it and for that he had to be alive. A real bullet would have been quick and painless and he'd never have known what happened. I wanted him to know the truth and feel pain the way everyone else did. I wanted him to be one of us."

Vincie had to sit down. She was feeling sick inside. Was this what Vernon had felt, sagging into a chair with the gun in his hand?

"Why didn't you stop him, then? I'm surprised you didn't try to keep him alive, so that he would go on suffering for as long as possible. You'd succeeded. You'd breached the castle wall. Why didn't you follow up your advantage? Why didn't you stop him?"

"How was I supposed to stop him, once he'd decided?" Chad said. "Dad never changed his mind about anything, not after it was made up. And I could tell his mind was made up, from the way he told me to leave. What was I supposed to do, go back and say, no, I made a mistake, Mom's death had nothing to do with you, you've always been a wonderful husband and father, and we're all as happy as can be. He would have known it was a lie, and anyway, it was too late."

Too late. She had been too late herself, coming to adulthood, coming to understanding.

"You could have stopped him, just by staying," she said sadly.

Had she ever stayed herself? Had she ever reached out a hand, as an equal, to offer comfort?

"He wouldn't have shot himself, with you in the room. If you'd just said, no, I won't leave, I'm staying right here. But that would have been too hard. You'd have had to go on facing him, alive, and that's a lot harder than ducking out and fleeing. So much easier just to cut the tie. You made him face the truth, you made that connection you said you wanted, but once you had it, it scared you out of your wits. As soon as you know you matter to someone, you're gone."

She looked at him, noticed that his cheek had a faint shading of stubble, that there were smudges of fatigue below his eyes. He looked bruised, and not in the least winsome.

"I've got some news for you, Chad," she said. "You matter to other people besides Dad. He wasn't the only one you could hurt. I love you. Darrell loves you. What you've done hurts us and always will. But I've got no plans to shoot myself, so you'll just have to go through life knowing there's someone who cares what you do."

Chad turned his head and looked at her, uncertainly. "How can you love me when I'm such a shit?" he asked.

Vincie felt tears well up. "Maybe I can't help myself, any more than Dad could. You're wrong about him, not caring about you because he didn't care about money. He just loved you. Period. The money was irrelevant, whether you had two dollars or two zillion. And if he didn't ask questions or reach out, it was because he couldn't see what he possibly had to give to you. We all look at you and you seem like someone magic and shining, and how could you need anything from us? You seem like a firefly, or the northern lights, something that came into being to be a source of delight to everyone who looks at it."

"How can you say that, after what's happened? How can you not hate me? Doesn't it bother you?"

"Of course it bothers me!" Vincie cried. "Maybe I do hate you. A person can feel more than one thing. Maybe I'm just Mom with the damned cowbirds you were talking about. You know how she would practically spit fire when she saw one laying an egg in some other bird's nest, knowing that its young would take the food that was meant for the others. But then an hour later she'd see a couple of them riding around on a cow's back, a couple of comedians, and she'd laugh and think they were the most enchanting creatures on earth."

30

Sleep still came hard.

It was three in the morning. The night had reached its solstice, the hour of deepest stillness, dark and cold. Soon the body would sense a change, not seen, but felt, a signal that sky and air were preparing for the approaching sun, a signal to insomniacs that their restless minds might finally be granted a brief blessing of sleep. Vincie, lying in darkness, felt her previous life receding with the night, but could not yet discern the shape of what might lie ahead. Her mind strained for the first faint outline of an object emerging out of dark.

Shedding a present life told her nothing about the future. If she was not bound to follow a course at right angles to her previous direction, then how was she to choose among the three hundred sixty degrees of the compass that became possible? How did a sailor choose a course when open water lay on all sides? By knowing what lay beyond. And she did not know what lay beyond.

But neither was she surrounded by pathless water. She opened her eyes and looked around at the shapes dimly visible in the room, the bureau, the dark square of a painting on the wall, the line where the solid gray of wainscoting met the patterned grays of wallpaper. It was the earliest landscape her mind had known, her bedroom in near-darkness. She was surrounded by landscape, not water. At seven degrees north of east, Chad lay asleep in his room.

At thirteen degrees east of south, Darrell and Georgeanne were asleep, too, or perhaps still awake talking. Directly below stood her father's desk, where he had added up the numbers that ended in financial extinction. Almost due west lay the university, and blackboards full of equations, complex and absolute, offering stability to a restless mind. In all directions lay fields she had plowed, cities she had visited, a museum she longed to see, the work she could do or could be taught, her parents' graves, books, newspapers, computers, and a multitude of sparrows and warblers that Phoebe could have identified but Vincie had yet to learn. She did not lack for paths and landmarks. She had only to choose her route among them.

She remembered Darrell's teasing command. Absolutely, definitely, without a doubt…She smiled a little. Not likely.

After a time, the square of sky in her window changed, sending its invisible signal to the sleepless, and she slept.

She awoke to a shadow, the branch of a tree snaking across her bedroom wall. If there was a shadow, then there was sun. She leapt out of bed and opened the window to lean out.

It was exactly the day that Darrell had described. The sun had topped the hills to the east, the sky was blue and wisps of fog wreathed the fields along the river. The wooded hillsides were tinted with the rusty red of budding leaves. Close to her window, a blackbird perched in the top of a maple, sending forth his proprietary warble and trill. Across the yard, another answered. The voices argued back and forth, negotiating possession of some blackbird's equivalent of the Alsace-Lorraine. Down below, the glossy leaves of the rhododendrons had uncurled and spread themselves wide. The fields were still brown, but the air smelled green.

It was a day when her mother would have pulled on rubber barn boots and rushed out with a gardening fork to clear the last mulch from her daffodils and poke the soil here and there, not to any purpose, since it was all still mud, but simply because her eagerness needed an outlet. Her father would have watched and shrugged, and might even have smiled. He would have tinkered with machinery, greasing and sharpening and changing fluids, but casually, free of the urgency that would overtake him in just a few short days when the work of springtime truly began. The day was a kind of happy sigh, a just-waked creature pausing to stretch itself before setting about its business.

Vincie gazed at the rust-tinted hills, and suddenly saw colors, cascading before her eyes. The hint of rust gave way to a multiplicity of green, the spectrum collapsed to a single color and redivided into a whole new spectrum, an infinity of greens, transparently pale, and vivid emerald, and deep, cool bluish tones. The greens merged into a single dark dusty one, mid-summer green below warm blue skies and purple black thunderheads. Quite suddenly, a tree here or there dipped a branch in red-orange, and all the trees followed, and the entire spectrum fanned out across the hills and sky, red, orange, yellow, green, blue, a blazing display that must pass quickly before senses grew numb. Retreat began, first to rusty browns, then to subtle tans and grays and ochres, and finally even tan departed, leaving pure white and soft gray and a green so dark the eye saw black. And then, just when the eye thought no further reduction was possible, white, too, departed, and gray descended, and the palette was churned together into a single, nondescript shade of mud.

And then this day arrived, bringing blue and rust, and the smell of green, and the world opened its eyes and stretched.

Fully awake now, Vincie felt her parents' absence with a new and sharper pain. Now it was not the loss to herself she felt. She was growing used to that. It was the loss to them, her mother's loss, not to be out searching for the first green shoots of crocus, and her father's loss, not to unhitch the stanchions and open the barn door and watch the cows' first gleeful, udder-flapping gallop out into the sunshine.

Chad was right. She did not know what their dying meant to

them. She could not live it with them, and they could not even try to tell her, as they might once have tried to tell her about other unknowable things. Yet the pain was real and the loss as vivid as if it were her own. She could feel the joy they would have felt, and the wrenching pain of that joy denied.

But I am alive, she thought. I smell the air and see the light and shadows and feel the joy. You are in me, so let yourself see what I see and feel what I feel. Stay alive in my life. My heart is strong, my nerves are electric, my blood is a flood tide, my mind can hold the universe, there is room in all of them for you, too. Stay in me, live in me. I welcome you.

For just a moment, she felt herself once again small, standing beside her father. Her hands gripped the metal railing of a pen inside the barn. She and her father were both watching, intently.

In the pen, a cow lay on her side panting, in straw that had begun clean but had since been dampened and dirtied with manure and spurts of urine and the first bursting sack of birth fluids, all of them churned together by the cow's hooves as she circled and lay down and got up and circled some more and lay down again. From under her outstretched tail, two hooves protruded, two small whitish pads poking out of a gaping red gash.

The cow moaned. Her body stiffened and she began to push, laboring with grunts and panting gasps. The hooves squeezed out an inch, slowly, then another. The cow relaxed and the hooves retreated, almost back to where they had been before.

It's taking so long, Vincie thought. It's so hard. Can't he do something?

The cow pushed again, the hooves inched outward and fluid dribbled out around them. She grunted and stretched her neck forward, her whole body straining. The feet squeezed out another inch, the red gash grew wider, and then the nose could be seen, and the tongue hanging limply out between the jaws. Vincie watched the tongue, too limp and still, and began to feel frightened.

"The calf doesn't look right," she thought. "Why doesn't he do something?"

Again the cow relaxed. The nose retreated, but not completely. Vincie could still see the tongue lying inert between the jaws.

The cow panted for a while and began the painful, grunting push again. The nose squeezed out again. The cow moaned and strained and slowly, slowly, the rest of the head squeezed out between her bones and through the tightly stretched gash in the skin. And then, quite suddenly, the whole body followed the head, slithering and squirting onto the ground in a gush of fluid and blood and membranes.

The calf lay still, too still. It lay in a crumpled tangled heap, slick with membranes, streaked with blood and manure. Nothing moved. Its head lay twisted sideways, not moving. Its eyes were open, glassy and staring, horribly fixed.

"It's dead!" she cried. "Dad, why didn't you do something? Can't you do something? Can't you help it?"

All that painful labor, all that blood, and for nothing. The cow lay panting, exhausted. Behind her rump, the calf lay inert in a sticky pool of fluid.

"Dad, do something!" she cried again. "How can it be dead? It's not fair!"

He didn't move. "Wait," he said.

Wait for what? Vincie thought, but did not dare protest again.

Her father stayed very still, watching, and she watched, too, but with rising terror and grief. Her gaze was fixed on the raglike limpness of the tangled legs and the lifeless stare of one wide-open glassy eye.

Then, suddenly, she saw what he was watching for. The eye blinked.

She held her breath and gripped the fence rail more tightly.

The eye blinked again. A nostril twitched. The head bobbed up an inch.

"Did you see?" her father asked.

She nodded and felt tears of astonishment and relief and joy start up in her eyes.

He put a hand on her shoulder, gently, and said, "It's hard work

265

being born, you know. It's no wonder they look dead at first."

The calf snuffled air out its nostrils and shook its head, like a swimmer surfacing and blowing the water from his nose and shaking it out of his ears. At the sound, the cow scrambled to her feet and whirled around to smell the calf. She set her tongue to the task of cleaning, licking with rough vigor and nudging and crooning encouragement, and then losing patience and bellowing a command that it was time to be up and about. The calf struggled and flopped and somersaulted, over and over, until finally it stood swaying on all four legs and gazing about in half-blind bewilderment. It took a wobbling step, then another, then wobbled too far and tumbled to the ground. It lay for a moment, gathering strength, and then, single-mindedly, began the struggle all over again.

Twenty minutes old, its eyes could see only shadows. Yet it seemed to know that those dimly seen shadows were its first glimpse of a world full of wonders and dangers, and that there was no time to be lost in setting forth.

Thirty-five years old, Vincie still struggled to see clearly, but for one moment she saw her father emerge from shadow and felt grateful to him. He had not rushed in with explanations to calm her child's fear. He had stayed close by but silent, some might say hard, and let her feel terror, because only then could she feel the whole miracle for herself.

About the Author

Edith Forbes grew up on a ranch in the West. For the past nine years she has lived on a small farm in Vermont where she raises cattle and writes. She is the author of *Alma Rose*, a novel which takes place in the West of her childhood. She is currently at work on a new novel.